BELOW THE LINE

BELOW THE LINE

A Hollywood Crime Novel

LOWELL CAUFFIEL

ARCADE
CRIME WISE

An Arcade CrimeWise Book

For Machine Johnny, Bobby, and all the boys in the playhouse.

First Arcade CrimeWise Edition

This is a work of fiction. Names, places, characters, and incidents are either the products of the author's imagination or are used fictitiously.

Arcade Publishing books may be purchased in bulk at special discounts for sales promotion, corporate gifts, fund-raising, or educational purposes. Special editions can also be created to specifications. For details, contact the Special Sales Department, Arcade Publishing, 307 West 36th Street, 11th Floor, New York, NY 10018 or arcade@skyhorsepublishing.com.

Arcade Publishing® and CrimeWise® are registered trademarks of Skyhorse Publishing, Inc.®, a Delaware corporation.

Visit our website at www.arcadepub.com.

10 9 8 7 6 5 4 3 2 1

Library of Congress Cataloging-in-Publication Data is available on file.

Cover design by Erin Seaward-Hiatt
Cover artwork: © LPETTET/Getty Images

ISBN: 978-1-956763-48-5
Ebook ISBN: 978-1-956763-49-2

Printed in the United States of America

1

THE JOB WAS IN LA—A city he considered highly overrated. Above all he loathed the traffic. Everyone in a goddamn competition. Cars blasting their horns, switching lanes with no signal, fighting for a lousy car length in yet another five-mile-an-hour freeway backup.

Warren Poole thought, the laid-back, Southern California lifestyle?

Shit, man, that ended at the asphalt.

He was lost.

And pissed. He'd sped across 250 miles of desert on the I-15 in three hours from Las Vegas, only to crawl for another three on the I-10 for the last sixty miles into Los Angeles. When he finally reached downtown, a web of interchanges and confusing signs spit him out into a neighborhood past the Los Angeles Convention Center. Now he was driving around in circles in the dark, looking at street signs and trying to get back on the I-10 to Santa Monica.

He was looking for Figueroa Street.

The theme for *The Good, the Bad and the Ugly* was distant at first: the flute open, followed by the vocal *wah wah wah* part. Not the whole song. Only two bars of it. It became louder when he turned onto a street of run-down storefronts, Latinos on the sidewalk and a couple of soul brothers on the corner. He had no problem with the scenery. He worked with a Mexican and a black dude on his first crew back in the day. If you were going to operate in certain neighborhoods, you had to employ some diversity.

Warren Poole heard the theme again.

Poole buzzed down his window. Now he not only could hear the song but muddled words that followed. It was coming from a loudspeaker somewhere. He looked around, guessing it was from a storefront. But he was doing twenty-five and the tune was following. He checked his mirror, a Chevy truck behind him. The theme maybe coming from behind the truck. And then he clearly heard the words after the music:

"Move it along, dog."

A red light ahead, Poole stopped. The truck rolled by him and took a right at the cross street. He turned on his dome light and looked at map he got from the Auto Club, trying to figure out where the hell he was. People told him he should get a smartphone with navigation. But he liked burners. He didn't want a number tied to his name, let alone anything that could track him.

He looked up from the map and noticed lights in his mirror. A white Chrysler 300. Pimped out with a chrome aftermarket grill and blue undercarriage lights.

The theme sounded loudly as the Chrysler pulled up. Then, "Move it along, dog."

Pool realized the music was the horn on the 300. He'd seen horns like that once in a car stereo shop, the kind of place where people bought novelty add-ons for their rides. He saw a horn that had the roar of Godzilla and another with cartoon sound effects.

The light still red, Poole looked at the map again, his eyes straining to find Figueroa in the maze of lines and street names.

The car sounded its novelty horn. "Move it along, dog."

Poole looked up at the signal, the light green.

They moved forward together, Poole driving slowly, looking at street signs, the 300 so far up his ass he could no longer see the grill or the glow on the pavement from the undercarriage lights.

The horn: The flute and *wha wha wha*. Every couple of seconds now.

Move it along, dog.

Poole slammed on the brakes, the Chrysler screeching to a stop behind him. He took a deep breath and thought about the situation for a few moments, weighing the options. Finally, he decided. He reached down under his pant leg and removed a Beretta Tomcat from his ankle holster and slid the .32 into his windbreaker.

He walked slowly to the 300, his eyes scrutinizing the driver. He was going to rap on the tinted side window with his knuckles. But the driver beat him to it, buzzing it down, a cloud of pot smoke wafting out.

The soul brother's dreadlocks hung off the back of his head down to his shoulders, the front part of his skull bald. He had a microphone in his hand. This asshole wasn't satisfied with only the horn, Poole thought. He also had PA wired into the Chrysler. Poole glanced at a light-skinned sister in a tight black dress in the passenger seat, a blunt between her fingers. She seemed harmless.

Poole said, "You in a fucking hurry? Or do you always jerk off with your horn when you smoke that shit?"

The driver slowly turned toward him, then back to the girl, saying, "The man a little out of his element, don't ya think?"

Poole watched the guy place the mike into its clip on the dash, doing it like he was in no hurry. Showing he wasn't rattled, that now he was going to tell Poole how it was going to be. But when he saw the driver casually reach for the glove box, Poole didn't wait for his fingers to touch the latch.

He grabbed a handful of the driver's dreads.

And slammed his face into the steering wheel.

Hard.

The flute. *Wha wha wha.*

No "Move it along, dog" this time.

The girl dropped the blunt in her lap and recoiled against the passenger door. Her hands swept her lap as the embers burned a hole into her dress.

Poole slammed his face into the wheel again.

And again.

The movie theme playing each time.

"I'm really fucking tired of that song," he said after one.

"I'm really tired of the fucking traffic," he said after another.

"And I'm really tired of this long fucking drive," he said as he slammed the driver's face into the wheel one last time.

Blood streamed into the soul brother's eyes, his arms limp at his sides, the soul sister shrunk into the corner of the door and her seat.

"What do you want?" she said, screaming it.

He wanted to drop in on an old girlfriend. Then he wanted to get settled. He wanted to get a decent night's sleep before the job ahead. But he didn't tell her that.

Warren Poole leaned close to the driver and spoke in a soft voice.

"Say, dog, you wouldn't happen to know where Figueroa Street is, would you?"

2

EDWIN BLAKE'S BIG BREAK INTO show business came in Detroit five years ago because somebody chopped up two drug dealers and a crack whore.

He was working homicide, the second shift on Squad Seven, called to investigate a multiple murder involving a Roto-Rooter van abandoned on Detroit's east side. A reporter named Rick Quigley from the *Detroit Free Press* showed up just ahead of three TV crews minutes after Blake's partner, Al Henderson, strung tape between two maple trees to establish the curbside crime scene. Blake detested the stories Quigley wrote about his unsolved cases. He decided Quigley's reporting had nothing to do with his skills as a detective. He concluded it was because Blake was six feet tall and Quigley was hardly five-two. So, Blake decided he'd give the reporter an exclusive. He told him to duck under the tape and follow him to the Roto-Rooter van. A couple of TV crews bitched that Quigley was getting special access.

Blake ignored them. He wanted Quigley to have his moment.

When they reached the back of the van Blake said, "Ricky, I'm going to let you see what we got." He swung open the doors, telling Quigley to step inside, Blake following. Al Henderson, who everyone called Hendo, stood outside the door, watching. He knew what was coming.

Blake shined his flashlight around the interior of the van, saying, "I know it doesn't look like much. But we've got a triple here."

"All I see are garbage bags," Quigley said.

"Look closer," Blake said.

Quigley bent over one of the bags.

That's when Blake reached into a Hefty sack and handed Quigley the severed arm of a thirty-two-year-old African American male.

"Here," Blake said. "Let's give a hand for the little guy."

Quigley jumped, slamming his head into the roof, only to trip over a router as he scrambled out the back door. Hendo later told everyone on the fourth floor of police headquarters that Quigley tossed his dinner in front of the TV crews. Blake didn't see that. But he didn't contradict him.

It was a good story, no matter how you told it.

The next morning, the inspector in charge of the homicide section woke Blake up, telling him to get his ass downtown. Quigley had complained to the deputy chief. Blake figured his boss was going to dress him down and note the incident in his personnel file. Instead, when he arrived at headquarters, the inspector said he wanted to personally congratulate him, saying, "It's about time someone did a number on that short stack sonovabitch."

While Blake was downtown, he decided he might as well say hello to the Squad Seven day crew. But he found the squad office filled with a half dozen people he'd never seen before. Somebody said they were from Los Angeles and were rehearsing for a cop movie they were shooting in Detroit. The location scout liked the police headquarters building at 1300 Beaubien because it was built in 1923, was gritty, and some scenes in *Beverly Hills Cop* were filmed there.

Blake poked his head into the doorway. Two actors were sitting at a desk, reading from a script. Blake could see the scene was an interrogation, a detective threatening a murder suspect with the death penalty unless he confessed to a homicide.

When they finished, Blake said to no one in particular, "Excuse me. We don't have that here."

"Don't have what?" said a guy in a baseball cap and T-shirt. He was sitting at another desk in the far corner of the room.

Blake told him that Michigan was the first English-speaking government in the world to abolish the death penalty in 1846. First-degree murder carried a sentence of mandatory life.

The guy in the ball cap said, "And who are you?"

"Detective Sergeant Edwin Blake."

"You work here?"

Blake said, "You're sitting at my desk."

Blake later learned the guy in the cap was the director. But he looked more like a fresh-faced counselor at a kid's summer camp. He asked Blake if he had any more suggestions, sarcasm in his voice.

"Since you asked, a homicide detective would never interrogate a suspect that way. In fact, he wouldn't use this office. He'd put him in the box, the little room down the hall. Let him sit there for a good hour and wonder what the score was. Then he'd drop by to say he'd be right back and let him sit another hour."

Blake figured at that point the director would tell him to fuck off. Instead, that night he took Blake to dinner at the Pegasus Taverna in Greektown, showing up with a satchel and still wearing the ball cap. After three glasses of retsina, that Greek wine fermented with wine sap, he started confessing. This was his first feature film, he said. He'd only directed TV episodes before. The script had a decent story, he said. But the dialogue was lousy. The producers wouldn't pay the writer for another pass. And he didn't think the writer could fix it anyway. He said he could polish it himself but was up to his ass in other problems. That's when he reached into his satchel, slid the script across the table and said, "You're just the voice of authenticity I've been looking for. Can you give me notes?"

For the next three weeks they met a couple times a week. Blake suggested realistic dialogue, flagged factual errors, and even came up with a couple better locations. Blake figured the screenwriter had never met a real detective and had gotten all his ideas from watching movies. He told the director, "This thing reads like it was written in a coffee shop."

The director said, "If you want to get specific, it was a Coffee Bean on Wilshire."

Blake came to like the director and decided to show him around. He introduced him to assistant prosecutors over drinks at a downtown bar and let him tag along on a homicide scene. He toured him through the crumbling Packard plant and cruised down West Jefferson to see the blast furnaces on Zug Island at the mouth of the Detroit River. The director got fired up seeing a world they didn't tell him about in film school.

The day the film crew left town the director told him he'd be in touch. Blake didn't hear anything for six months. Then one night the director called to tell him ABC had picked up a series from a pilot he'd directed, a cop show. The executive producers were looking for a technical consultant and he wanted to recommend Blake for the job. It would require that Blake move to Los Angeles.

"I'll have to think about it," Blake said.

"It's pays $3,500 a week," the director said.

Blake told him he'd get back to him in twenty-four.

He'd worked in homicide for ten years. He'd seen other dicks cite the weekly array of bodies and leave with mental disability claims. But the carnage never rattled Blake. He liked homicide because he was his own man. He liked being on crime scenes without a supervisor looking over his shoulder. When he was at 1300, he liked working suspects in the box. His partner claimed he was a master at working "the religion angle."

"I'm not a churchgoer," Blake said.

"You know what I mean, Eddie," Hendo said. "You get these scumbags to believe in redemption. That they could become the solid citizen they were always meant to be by copping to first-degree murder."

On the other hand, homicide wasn't the same outfit as when Blake signed on. The old-school dicks, the detectives who showed up in suits, starched shirts, and expensive leather shoulder holsters had all retired. With them went their tactics. Those cops didn't spend much time on forensic evidence. They just rounded up people, most of whom already had sheets or warrants, and locked them up until somebody gave somebody up. But a US Department of Justice probe put an end to the practice. Without those moves, everyone had to rely more on an understaffed evidence collection unit as the city skidded towards bankruptcy.

Family wasn't tying Blake to Detroit, either. His mother had retired to Tampa. His first wife lived in South Carolina. They hadn't talked in years. His second wife worked in the domestic violence unit. She left him after five years for a female chief who ran a firehouse on the northwest side. Blake wrote it off to her working with battered women, which had brought her to the conclusion that most men were just no goddamn good.

Blake decided to take two days off and fly to LA to meet the showrunner and a couple of ABC executives for the new series. He liked the way they sent a Town Car to the airport to pick him up, the driver waiting in the LAX baggage claim with Blake's name on a sign. He liked that he'd left streets packed with dirty snow and in five hours was seeing palm trees as smooth jazz played on the Town Car's radio. He liked walking around the Warner Brothers lot where he spotted the names of films like *Dirty Harry* and *Blazing Saddles* on plaques outside the sound stages, informing people what movies had been shot there.

"Do you like their offer?" the director asked afterwards.

"No," he said. "I loved it."

Blake was forty-seven years old. He returned to Detroit, filed for his pension, and drove back to LA with a couple of suitcases, his record collection, and all the possessions he could jam into a Jeep Grand Cherokee.

He never expected the adjustments he had to make to his new work environment. His first day on the job he wore his best suit. The receptionist thought he was an attorney. He told Hendo, "Only agents and attorneys wear suits. I feel like I'm back in narcotics." He switched to jeans, Frye engineer boots, and a collared shirt, untucked.

From the go, Blake began laying out stories and investigative tactics to the room of eight writers. But he quickly noticed that his sarcasm, cop shop humor, and general attitude wasn't landing well. Once, he joked that he had to let a handicapped suspect go because he couldn't figure out how to cuff a one-armed man. The writers thought he was serious. "My brother is handicapped," a female writer said. "I find that offensive."

Blake began wondering if his days were numbered.

That's when Carla stepped into the picture. They met on the Warner Brothers lot. She'd shown up to counsel a newly sober actress who panicked when the network sent a congratulatory bottle of Cristal to her trailer. Blake happened to be walking by when Carla emerged from the Star Waggons trailer. She handed him the $300 bottle of champagne, saying, "Hey, big guy, do something with this." He told her they could share it at his place that night, half expecting her to blow him off. Instead, she said, "I don't drink. But you can buy me dinner sometime." He found out on the first date she was a member of Alcoholics Anonymous and sponsored a lot of women she called her "pigeons." On their third date he invited her over to his apartment for some pasta he put together. He told her that things weren't going well in the writers' room.

"I'd really like to succeed at this," he said.

Carla said, "There's two kinds of people in this world, Eddie. Those chasing cash and prizes. And those simply trying to do the next right thing. Both have their own definition of success." She knew quite a bit about the industry. She explained her late dad was a top Hollywood entertainment attorney.

They ended up in bed. Afterward, she used the bathroom and left, saying she had to meet one of her pigeons at a midnight AA meeting. When Blake hit the head later, he found she'd written something in lipstick on the mirror:

Eddie, Tap the Brakes.

He called her. "Carla, sex was your idea."

"Not that," she said. "Your job. Just tap the brakes. Or you're going to scare these industry people to death."

He came up with a plan. He decided to apply what an old homicide dick used to say: "You can lead a horse to water, but you can't make him drink. But you can make him goddamn thirsty." He kept his mouth shut. Became aloof, mysterious. The writers had to pull the stories and tactics out of him. When they used an idea, he told them how original they were. Soon the showrunner was making full use of him. He often sent Blake to the set to help directors block scenes or advise the stunt coordinator on action sequences.

In his first year in LA, Blake traded in the Jeep for a new Dodge Challenger SRT and spent hours driving the muscle car around and discovering the spots he'd seen in his favorite films. He passed a

Saturday afternoon up at the Griffith Observatory where they shot *Rebel Without a Cause*. He spotted the office building they used in *Die Hard* in Century City. At night he watched dozens of shows and films on TV, spotting scenes with streets and commercial strips he'd driven through only days before. He found it all exciting.

One night over dinner, Blake told Carla, "I feel like I'm living in a film."

"You are, Eddie," Carla said. "It's called Narcissism Ground Zero. Everyone here is the star of their own movie."

The last thing he expected was his to flop.

3

HE ARRIVED AT DAGNEY'S in Santa Monica just before 11 p.m. She greeted him from behind a locked screen door, one hand on her hip, dressed in a pair of tight black yoga shorts and a white smock top cut just above her navel. Warren Poole expected she'd give him shit for showing up with no warning.

She did. "You can't call first, Warren? Or did you run out of minutes on one of those lousy pre-pays. You can't stay here."

"I've booked a room," he said.

She swept a lock of hair away from her eye. "That's not what I'm saying. I'm working."

"You shooting fuck films in your crib now?"

"I told you I was hanging it up the last time you were here. When was that? Two years ago? Maybe three?"

Poole shrugged. "Just open the door, Dagney."

She hesitated but then clicked the latch. He walked right past her and stopped in her living room, looking around. He knew she'd bought the Craftsman bungalow when prices tanked after the Northridge quake, back when she was a big adult star rolling in the porn bucks. The place had changed since he was there last. Gone was the clutter. Gone was a salt-and-pepper shag carpet, replaced by hardwood floors. Gone, too, were any film posters, replaced by a large print of a hot air balloon rising over a foggy city in India. It hung over an overstuffed couch. She'd also added a flat screen TV and a book cabinet with glass doors. There was an odd-shaped glass coffee table, covered with two stacks of hardcovers and paperbacks.

Poole picked one up and read the title: *Women Who Run With The Wolves*.

He tossed it back on the table and said, "What's that smell?"

She was standing at the threshold of the living room with her arms crossed. She uncrossed one arm and pointed to a cone-shaped device on a credenza, a stream of vapor coming out of a hole on the top. "It's jasmine. Aromatherapy. It elevates your mood and reduces stress."

He plopped down in an IKEA easy chair. "I'll stick with bourbon."

"I don't keep hard liquor around," she said.

"Make it a Heineken."

"That, too."

"Christ, Dagney. It's been a long drive. Whataya got?"

"Kombucha."

"Kom what?"

"It's fermented, made from a Manchurian mushroom. I drink it before my Tai Chi and Kung Fu classes."

"You're doing that now?"

"I got sick of having my ass grabbed. Some guy recognizes me in an elevator and tries that? He'll want off on the next floor. Not to mention stalkers. One of them shows up here I've a got a surprise for those sick sonsabitches, too." She paused. "The Kombucha will give you a lift. And it aids in digestion."

"There's nothing wrong with my gut."

"Looks bigger than last time."

"And what happened to you?"

She uncrossed her arms, walked across the living room to the doorway of the kitchen and turned around. "My back was killing me. The implants. My accountant said I could write off the reduction as a business expense. He put it under repairs." She pushed a strand of her blond hair behind her right ear. "You want what I got or don't ya?"

"I'm always good for a tumble," Poole said, his back straightening.

She rolled her eyes. "The *Kombucha,* asshole. It does have *some* alcohol."

"Bring it," he said.

When she returned from the kitchen, she handed him a bottle that looked like a long neck beer. He took a sip. It didn't taste like tea. It was tart, like weak vinegar. Dagney sat down on the overstuffed couch and crossed her legs, swinging the top leg up and down. He liked her long, slim legs, and the way they rose to her peach-shaped behind. He was thinking her smaller tits were just fine, losing her old Jessica Rabbit rack. Almost fifty now, she still looked good. And, he decided, any physical flaws she may have developed with age would be more than compensated by her cinematic skill set. He'd never slept with her after she started doing adult films. It was the reason he'd dropped by to see her. He wanted to find out what he'd been missing.

But getting there might take some time.

"So, Warren," she said. "To what do I owe the pleasure?"

She sometimes talked formal like that. Odd, considering he knew she dropped out of school in the tenth grade. His theory was that she picked it up from dialogue back when skin flicks actually had scripts and story plots.

"Here on a job," he said.

"A job? I didn't see a truck outside full of hot merchandise." She pumped her leg a little faster. "On second thought, I don't want to be involved. Whatever it is, don't bring it here."

"It's not that kind of job."

He wasn't going to tell her anyway. This line of work, you keep the circle tight.

He took a pull on the Kombucha. He was acquiring a taste for it. "Just thought I'd drop by and say hi, Dagney. I went through a lot of shit to get here. You gotta be fucking crazy to live in this town. Vegas ain't no picnic. But at least you can get the hell around. Fucking city of angels? Bullshit. Far as I'm concerned, that fat fuck Korean lobs a nuke and glasses off the place, it would be no big loss."

She stared at him for a couple seconds, then uncrossed her legs and leaned forward. "You know what your problem is, Warren?"

"Here we go."

"You focus on the negative."

"I'm just realistic."

"No, there's a difference. You're a negative person. Ever since I've known you."

"We had a couple good years."

"Yeah, you were nice—to me. Everything else, you complained. Frankly, it wore on me."

Frankly, he thought. Using those clever words again.

"Warren, listen to me," she said. "Ever think why you've been running in place all these years? Doing the same old chickenshit jobs? What you don't realize, you *manifest it* with your attitude. Only when you develop a positive mental attitude will you attract positive results."

Poole said, "What, like sucking a mile of cock on film?"

"Two miles, Warren. And fuck you, too." She got up from the couch. "You see, this is exactly what I mean." She walked over and sat down on the ottoman just a couple feet from his chair. She reached out and touched his knee. Her tone softening. "Listen to me. It's like this. You wear your talisman on the wrong side."

"I don't wear jewelry," he said.

"No, your *mental attitude*. That's your talisman. On one side is a positive mental attitude. On the other, a negative attitude. People sense it. You wear the negative side, you will attract the negative. You wear the positive, you attract the positive. Think of it that way."

She told him a story. How competition had killed her career. How when she started in the business there weren't many gorgeous female performers. How agents would mine the clubs and have to convince girls to take the leap into adult films. Get them first to do nude spreads. Then solo work or with another girl on camera and slowly lure them into hard core. Now girls from all over the country were flying into LA and lining up outside the porn agencies on Monday mornings. Others were working in their homes with inexpensive high-def cameras, shooting scenes with their boyfriends and posting content online.

"Even so," she said. "I had a good run with the MILF thing. But then even that work dried up. I could have gone negative, Warren. Given up. But I didn't."

Poole said, "You said you were done."

"That's right." She smiled. "Now I'm an entrepreneur." Saying it like a business school had bestowed the title on her. "I'm going to launch my own website."

Poole shook his head. "Nobody pays for porn anymore, Dagney. It's free."

She took her hand off his knee. "What? Now you're an expert?" She leaned forward, his voice going softer like she was telling a secret. "Depends on the content. Actresses with a name, they're pulling down big bucks with their own pay sites. No agent cut. No studio bullshit."

Poole took another pull on the Kombucha. "What kind of *content?*"

She stood up. "You'll see when I get it up."

Dagney sounded like she had an angle. "Maybe I'll be interested in a piece," he said.

She shook her head. "Sorry. It's going to be *all mine*. But that's good. I like the way you're thinking. See, that's *positive*. That wasn't so hard, was it?"

He wasn't in the mood for a self-help lecture. He finished the Kombucha and placed it on a side table. "It's late, Dagney. The hotel is probably wondering where the hell I am."

Dagney popped to her feet, saying "Hang on." She walked across the living room to the book cabinet, opening the glass doors, her fingers running across the titles there. She returned with a paperback and sat down on the ottoman.

"You need to read this."

She took her time telling him about the book. She said the author landed an interview with Andrew Carnegie in 1908, expecting to write an article about the industrialist. Instead, Carnegie challenged him. He'd pay his expenses to interview all the big shots of his day. People like Rockefeller, Ford, and Edison. Find out the secrets to their success and write about it. His name was Napoleon Hill and he ended up writing one of the top best sellers of all time.

"He wrote this one in 1960," Dagney said. She held up the paperback like it was a sacrament. "It's just as powerful today. This will put it all together for you."

She held out the book.

He hesitated. He was never much of a reader. The last book he tried put him to sleep.

She touched his knee again and said, "Warren, it's a fucking *life changer*."

Poole rose from the chair, her face now in front of his groin. He looked down, fantasizing about what she could do in that position as she looked up with imploring eyes.

He reached for the book.

"Read the cover, Warren."

It was bright white, the author's name at the top: Napoleon Hill, also the author of *Think and Grow Rich*.

The title was in large, bright red print. The subtitle was smaller in royal blue. It read:

Success

Through a Positive Mental Attitude

Poole looked at his watch. It was nearly midnight.

"I've got business tomorrow," he said. "Maybe I'll get to it after."

4

Edwin Blake was expecting the doctor's appointment to result in a clean bill of health, a one-hour session to satisfy Carla. But it wasn't going that way.

Blake said, "Let me get this straight, doc. I spend ten years in Detroit homicide. See people's brains and guts blown out week after week. But, hey, I'm okay with that. Never had an issue. But then I come out here. Work five years with these Hollywood people. It's all make-believe. And you're telling me at the age fifty-two I've gone mental?"

The psychiatrist was named Dr. Evan George, sixty-something with silver hair. He was sitting on a red upholstered chair, a clipboard in his lap, Blake sitting upright across from him on a black leather couch. Blake had responded earlier to a series of his questions: Had he lost interest in daily activities? Was he experiencing sadness or feelings of being down? Was he having trouble concentrating and making decisions? Was he avoiding social activities? Blake had answered yes to those but denied he was having sleep or eating issues. He'd tried to answer honestly. At four hundred bucks an hour, he figured he should get his money's worth.

"How about hobbies?" the psychiatrist also had asked.

"I collect postwar blues records. Vinyl. Seventy-eights, preferably." Blake said. "You know. Otis Rush. T-Bone Walker. Early B. B. King."

"When's the last time you listened to one?"

Blake couldn't remember. Maybe a year. Maybe more.

Dr. George said, "The medical term is dysthymia. It's less acute, less severe than a major depressive disorder. And you're certainly not bipolar. That would be very disruptive. No, what I'm hearing is dysthymia." He looked down at notes on the clipboard. "And based on your responses, it appears you've been suffering from it for at least two years." He looked back up. "But I've got good news. It's treatable."

Blake said, "Doc, I haven't exactly been on a winning streak lately. Who wouldn't feel a little out of it?"

The psychiatrist smiled, as if he'd heard that before. "This sort of thing can't always be attributed to life events. It can be a constellation of factors. There's some evidence of genetic disposition. You also told me you don't even feel motivated to work. But it's like, what came first?" He looked down at the clipboard again. "You told me your late father worked into his late sixties before he lost his machine shop." The psychiatrist looked up. "How did that happen, anyway?"

"GM sent his work to China."

"And how did he pass?"

Blake hesitated. He didn't want to get into it. But he could feel Dr. George pressuring him with his eyes. "Sitting around didn't suit the old man. He started hitting the bottle."

"And?" Dr. George said, still eyeing him.

"My mother found him in the garage. The car running. He'd handcuffed himself to the wheel and tossed the key. God knows where he got the cuffs. To this day my mother claims he was murdered. But the man had no enemies."

"Was there an inquiry?"

Blake nodded. "I pulled the file after I joined homicide. His BAC was off the charts. Suicide was an easy call for the ME." Blake glanced down and then up. "I gotta say, doc, we never saw it coming. He was always one tough sonovabitch."

The psychiatrist made another note. He looked up and said, "Like you?"

"Not even close."

Dr. George leaned back, crossing his arms. "Everything you've told me. You have a secure job in homicide. You say you were not impacted by the dark nature of that work. But then you take a big risk. Come out here. Take on a new career with no safety net. That's a pretty tough guy."

"Never looked at it that way," Blake said.

Dr. George half-smiled. "The only trouble with tough guys is they suffer in silence." He leaned back in his chair. "Edwin, it's good you came to see me."

Blake was sure Carla thought it was good. She drew the line a week ago, saying he was different than the guy she met. She said he spent too much time "isolating." She complained they never went out anymore. She told him it had been five months since they'd made love. It's not that she wasn't desirable. Sex just seemed like too much work. He didn't tell her that. When he couldn't come up with a believable excuse, she told him he needed to see this shrink in West Los Angeles who'd helped a couple of her AA pigeons. "And if you don't, Eddie," she said. "Then we're finished."

Blake said to the psychiatrist, "You're different than the Detroit Police Department psychologist I saw twenty years ago."

"And that was for?"

"A felon with three warrants pulled a .357 on me during a traffic stop. He apparently never spent any time at a range. But I had.

Department policy: you visit a shrinker after a fatal shooting. Saw her once. She hardly said a word. At least you talk."

Dr. George smiled, set his note pad on a side table and said, "Let's see what we can do about your situation. Presuming you're willing to embrace a therapeutic solution."

Blake didn't answer.

The psychiatrist got up, walked over to a desk, and sat down in front of his laptop. Blake watched him scroll through a couple of screens and then write something on a prescription pad. He walked the slip over to Blake, handed it to him and sat back down in his red chair.

Blake looked at the script, trying to make out the writing.

"It's an antidepressant. Think of it as just a little helper. You take one in the morning and one at night. You're not going to feel drugged. Sometimes there're a few side effects. Dry mouth. Insomnia. Tremors. Perhaps feelings of irritation. But they should pass."

"Then what?"

"It's subtle, actually. You'll find your mood will be elevated. More mental clarity. A sense of well-being. I had one depressed patient who said he was sitting on his couch one afternoon when he realized the sun was shining through the window. He realized he hadn't noticed that in years."

Blake didn't like that word *patient*.

Blake said, "I've got to be honest with you, doc. I don't have the kind of money to sit on your couch week after week."

Dr. George smiled. "I don't do psychotherapy. As I was saying, it's the most treatable mental disorder. I don't want to see you for a month to see how you're adjusting to the medication. Of course, if there're any problems—suicidal thoughts, fits of rage, allergic reactions, that sort of thing, which are rare—please call me."

Mental disorder. Blake didn't like that word, either. He was happy his hour was up. He stood, tucking the script in his shirt pocket.

Dr. George stood, too. "I'll walk you out," he said.

The psychiatrist's office was on the first floor, a separate entrance on Santa Monica Boulevard. As they stepped onto the sidewalk Blake glanced up the street to where he had parked his car at a meter a little more than an hour ago. From his angle, the parking space looked empty. He thought maybe he'd forgotten where he'd parked the Dodge. "Doc," he said. "Can this depression thing affect your memory?"

"Absolutely," Dr. George said, putting out his hand. "I'll look forward to seeing you again."

The psychiatrist disappeared back inside.

Blake walked to the spot where he thought he'd left the Dodge and stood for a moment, gazing at an empty space. Then he walked east a half block, returned, and walked a half block west. He was sure he'd parked it on the street. He checked the parking signs. He didn't see any postings of a tow-away zone. No signs with a number you called when a truck hauled your car. Still, he knew throughout LA there were predator towing companies that concocted excuses to impound vehicles.

He spotted a homeless man in an M65 surplus jacket, beard, and a ponytail. He was sitting on the curb not fifteen feet away from where Blake now was sure where he left the car. He walked up and pointed. "My car was parked right here, a dark grey Dodge," Blake said. "You happen to see it?"

The guy looked up and said, "Sure did."

"It get towed?"

He shook his head. "Car had a real nice sound when he started it."

"Who started it?"

"A guy."

"Parking Authority?"

"No, sir."

"What did he look like?"

"Young guy," the guy said. "Colorful."

"Colorful?"

"Yeah. He had lots of ink. Took off fast, too. That car can move."

Blake's eyes scanned up and down Santa Monica Boulevard. He looked back at the homeless guy. The vagrant hadn't asked for a dime. But Blake peeled off a ten-spot anyway and handed it to him.

Blake looked back at the vacant parking spot. He must have stared at the 120 square feet of dark pavement for a good minute.

It looked like the emptiest spot in the world.

5

"THE ODDS ARE WITH YOU," said the uniformed officer sitting behind a computer terminal. He had a blond crew cut that glistened under the fluorescent lights of LAPD's West Los Angeles Community Police Station. "We recover most stolen vehicles. Only catch is half are damaged or stripped for parts."

The young cop typed, then handed back Blake's proof of insurance, which had the Dodge's vehicle identification number. Blake didn't have the registration. It was in the glove box. He had walked the six blocks to the station rather than phone in a stolen vehicle report.

Blake said, "I've got a witness. He said the asshole who took it had a lot of tattoos. Late twenties. About five-ten. Dark brown hair." Blake handed the officer a slip of paper. "The witness is homeless but has a cell."

The cop typed some more, then handed the slip back. "Do you know anyone who matches the suspect's description?"

"Can't say I do."

"Where were you when it was stolen?"

"Doctor's appointment."

The officer looked back at his terminal, asking Blake, "Color of the Dodge Challenger?"

"They call it gunmetal. Black rims."

He typed again. "Don't see many American models like that around here."

"It's an SRT. Special edition. They only made four hundred of them that year."

"How much that set you back?"

"Sixty-five out the door."

"Still paying for it, sir?" The officer's eyes were still on the screen as he said it.

"I have a clear title."

Blake knew where the cop was going. People get behind in their payments. Get some stupid ideas. Have the car jacked or torch it themselves and let the insurance company pick up the balance. Blake's first thought was to tell the young cop to fuck off. Tell him he wasn't some dummy that he could practice on for a detective's exam. But Blake had been through enough contentious situations as a police officer to learn that his first thought was usually the wrong one. It only created more problems.

He went with his second. "Look, I appreciate your being thorough. But if I had caught the sonovabitch, you would never have heard from me. You would be getting an incident report from the EMTs who had to scrape him off the street."

The cop leaned back in his chair, nodding, looking at Blake differently now. Looking at him like he wasn't just another Angelino who'd walked through the door with a problem. He said, "It's never a good idea to take the law into your own hands, sir. But I can understand why you might feel that way." He paused again, then said, "Hopefully, you'll get lucky."

Blake said, "Where I'm from, a car like that would go straight to a chop shop."

The cop picked up Blake's license off his desk, looking at it "The Pacific Palisades? That's a long way from the hood."

"Detroit originally," Blake said. "There they just walk up to your car at a stop light and put a gun to your head."

The cop looked up, saying "I guess I won't be vacationing there anytime soon." His hands went back to the keyboard. "Okay, anything else? Any valuables in the car?"

Blake thought about the question. He didn't want to answer. He knew more questions would follow. But if he was typing the report, he'd want to know.

"Nothing in the trunk," Blake said. "Nothing visible through the windows. But there's something under the front seat."

The officer looked up. "Something?"

Blake scratched his temple. "Yeah. A Smith & Wesson CS45. Chief's Special. And it's loaded. Six in the mag. One in the chamber."

The cop's brow furrowed. "And what was it doing there? In the State of California, a firearm must be unloaded and placed in a case in the trunk of your vehicle."

"I've carried it since the deputy chief promoted me to the Homicide Section of the Detroit Police Department."

"You're here on the job?"

"Not for the last five years."

Blake reached for his wallet and handed the officer his Los Angeles County conceal carry permit. On the back he'd scrawled the serial number of the pistol. The cop looked at both sides, then typed again.

The officer handed it back and said, "Private security?"

"I'm registered with the state bureau," Blake said. "But mainly I do consulting."

"What kind of consulting?"

"Movies. TV shows. I help writers and directors get the details right. You know, so guys like you and me don't sit in a movie with our popcorn, saying, hey, a cop would never do that."

The cop said, "That doesn't sound like dangerous work."

Blake said, "Only if you tell a producer what you really think of his film."

Warren Poole slept with his Beretta Tomcat. It was an old habit. The feel of the pistol's steel under his pillow always relaxed him and put him out. He'd been sleeping that way for years, ever since some high desert trash broke into his Las Vegas condo and surprised him in bed at 3 a.m.

His boutique hotel was near Universal Studios. The BLVD Hotel & Spa seemed a good location, not too far from downtown and a straight shot on freeways to the coast. He slept in. When he finally rolled out of bed, he saw Dagney's Napoleon Hill book on the nightstand. He considered taking it with him to the toilet. Instead, he took the hotel's brochure to read about its perks. Five minutes later, he put on the room's complimentary slippers and bathrobe and walked to a hotel amenity called the Viya Spa.

Poole figured he was about to get busy. If there was a time to treat himself to some luxury, that time was now.

He chose a treatment called the Viya Signature Massage, the massage therapist saying she was customizing it just for him. The gal wasn't bad looking. But she was older, slightly overweight and wore no makeup. Working with him on the table she said she was increasing oxygen flow and releasing toxins from his muscles. He didn't know about that. Near the end she put heated stones on his back, saying they would impart a *powerful vibration* to his being. He didn't know about that, either. They just felt like hot rocks.

He charged the $150 to his hotel bill and handed the gal a twenty. "Here, hon," he said. "Go buy yourself some makeup, some lipstick. You're in the hospitality business, if you know what I'm saying."

On his way back to his room he picked up a breakfast sandwich and a coffee from the hotel café. He ate it at the small desk near the window, eying the thick traffic on Ventura Boulevard. When he was finished, he plopped on the bed and called Dagney.

She said, "Have you been reading the book?'

"I'm busy," he said.

"Doing what?"

"You said you didn't want to know anything."

"I said I don't involve me."

"I have to meet with some people. That's all."

"What kind of people?

"Just people."

"Well, I'm sure it's something shady."

"What makes you say that?"

"If it wasn't, it wouldn't be one of your jobs."

Poole changed the subject. "Look, I get things handled, maybe we could grab a bite." He was determined to eventually make a move on her. When the time came maybe tell her it was for old time's sake.

"I'm always good for dinner," she said. "Presuming you're picking up the tab."

"Of course."

"With no expectations."

"Did I say anything about that?"

"Answering with a question. The sign of a liar."

Poole glanced over at the nightstand, the Napoleon Hill book there. "We could talk about the book," he said. "I'm sure I'll have some questions."

"If you read it."

"I promise."

"Promises. Promises. Another sign."

"Hey."

"Look, I have to go," Dagney said. "I'm working on my website. Call me when you wrap things up and we'll see."

Poole decided to leave it there, take it slow with Dagney. Time was on his side. He didn't have to meet with a bunch of people, like he told her.

You didn't do that. Not when you were a hired gun.

6

BLAKE WAITED TO CALL CARLA until he was done with the report. He didn't want her inside the station, asking the police questions, making a scene. Now, sitting next to her in her Mini Cooper, he could tell by the way she was gripping the wheel that she was going to have a lot to say. She was wearing a floral print blouse and a pair of yoga pants, which she could still pull off despite being forty-five.

Blake said, "Why is it when I'm in this car I feel like a decapitation waiting to happen?"

She swung onto Santa Monica Boulevard, turned and said, "So, did you lock it?"

"No. I also wrote 'Please steal me' in the dust on the back window."

"See, this is what I've been saying," she said. "I ask you a simple question and you automatically go dark."

"I thought I was just being a smart-ass."

"Faith, Eddie. You'll get it back."

"My winning personality?"

"Your car." She paused. "Speaking of, did you like Dr. George?"

"He was okay."

"And what did he say?"

"He asked a lot of questions."

"Like what?"

"About my general health."

She looked over again. "Did you tell him your diet? Carbs, red meat, and not enough fruits and vegetables. You know that stuff turns to acid. And acid causes inflammation. And inflammation causes aches and pains. Diseases. Even brain fog."

"That pimply kid in the vitamin aisle at Whole Foods tell you that?"

She squinted. "Fuck you, Eddie."

"Keep your eyes on the road, Carla. You can swear without eye contact."

She looked back at the road but then turned again. "Don't bullshit me, Eddie. Dr. George isn't a GP."

Blake didn't want to get into it. But he knew she'd be relentless. "He says I have some form of depression. I can't remember the name."

Carla nodded, a self-assured nod. "I knew it. Did you know one in four recovering alcoholics suffer from clinical depression?"

"I'm not an alcoholic."

"I'm just saying. I'm very familiar with it. Dr. George helped a couple of my pigeons after they cleaned up." She let a few seconds pass and looked over again. "Eddie, there's no shame in it."

He wasn't feeling ashamed. He just wasn't sure the psychiatrist was right.

Carla said, "Okay, which drugstore?"

"What makes you say that?"

"We'll stop."

"For what?"

"Eddie, goddamnit." She motioned with her fingers. "Let me see it."

"See what?"

"The script."

She knew him too well. He reached in his pocket and handed it to her.

She glanced at it. A long glance.

"Carla, keep your eyes on the road."

She handed it back, saying, "Okay, you're going to stay with me for a couple of days. And, Eddie, don't give me any crap."

"Why would I stay with you?"

"Sometimes there're side effects."

Blake said, "I'm expecting calls. On my land line."

"What, from phone solicitors? For months you've been telling me you haven't been doing shit."

"Look, Carla. I know what it's like over there. Your phone always ringing. Those girls you sponsor. Your pigeons. People coming and going night and day."

"You make it sound like I'm running a whorehouse."

"It wouldn't take much more to get it there."

"Eddie," she said slowly. "That was uncalled for."

Blake knew nobody was turning tricks. Carla's passion was sobriety. She sponsored at least a dozen girls, half of them living with her in what she called her "sober living" home in Studio City. She guided them through the Twelve Steps and one calamity after another. That guaranteed that Carla dealt with a crisis pretty much every day.

Carla seemed to thrive on conflict among women. She revealed her checkered past on their first date. That immediately made him like her, that she was straight up. Her gin and Percocet addiction developed during her ten years on the pro roller derby circuit. Carla skated under the derby name Ronda Rumble, first with the final matches of the Los Angeles Thunderbirds and later with Texas teams. Ronda Rumble's crowd-pleasing specialty was the "can opener." He'd seen her do it on some old footage she'd shown him.

At full speed she squatted like a compressed coil and threw a violent, upward torso check led by her forearm. It often sent a competitor airborne over the track barrier. The free gin came with the afterparties. The Percs soothed numerous injuries but continued well after she stopped skating. She hit bottom when an undercover Ventura County cop ended her run in an Oxnard bar where she was slinging gram bags of crystal to pay for her opioid habit.

Blake admired the way Carla had turned her life around. But she often went to extremes. She was always looking to "be of service." Always on the hunt for a new rehabilitation project, whether alcohol was involved or not.

Now he was her target.

"I'll swing by the pharmacy," she said. "Then you can pick up some clothes and we'll head over the hill."

"Carla, I'll be fine."

"What if you have a seizure?"

He turned to her. "I'll stick something in my mouth."

This time her eyes stayed on the road. "Oh, so is that why I haven't been getting laid? You been sucking your own dick?"

He laughed. He was surprised he did. He couldn't remember the last time he'd laughed. But he had to get her off this idea of staying at her place. Maybe if he gave her something to do.

"Look, I'll check in every couple of hours," he said, "Just like your pigeons do. And you can come by in the morning. Make me breakfast if you want."

"I've seen your fridge."

"Then bring me something good. Something organic."

She nodded, thinking about it.

"And maybe you could do me a favor right now."

"What's that?"

"Go into the drugstore and fill the script for me."

"Sure. But why?"

"Something like this, I'd prefer not to put it on the street."

Fifteen minutes later, the prescription bag in her lap, she pulled to the curb at his building off Sunset Boulevard. He leaned across the console and gave her a kiss on the cheek.

But she swung her door open and followed him inside.

She took out her cell phone as they walked into his apartment. "You're going to need a car," she said.

Soon, she was talking to the Enterprise Santa Monica office. He tried to give her his credit card. But she waved him off, insisting on paying. She was that way with money. Her late father had left her a generous trust fund contingent on her staying sober. Blake asked her to reserve a full size. When she finished with the rental, she went into the kitchen. She returned and handed him a glass of water. Standing over him, she held out her hand.

"One of these," she said. "Twice a day."

Blake stared at the small pink pill in her open palm. He picked it up. "Let's go get the car," he said.

She said, "A full size won't be available until tomorrow."

Her cell phone rang. When she turned away from him to answer, he slipped the pill into his shirt pocket but drank the water.

Carla paced as she talked. He could tell by her conversation it was one of her pigeons. When she circled back to the couch, still talking, she looked down at him, spotting the empty glass he was holding.

She smiled.

A couple seconds later she was at the door. She covered the phone with her hand and said, "A problem at the house. Call me."

He gave her a thumbs up.

And she was gone.

Blake waited a minute and then replaced the water glass with a cold Corona in the kitchen. He'd developed a headache. He briefly pressed the long neck against the base of his neck. Then he twisted off the cap, but it bounced off the mound above the rim of the kitchen trash can.

On his way to the refuse room with the cinched garbage bag he stopped by the floor-to-ceiling mirrors next to the elevator. He found himself staring at the guy looking back at him with a trash bag in his hand. He wasn't grey. And his age lines were not deep. But his eyes looked vacant. They reminded him of the look he'd seen in a hundred mug shots.

Blake dropped the trash in the refuse room, returned to his apartment, and plopped down in the chair at his desk. Carla was right. He wasn't expecting any calls. He hadn't even heard from his agent in two months. He was convinced his career took a dive when he turned fifty, when his agent still was booking weekly meetings. Most of the network executives who did the hiring were young women or gay men. He couldn't shake the feeling that he reminded them of their fathers, with all the emotional baggage that came with that.

"When's the last time you worked?" Dr. George asked earlier.

"An indie that never made it to the theaters," Blake said. "And I got fired."

"What did you do?"

"My job. Halfway through the shoot, the director asked me to show the lead how a cop cleared a room with a sidearm. The actor refused to learn trigger discipline. And then he wanted to brandish his pistol horizontally, gangster style. I told him he was being stupid and couldn't hit a parked Budweiser truck that way. The actor complained to the director. I was gone before they even filmed the scene."

Blake remembered what his agent said. "Eddie, the director said you weren't being collaborative."

"That's bullshit," Blake told him.

"This whole town runs on bullshit," his agent said. "You don't want to get the reputation of being *difficult*."

That was nearly two years ago. Blake had to downsize to a studio from the one bedroom he had facing the ocean when the money was good. He still had his Detroit police pension. But that didn't go far in one of the most expensive cities in America.

No work. Carla threatening to leave him. A trip to a shrink. And now his car was gone. Blake took a swig of the beer and thought, he might as well just give up. Vegetate on a couch and eat bad food until he dropped dead of a heart attack. That didn't sound that bad, actually.

It was a disturbing thought.

He reached into his shirt pocket and pulled out the pink pill, staring at it for couple moments. He remembered what Dr. George had said about one of his patients and the sunshine. He was in Southern California. And he hadn't noticed the sunlight either for months.

He popped the pill and chased it with the Corona.

And found himself thinking about Carla. She came on strong, but she had his best interests at heart. He wanted to call her. He'd forgotten to thank her. For the ride. For getting the script. For booking the rental car.

He reached for his land line.

Only then did he notice the red voice mail light blinking on the handset.

The message was short:

"Hello, this is Lindsay, Jason Perry's assistant. JP would like to set a meeting with you. Tomorrow. At his home. Two o'clock works for him. Please confirm. He wants to discuss a television project he has for you."

7

THE NEXT MORNING, BLAKE CANCELLED breakfast with Carla and booked an Uber, eager to secure wheels for his meeting with Jason Perry. He was feeling agitated. He looked at the sheet that came with the prescription. It confirmed that was a possible side effect. He also saw he shouldn't drink alcohol while on the medication.

The only full-sized vehicle on the rental lot was a white Dodge Ram pickup. He didn't mind a truck. In fact, he liked sitting high above the BMWs and Priuses that proliferated LA. But the pickup's white finish was a concern. In Southern California most Mexican workers drove white pickups. Movie people drew conclusions based on your wheels. And he had a meeting in the Malibu hills with one of the most ostentatious producers in town.

Jason Perry—or JP, as everyone called him—had built his career by attracting attention to his money and persona. Across three marriages, *People* and *Us Weekly* regularly tracked Perry as he dated beautiful film and pop stars. He promoted his movies on late-night talk shows and was regularly sought out for comment by the trades. He was a household name for a couple of decades, but in recent years his profile had shrunk to the inside pages of Los Angeles lifestyle magazines when event photographers snapped his picture at charity events.

JP also was the executive producer of the TV series that brought Blake to LA. But Blake rarely saw him on the set or in the writers' room. Still, the writers blamed JP for killing the show. They'd predicted the series would go a hundred episodes, which meant five years of steady work and residuals for everyone. But JP never read a single script. Rumor was he had dyslexia. So, JP made the showrunner come to his house to screen the first cut of every episode. Then he would give notes. Often an episode would have to be recut, or worse, new scenes shot. By the end of the second season JP was convinced his wife had the hots for the showrunner. It was a ridiculous notion, Carla said. The showrunner made well under a million a year. She said, considering the wife's tastes, this automatically disqualified him as a long-term threat. JP fired him anyway. The best writers followed the showrunner to another series. The network cancelled the show two episodes into season three.

As he steered the Dodge Ram through the curves on Kanan Dume Road, Blake decided JP was a big contributor to his failing Hollywood career. Despite that fast start, in the years since, he'd accumulated only a half dozen more credits on the Internet Movie Data Base, or IMDB, the website people checked to see if someone was the real deal or just a wannabe.

Blake decided, JP owed him. Today, he expected to collect.

A few minutes later, Blake wheeled the truck through the tight curves of Mulholland Highway, a two-lane road in the Santa Monica Mountains above Malibu. A mile later, he pulled the white Ram up to a stainless-steel gate at the foot of a long, steep driveway. He pressed the call button on the intercom, glancing up at a security camera aimed at the truck.

A woman answered and said, "*No bueno*. Gardeners go to the back gate."

And hung up.

Blake pressed the call button again. When she picked up, he said, "It's Edwin Blake. I have a two o'clock with Mr. Perry."

The gate slowly swung open, its electrical motor humming. Blake drove up the driveway, the house revealing itself on a meticulously landscaped lot as he came over a crest. The home was an ultra-modern design, an angular one-story structure of stone, glass, and steel—the kind of place that Blake thought would be as cold as a meat cooler in a Michigan winter. But it was the kind of house he expected for a player like Jason Perry. Blake parked on a stone turnoff, a good hundred feet away from a Bentley, a Ferrari, a Tesla, and a BMW parked on polished grey travertine in front of the garage.

A girl with red glasses and stringy hair greeted him at the door. She looked hardly out of college. She introduced herself as Lindsay, the assistant. "JP's in the living room, down the hall to the right," she said when he stepped across the threshold. "Would you like regular water or sparkling?"

"Do you have any coffee?"

"JP doesn't drink coffee."

He told her to bring whatever she had.

"Room temperature or chilled?"

"It doesn't matter," Blake said.

Blake walked down a long hallway, his boot heels clicking on a marble floor. He passed a well-appointed home office, a housekeeper dusting off its sculptural desk. Abstract paintings hung on one side of the hallway, lit by ceiling lights. He stopped momentarily to look at one, white canvas with little more than random brush strokes in black.

At the end of the hall, he turned right into a room that had glass walls on three sides, one with a distant view of the Pacific. At first, he thought he'd made a wrong turn. He saw a guy sitting on a modern, L-shaped white leather couch. He was wearing a hooded brown bathrobe and a pair of sheepskin Ugg boots, nothing above them but his hairy legs. His knees were spread, revealing black bikini underwear that covered his crotch.

"Excuse me," Blake said. "I'm looking for Mr. Perry,"

The guy glanced up. "Edward, right? Sit down."

Only then did Blake recognize Jason Perry, a quite different version of the producer he remembered from his cop show. JP's skin was pulled from a facelift. His hair was dyed dark brown and shoulder length, a style suitable for someone forty years younger playing in a heavy metal band. The shaggy cut appeared starkly at odds with an unkempt white beard that gave away JP's sixty-six years.

Blake sat in the only seat available in the minimalist decor—a pea green fabric egg chair. When he leaned back it surrounded his shoulders and made him feel like a captive. He slid forward and sat on its edge.

Blake said, "It's Edwin, Mr. Perry. My friends call me Eddie."

JP didn't look up. His eyes were riveted by a slip of paper he gripped between his hands. He said, "You know my wife, Corrina, we're no longer together."

"I seem to remember reading that," Blake said.

JP kept his eyes on the paper, explaining that Corrina was now seeing the owner of one of the world's largest hedge funds. When he looked up, he said, "Fucking guy is nearly ninety. Can you believe it? And get this, he comes over to her house last week. Sits on her couch in the house I paid for in Beverly Hills. And you know what he does? He shits his fucking pants. He literally loses control of his goddamn bowels all over a six-thousand-dollar couch."

JP held up the paper. "This is the bill."

"A bill?" Blake said.

"Five hundred and fifty-two bucks. I pay twelve grand a week to the woman. Alimony. And what does she do? She sends me the fucking dry cleaning bill. That corpse she's fucking has a net worth of six billion. But I have to pay to clean up his shit?"

Before Blake could think of an answer, the assistant Lindsay came in and handed Blake a Pellegrino. It was room temperature. When he reached for it, he noticed his hand was trembling. Another side effect. He left the bottle capped, concerned the sparkling water might spray all over the egg chair and a white cashmere rug on the marble floor. He stuck the Pellegrino between his legs and stilled the tremor by sliding his hand under his leg.

"So, what can I do for you, Mr. Perry?" Blake said. He wanted to get to the business at hand.

The producer ignored him, his eyes following Lindsay as she left. After she disappeared, JP reached into a small teak box on a low chrome coffee table and pulled out a hand-rolled smoke. He lit it, inhaled, and held in the draw.

"Medical," he said, exhaling. "Fucking ortho at Cedars says I need a hip replacement."

He held the joint out to Blake.

Blake smiled and said, "My hips are good."

The weed seemed to calm JP down. He tossed aside the cleaning bill and leaned back on the couch, spreading his legs even wider. "So, Edward, my people tell me you did some great work on my ABC show. Former top cop, huh? Originally from Detroit. Jesus Christ, I shot a 50-million-dollar feature there back in the day. The city is a fucking crime theme park. They ought to charge admission just to drive around." He took another hit and said, exhaling, "So whataya got going these days?"

"I'm looking at a couple of shows as soon as pilot season wraps," Blake said, using some industry jargon. Guys like JP thought you knew something if you knew the buzzwords. Blake also knew never to look desperate.

Producers like JP could smell desperation.

"Good. Good." JP said, nodding and taking another hit. He exhaled. "Home viewing. That's where it's at now. Fucking features are an international distribution game. All comic book crap—mindless bullshit kids watch in the States. And the Chicoms can't get enough of that shit. Nobody's making anything that will stand the test of time. I'm done with features. TV, my man. Cable or streaming. I've got something in play with Warner Brothers. Something *original.* A buddy cop show with a twist."

JP leaned forward. "How about this," he said, outstretching his hands, both thumbs up. "A tough guy detective takes on a convict as his partner. Oil and water. They can't stand each other. But they make one hell of a team."

"Reminds me of *48 Hrs.* with Nick Nolte and Eddie Murphy."

"It *is 48 Hrs.*, Edward. I optioned the goddamn thing. As a series. And, from what my people tell me, you're perfect for the inside cop stuff."

"When do you start shooting?

JP took another hit off the joint, shaking his head. "The writer hasn't written the pilot yet. He's in Vancouver, finishing up something for FX. But when he gets back, I want to hook you and him up. Like I was saying, you're perfect."

Blake began thinking a few things weren't making sense. The show idea was hardly original, but he wrote that off to the weed and JP's hyper salesmanship. However, any work for Blake would be months away. And even if it was at hand, a producer with his star on the Walk of Fame wouldn't have summoned someone of low stature like Blake to his home. Also, that morning, Blake had looked up Jason Perry on IMDB. He'd only done one movie in the past three years—a comic book movie. And it bombed.

"Mr. Perry," Blake said.

"Call me JP. All my friends do."

"JP, you have a beautiful home here. Very private. But remote. I'm just wondering, is there also something else you had in mind by inviting me here? Maybe a security issue?"

JP snuffed out the joint in a polished metal ashtray, leaned forward and pointed his finger at Blake. "I like you, Edward. You're a smart guy. My people said you were smart. Real smart." He leaned back on the couch, nodding, smiling, like Blake had said something profound. After a long pause, he said, "So tell me, when you were with LAPD, I presume you had to find people."

JP now getting both his name and where he served wrong.

Blake said, "You mean Detroit homicide. But yes, we had to find suspects, witnesses."

"How about people who did not want to be found?"

"Most of them didn't."

"Were you good at it?"

"The department thought I was."

"How did you do it?"

Blake leaned forward, crossing his hands and resting his elbows on his knees. "People leave a trail. They use a credit card. Or make a phone call. Get a parking ticket. You start with a big circle and shrink it down. You hit the street. Sit on a location. The scumbags on the run? They eventually always pay a visit to mom."

JP nodded, spreading his legs wider, the robe open, his junk bulging in the bikini underwear.

Blake forced his eyes elsewhere and came right out with it. "Mr. Perry, JP, exactly what do you need from me?"

"It's a favor," he said matter-of-factly. "Not for me. A favor for an old friend. Actually, *his* friend. From Chicago. That's where I'm from, you know."

"Seems I read about that, too."

"I came out here as a punk kid with nothing but a rusty VW bug and a suitcase. And now look at all this." He spread his arms, palms up, scanning the room and its view. "I think it's good when you give back, don't you? Especially me. I have no family, no heirs."

Blake nodded, doing his best to smile. Then he said, "Did you say a friend of a friend?"

"It's complicated," JP said.

Blake decided not to press him how the favor landed with him. He wanted to see where JP was going.

JP continued. "I guess it was one of those nasty divorces. Something I certainly can relate to. Wife takes the guy for everything. Takes his daughter, too. Then they move out here. The husband says his ex develops a drug problem. Falls in with the wrong crowd. And now she's disappeared. The daughter, too. He needs someone to find them."

Blake offered some standard advice: "The ex-husband should start by filing a missing person report with LAPD for both the mother and the child. Have him contact the juvenile division, too. It would be helpful if he had some paperwork from the court detailing their custody arrangement."

"I'm not sure he has time for that," JP said.

Blake said, "I can check around and find a good private investigator."

JP popped to his feet. "Fuck no. I hired one those assholes to check out one of my producing partners. And guess what? He ended up tapping my goddamn phone and selling information to my competitors. Do you have any idea what that did to my leverage?"

"But it's not about you, JP."

JP waved his right hand back and forth. "Doesn't matter. Everybody talks in this town. You try to do something for somebody. They twist it all around. Next thing you know, you're in the goddamn

National Enquirer. I need to hook this guy up with someone I can trust. Someone like you."

Blake knew it was coming. He said, "What makes you think you can?"

JP plopped back down on the couch. When he had Blake's eyes, he said, "Because, Edward, you'd like to get back to work."

Blake realized JP had looked him up on IMDB, too.

Blake thought about the proposal for a few moments. He knew it was something he could do. Work a couple of databases. Talk to some neighbors at the ex-wife's last known address. Routine stuff. But it could be time consuming. He said, "Something like that, finding these people, it could go quickly. Or it could take days. Even weeks. But it's not the kind of thing someone does without compensation."

JP said, "Like I said, this friend has no money."

"So, I guess that's on you then," Blake said.

JP looked surprised. "Edward, the studio hasn't given me any god-damn money. That doesn't kick in until we get a development deal."

Christ, Blake thought, skip tracing isn't industry work. But producers like JP were used to getting everything done on somebody else's dime. Blake thought, he's paying his ex-wife twelve grand a week and has a Bentley and a Ferrari parked on that travertine drive-way, but he wants me to go to work on the promise of a future deal? It was a typical Hollywood business proposal. Blake wanted to get up and walk. But that was his first thought.

He went with his second. Blake said, "This ex-husband, he's in Chicago?"

"He just landed at LAX." He pointed both index fingers at Blake. "Look, just go meet with the poor bastard. Go from there. What happens after that?" He held out his hands, palms up. "I'll leave that to you. If you're able to find her, hook the guy up with his family, let my assistant know. Better yet. I'll give you my cell."

Blake took a good look at JP. No longer magazine cover material. The guy waking and baking, stoned before mid-afternoon. He looked like a cross between a badly aging rocker and a Carmelite monk. In any other city he'd be considered a freak.

In a way, Blake felt sorry for him.

Blake said, "I suppose I could look into it."

JP jumped to his feet again. "Good. Good. Like I said, we all need to give back." He pointed at Blake, his thumb up, like his hand was a gun. "I'll tell you what I'm going to do. Associate producer's credit. When we go to series. You could even write an episode. They'll rewrite it, of course. But you'd be right there above the line with the other writers and the talent. Handle this, and it's no more below-the-line for Edward Blake," JP still getting his name wrong.

Blake asked, "Isn't creative consultant above the line?"

"You know what the hell I mean," JP said. "Do you have any idea how many careers I've made in this town?"

Blake didn't get a chance to answer or finally correct him on his name.

JP walked out of the room.

Blake remained in the chair, cradling the warm Pellegrino. After two or three minutes, he started to wonder if Jason Perry was even coming back. Finally, the assistant Lindsay entered, carrying a folio, saying she was going to show him out.

When they reached the front door, she pulled an envelope out of the folio and handed it to him, saying, "JP says everything you need is in here. Good luck."

Blake held out the bottle of Pellegrino. "Here, I never opened this."

Her eyes went to his hand. It was still trembling.

"Take it with you," she said. "It's on JP."

8

WARREN POOLE WAS PARKED AT a scenic turnoff, spot reading *Success Through a Positive Mental Attitude* by Napoleon Hill while intermittently checking out cars approaching on Mulholland Highway. He decided he wouldn't read the entire book. He figured it was more efficient to go the table of contents, find the material that interested him and read those sections. That way he could impress Dagney. She'd think he was being appreciative. And everything would flow from there.

One line in the book stopped him and made him think. It was a principle presented by the author, a way to adjust one's attitude. It went: *Within every adversity is the seed of an equal or greater benefit.*

Poole had seen his share of adversity in his fifty-four years. But the way he saw it, he didn't experience much benefit. Growing up in a one-bedroom flat with two sisters hadn't given him a head start. A month in a juvenile detention center woke him up long enough to graduate from high school. But when he told his father he was thinking about applying to a college, the old man said that was for rich people. The Marines bounced him out of boot camp after he objected to the DI calling him "Poole Tang" and broke his jaw with the stock of an M-16. After he turned a couple of grand running numbers for one of his uncle's pals, he stole a car and decided to drive to California to ditch those Chicago winters. He was eighteen. He never made it. Approaching south on the I-15, he saw the glow of Las Vegas, took an exit and lost his savings on a roulette wheel at the Sands. When he thought about it, maybe a few good years came out of that adversity. He stayed in Vegas after his uncle vouched for him and hooked him up with a crew. But by his mid-twenties the feds had cleaned up the casinos, all the ownership going legit.

Dagney had it right. Now he was mostly bottom feeding for the Russians: Collecting markers. Hammering pimps trying to poach their escort services. Snagging drops from corrupt vice cops. He'd done a half-dozen big jobs for the Italians over the years. Heavy stuff in Toronto and New York. But they were few and far between and carried a lot of risk.

Poole closed the paperback and looked out at the Pacific Ocean and the large Malibu homes dotting the hillsides below. He saw a young couple—they couldn't have been even thirty —coming out of one, pushing a baby stroller. He wondered how they could afford that kind of crib. He'd picked up a free local real estate magazine called *Diggs* and leafed through it at his hotel the night before. He saw cracker boxes in Santa Monica going for seven figures. He saw Malibu trailer park homes starting at a million. The Malibu homes like those on the hills below ranged from five to twenty-five million. He was pretty sure you needed more than an attitude adjustment to afford those cribs. You needed mommy and daddy to throw down. Or you were skimming with some sort of corporate scam.

The success book was bullshit, Poole decided—just as he saw the white Dodge Ram round the curve in his rearview mirror. He'd seen the pickup earlier when he was sitting on the property with the stainless-steel gate on Mulholland, the film producer's spread. He'd only caught a brief look at the driver behind the wheel.

Now the guy was on the move.

Poole tossed the paperback onto the passenger seat, waited until the truck entered the next curve. Then he pulled out onto Mulholland. A few seconds later he was following about ten lengths back. Maintaining that distance, he had to run a yellow after the Dodge turned toward the ocean on Kanan Dume Road. He followed another three miles, only pulling up directly behind the truck at the light on Pacific Coast Highway.

The heavy traffic made it easy for Poole to hide his tail on the coast highway. He was driving his silver Toyota Camry, nearly eleven years old. He had a Cadillac STS back in Nevada. But the Toyota was his job car. The color, the design lines, the ride didn't stand out. Driving, he looked like just another asshole grinding out a living trying to get from point A to point B.

By the time they reached the Malibu pier cars were bumper to bumper. Poole resisted the urge to pull alongside the truck and take a good look. But he also liked to get a read on somebody before he did a job. See where he lived. What he had going, especially on a job with as many moving pieces as this one.

Twenty minutes later, when the truck turned right off Sunset Boulevard onto a cul de sac with a three-story apartment building, Poole kept driving. He did a U-turn further up Sunset and came back to the cul de sac a couple minutes later. The white pickup was parked at the curb. Poole stopped, looked up at the apartment building, checking it out.

And saw the guy who he'd been told was named Blake. He was standing behind a floor-to-ceiling window on the second floor, a unit over the lobby doors. He seemed to be looking out at nothing in particular. A few seconds later he wandered away from the window.

Poole punched in the phone number he saw on a for-lease sign out front. A woman answered, identifying herself as the resident manager.

Poole said, "I was driving by and saw your building. What do you have available?"

She gave him a quick rundown of available two-bedroom units. Four to five grand a month, depending if you wanted a unit facing the street or with an ocean view. All utilities included. She had no one-bedrooms available. "They're in high demand," she said.

Poole said, "I like the one with the big window. The one over the entrance."

"Are you single?"

"Why do you ask?"

"It's only four hundred square feet. A studio. But it's rented. I can take your number—"

Poole hung up before she finished. And looked back up. The guy Blake standing there again, apparently lost in thought. A longneck beer dangled from his hand. The way he handled the bottle, the way he swigged it, reminded Poole of his old man, how he pulled on a cold one after swinging a hammer all day.

He thought, this guy Blake, fifty something. Nice neighborhood. But no house or condo. Not even a decent-sized apartment. Probably barely making his rent. That new white truck probably siphoning off a big piece of his monthly nut.

Poole told himself, let Blake do the grunt work. Then take care of business. Tag Dagney and then head back to Vegas. Drive after midnight when there was no traffic. He could do the three hundred miles in less than four hours.

He liked speeding through the desert in the dark.

9

EDWIN BLAKE BELIEVED YOU COULD get a good read on somebody if you met them at Philippe the Original instead of one of the pricy, pretentious restaurants in Brentwood or Beverly Hills. Find out if they liked a restaurant with some real character.

Located a block from Chinatown, Philippe boasted that it invented the French dip sandwich in 1918 when its French-born owner inadvertently dropped a sliced French roll into the roasting pan filled with juice still hot from the oven. The place looked as if it hadn't changed since it opened in 1908: A floor covered with sawdust. Communal dining on benches and long tables. People waiting in lengthy but fast-moving lines to get their sandwiches from women servers in old-school diner uniforms. And four oak phone booths. Blake speculated that they might be the only pay phones left in LA.

While they waited in line, Blake made light conversation with the ex-husband named Dale Rose, Jason Perry's friend of a friend. He was getting a feel for the clean-shaven guy with the small bald spot in the crown of his head. He was about five-ten and looked like he was his late forties or early fifties. He was wearing a pair of tan Dockers, Hush Puppies, and a polo shirt tucked in at the waist.

Standing behind him in line, Blake could smell his aftershave. He remembered that scent. It came in a green glass bottle with a pewter crown for a cap. He remembered trying it when he started shaving in high school. Royall Lyme, that was it. He was surprised it was still around.

Blake concluded Dale Rose looked like the kind of guy who got his hair cut for twenty bucks at a neighborhood barber shop and sold insurance at the Auto Club. He seemed harmless.

Rose said he was staying nearby at the Kawada, a budget hotel, another reason Blake chose Philippe. He took Blake's recommendation when they ordered. He got the French dip and a side of potato salad. Blake ordered the same with a lemonade. But Rose wanted a coffee. He couldn't believe a cup of coffee was listed at only forty-five cents on the large sign on the wall.

"Up until a few years ago it was nine cents," Blake said. "The *Times* actually wrote a story about it when they bumped the price. Called it the end of a tradition. But still under a half a buck, you can't go wrong."

They got around to what they were there for when they sat down.

"You see, Detective Blake," Rose said. "My wife, my ex-wife, Jackie, never had problems until she came to Los Angeles."

Blake said, "She wouldn't be the first."

He thought about correcting Rose. Tell him he was not a detective with a police department. Tell him he didn't even have a private investigator's license. But he decided not to burden the guy with details. Rose looked worried, or nervous. He was eating quickly between gulps of coffee. Blake also noticed he had a habit of frequently arranging his hair with his fingers over the bald spot, pushing it back so it was covered.

Blake asked him for a good description of his ex-wife and daughter.

"I have this." Rose handed him a snapshot of them both. "My daughter sent it to me back when we were in touch."

They were pictured standing in front of a formation of boulders. Blake saw a good-looking woman in her early forties, light brown hair, dressed in a pair of tight jeans and a halter top. The teenage daughter was dressed Goth—black jeans and black T-shirt that had the outline of a skull, the letters scrawled inside: DON'T LET THE BASTARDS GRIND YOU DOWN. She had dark lipstick, a ring piercing in her nose and a streak of purple hair that hung over one of her eyes. The girl didn't look happy. Or maybe she was just doing her best badass pose.

"I'd like to keep this," Blake said. "I'll get it back to you."

Rose nodded. "I was upset when Jackie took my daughter and relocated two thousand miles away. But I didn't have the money to challenge it in court." Rose pulled an envelope out of his pocket. "But I do have this."

He unfolded some stapled papers out of the envelope and pushed them across the table.

Blake looked at header:

STATE OF ILLINOIS
CIRCUIT COURT OF COOK COUNTY
DOMESTIC RELATIONS DIVISION

"I do have joint legal custody," he said. "I believe that lets me take my daughter if her mother is unfit."

Blake leafed through pages, just glancing at the legal jargon. He didn't want Rose to notice the twitching that still plagued his right hand.

Blake asked, "Let's back up a little. How do you know Jason Perry?"

"Actually," he said. "I've never met the man face to face."

Blake squinted.

"I was a bookkeeper. For a big Chevy dealership. The owner grew up with him. He always talked about the movies he produced. They'd hook up sometimes in Chicago. Sometimes in LA. But the owner sold the dealership and they laid me off. That was a year ago, right around the time the divorce was finalized."

"That's a bad year."

Rose nodded. "So, when I lost contact with Jackie, my old boss was the only one I knew who had connections out here. He put me directly in touch with Mr. Perry. But I've only talked to him on the phone. That's okay. He sent me you."

Blake wanted more details about his marriage and divorce.

"I met Jackie when she came into the dealership to buy a Cavalier. She was working as a bank teller when we got married. Everything was good until our daughter was born. She put on weight. It was no big deal for me. But it was for her. Then a couple years ago she found a way to take it off with this protein drink from a company called Herbalife."

"That's based out here."

"Right. Next thing I know, she's a distributor and is going to all these motivational meetings. Soon, she's telling me *I* wasn't motivated. That *I* was wasting my time as a bookkeeper and needed to develop a winning sales mentality like her. Start selling cars." Rose arranged his hair again with his fingers. "That's just not me. Our marriage went downhill from there."

"How did she end up in Los Angeles?"

"She was dead set on moving after she attended the Herbalife annual meeting out here. Funny thing, after she got money in the divorce, she stopped selling the stuff, packed up and left."

"She didn't get work in LA?"

"She had fifty thousand. Her share of the house."

"Friends or family? Any in California?"

"Her parents passed. No sisters or brothers. I checked with her aunt in Illinois. She hasn't heard from them either."

Blake said, "When exactly did you lose touch?"

Rose said Jackie's cell phone was disconnected a couple months ago. He said he recently called LAPD and asked them to do a health and welfare check at the address he had for her. "The police said she hasn't lived there for months. I also checked the Friend of the Court where I send her child support. They told me she was still receiving my payments through their direct deposit service. Beyond that, they wouldn't tell me anything more."

Blake handed Rose a small spiral notebook and asked Rose to write down his wife and daughter's full legal names, dates of birth and last known address. Rose also wrote down their social security numbers. The ex-wife's legal name was Jacqueline Margaret Rose. The daughter's name was Isabella, but friends and family called her Bella. She was thirteen years old.

Blake slid the notebook into his pocket and said, "Well, your ex-wife Jackie may not be missing. She may just not want to be found. Maybe she's just running from bill collectors. Fifty thousand doesn't go very far here."

Rose leaned forward, speaking in a quiet voice. "As far as I'm concerned, Detective Blake, my ex-wife is free to disappear. My daughter is my concern."

"When did you last talk to your daughter?"

"Jackie is a control freak. She took away Bella's phone. We'd email. But she hasn't answered me in weeks. The last one I got, she told me her mom was taking a lot of pills. Knowing Jackie, she probably monitored my daughter's email, read that one and shut it down. Jackie knows I'd come and get her. That's how I know she's avoiding me."

"What kind of pills?"

"I guess she got her breasts done by one of those Beverly Hills doctors you see on TV."

"That would cut into that fifty really quick," Blake said.

Rose nodded. "That's how it started. Painkillers. My ex-wife never could tolerate pain. She only knew how to dish it out."

Rose looked down, embarrassed, arranging his hair again. He looked up and said, "Can you find Bella, Detective Blake? I can only afford to stay a few days. And I need to take my daughter home."

Blake thought, Dale Rose calling him *detective* again. He decided to let him. He liked the way it sounded.

He always did.

10

BLAKE GOT RIGHT ON IT. Working helped him ignore the agitation he still felt from the antidepressant. He took Sunset from downtown and drove the five miles to Los Feliz to check out the last known address Dale Rose had given him for forty-three-year-old Jacqueline Margaret Rose.

The location was in an old LA neighborhood on a curved section of a street called Sunset Drive. Blake was familiar with the area. When he first moved to LA, he wanted to see Walt Disney's first Hyperion Avenue studio built in the 1920s. Nothing remained of the nearby studio but Walt's nearly century old Craftsman bungalow.

Blake parked the rental pickup on the street and took a couple dozen steps down to a small cottage-like guest house on the hillside below a larger home that bordered the street. When no one answered, Blake climbed back up and knocked on a neighbor's door. A hipster with short hair and a four-inch-long beard answered. He showed him the photo he got from Rose.

He shrugged. "I'd see them going to their car now and then. But we never really spoke. One day a small moving truck showed up and they were gone by that afternoon."

"When was that?"

"I don't know, man. Months ago."

Blake knew neighborhood friends were not easy to make in parts of Los Angeles. Unlike the older houses in Detroit that had porches, most LA homes offered little more than a door and a window where the blinds or curtains were typically drawn. Most Angelinos hung out on their backyard patios.

Blake was heading to his car when he saw a BMW pull up and park on the street. A dark-haired woman of maybe forty got out and went to the mailbox that belonged to Jackie Rose's former bungalow. She was looking through her mail when Blake approached.

"Excuse me. I'm looking for the woman and her daughter who used to live here. My name is—"

She interrupted, irritated. "Like I told the guy last night, I don't know the people who used to live here. I just moved here from Brooklyn. But here—" She thrust out a couple of letters. "Take 'em. I'm sick of schlepping their mail every day."

Blake looked at the envelopes, a bill from Nordstrom's and another from a dentist in Santa Monica. He looked up. "Do you have any more?"

The woman hadn't lost her New York attitude. "Do I look like I'm responsible for irresponsible people? Tell me, what kind of person moves and doesn't inform the post office? It's inconsiderate."

Blake nodded. "Absolutely, ma'am." Saying *ma'am* like he used to do when he was on the job. "I'd toss it, too."

She looked at him and seemed to soften. Maybe even seeing him as a detective now. "God," she said. "I must sound like a bitch."

"No," he said, "You sound like someone trying to get home in traffic."

"Oy," she said, glancing upwards.

Blake had noted what she said earlier. "You mentioned someone showed up here last night? Did he state who he was?"

"Yeah, came to my door. Ten o'clock at night. Looking for the woman. Said he was her ex."

Blake asked her for a description. She described Dale Rose.

She said, "He gave me the creeps. I didn't let him in."

Dale Rose never told Blake he'd been to the bungalow. He made a mental note to ask him about that. Blake said, "I'll make sure that doesn't happen again, ma'am. Make sure nobody bothers you again. LAPD was advised by loved ones worried about her welfare."

The woman's fingers touched her lips. "Oh, my God, you don't think she's been murdered or something, do you? Now I feel terrible. What happened, detective?"

"Blake," he said. Like Dale Rose, the woman assumed he was on the job. He hadn't worked the street in more than five years, but he'd instinctively fallen into his old persona and was speaking like a cop. People heard certain words like *ma'am* and *stated* and *advised* and it was as good as producing a shield.

Blake held up the two letters. "Look, I wouldn't be concerned. She's probably just trying to skate on her bills."

She waved goodbye when he drove way.

He drove a couple blocks to the closest commercial strip on Hyperion Avenue. He took an hour showing the Jackie and Bella Rose photo to clerks at Trader Joe's, a liquor store, and a consignment store called the Crossroads Trading Company, thinking maybe the girl Bella had outfitted herself there with vintage clothing.

He came up empty.

When he walked out of the consignment store, Blake spotted a discount drugstore across the street. A couple minutes later he stepped up to the female clerk behind the pharmacy counter.

"I'm here to pick up a prescription for Jacqueline Rose," he said.

The clerk's fingers went to a keyboard. "Date of birth?"

He had it memorized.

The clerk checked her computer and then walked over to a rack with prescription bags hanging on hooks. She returned with a small sack, dropped it on the counter and, looking in her computer screen again, said, "I don't see that anyone has been authorized to pick this up for her."

"Well, she's laid up," Blake said.

"Any other prescription, that would be fine. This is a controlled substance. And you have to present an ID."

Blake picked the script off the counter and saw it was for thirty, ten-milligram Percocet. He saw the name of a doctor in Culver City and committed it to memory. He suspected it was from a script mill. He'd check that out tomorrow.

He said to the clerk, "Well, she said nothing about that. When did she request the refill?"

She looked at her computer screen again. "Almost a week ago. Tell her she needs to pick these up sooner. We only hold a prescription for seven days."

Blake smiled and said, "I'm going to have her call you." He reached for his back pocket, as if he were looking for something. "I guess I left my phone in the car. I'll be right back."

He walked out and didn't return.

Blake decided during his drive back to the coast that this gal Jackie and her daughter were on the run. He thought, what addict doesn't pick up pharmaceutical quality dope?

In his apartment Blake sat down in front of his laptop and worked a couple of databases people used to find old classmates and lost loves. He found past addresses for Dale and Jacqueline Rose in Arlington Heights, Illinois. He found the address of the bungalow in Los Feliz but nothing more. He wished he had access to the law enforcement databases he used back when he was on Squad Seven.

He thought about calling a friendly contact he had in the Los Angeles Police Department, a detective named Paul Ricardo who worked in LAPD's Valley Bureau Homicide. He'd met the detective a couple years ago when researching LAPD's homicide procedures, which were different than Detroit's. He was working on the film where his advice to the lead actor got him fired. He thanked Ricardo by buying him dinner. They'd also met a couple of times for drinks. But he hadn't been in touch with him for months. And he would be putting the detective on the spot with what would amount to an illegal records search.

He decided to go for a swim instead. He changed into his trunks and walked out to his building's outdoor pool that overlooked the South Bay. He planned to swim fifty lengths freestyle, a half mile, which he tried to do three times a week. But he found himself losing count. He started thinking about Dale Rose. Wondering why he hadn't told him he'd visited the bungalow. Hell, he realized, he really didn't know anything about the guy. What if Rose had a sheet? Maybe he was obsessed with his ex, out for revenge. Blake had worked enough domestic homicides to know batterers could put on one hell of an act.

Walking back from the pool, Blake started questioning why he even took the job. He had few investigative tools. He could sniff out leads, pound the pavement, and talk like a cop. But it ended there. He couldn't get a warrant for phone or credit card records. He couldn't haul someone in and interrogate them in the box. In California, he couldn't even look up someone's vehicle registration, let alone quickly obtain an arrest and conviction sheet.

Back in his apartment he didn't even bother to take off his swim trunks. He sat down in his office chair and picked up the phone. It was 7 p.m., 10 p.m. Eastern. He knew his old partner still worked the second shift.

Al Henderson answered.

Blake said, "It's Eddie. I need your help on something."

Henderson said, "The family is just fine. And, yes, things are looking up in homicide. But it's goddamn ten degrees outside. Thanks for asking. I see you're still a decent guy cleverly disguised as an asshole."

"Yeah, I brought me with me. But don't tell anybody out here."

Hendo wanted an update. He always wanted one when they talked. Always asking about the weather. Always imagining Blake was walking red carpets, hobnobbing with big stars. He wanted to know if Blake had hung out with any of them lately. Blake told him it wasn't like that. He gave him the name of a well-known actress he saw buying a bathroom fixture in a plumbing store. He told him about a famous director he saw staggering drunk one night in Santa Monica's Third Street promenade.

That seemed to satisfy him.

Blake said, "Look, I'm doing a little side job as a favor. A guy looking for his missing ex. But I need to make sure he's legit, that he doesn't have a sheet."

Henderson launched into the by-the-book response. "You know very well, Eddie, that doing criminal background checks on the National Crime Information Center system and providing that information to unauthorized, non-law enforcement personnel is unlawful."

"How about this?" Blake said. "I'm a tipster. I call in and say I think a guy I know has fled to Detroit and I think he may have 86'd his wife. You'd run it then, wouldn't you? I sure as hell would."

"You're not six months from getting vested." The phone went silent for a few seconds. "Jesus Christ, Eddie. Name and DOB."

Blake gave him Dale Rose's name, adding, "I don't have a birth date. But he's mid to late forties. Maybe early fifties. Any hits likely would be in Illinois, Chicago area."

Blake waited as Henderson typed.

Thirty seconds later, he said, "Dale Lyle Rose. Age forty-eight." There were a few seconds of silence. "Only one entry of interest here, Eddie. His name showed up in the stolen vehicle file. Somebody jacked his car six years ago."

Blake was relieved. "Okay. I got one more."

"You're pushin'."

Blake gave him the name Jacqueline Margaret Rose, her date of birth, and the Los Feliz address. He listened to more typing, then silence, Hendo taking his time, no doubt reading entries.

"Interesting," Henderson finally said. "How long you been looking for this woman?"

"Only a day."

"Where's Ventura County? That close to you? The weather nice there, too?"

"It's an hour north. Up the coast. The weather same as here. C'mon, man. Whatya looking at? He says the ex has got a habit and she's got their kid. This guy Rose is frantic."

"I would be. She was arrested in Ventura County two days ago. Felony possession of a Schedule II controlled substance. Looks like you've found mommy dearest."

"You've got a current address?"

"You're slippin', Eddie."

"You're not making any sense."

"They pick her up. If it's anything like here, she spends the night in the station lockup. A day to transfer her to the main jail. Today is Friday. You know the drill. These judges and their precious half days on Friday. She doesn't have the kid."

"You don't know that. Make your point."

"She won't bond out until Monday, Eddie. Ten to one the gal you're looking for is still in jail."

11

Blake asked Carla, "How many times did you get locked up?"

Carla said, "Twice. When I was first arrested. Couple of days. Until I posted bond. Then, after my attorney made a deal with the DA, I pled out and served three months."

"Anything you couldn't handle?"

"The women's jail wasn't so bad."

It was Saturday night. They were sitting in Valentino, an Italian restaurant in Santa Monica. Pricey, Blake thought, but worth every dollar. Old school. Softly lit and quiet. A seven-course meal. No out-of-work actors trudging through their shifts, thinking about their next audition instead of getting an order right. Instead, journeymen waiters hovered on the perimeter of the dining room, anticipating every request. Blake wanted to do something nice for Carla for picking him up at the police station and hooking him up with the rental.

He also had an idea: a way Carla could help find thirteen-year-old Isabella Rose.

Henderson had most everything right. First thing in the morning, Blake checked the inmate directory for the Ventura County Pretrial Detention Center. Yes, Jacqueline Margaret Rose was still an inmate. And there was a bonus. Monday was President's Day, a court holiday. That meant she couldn't be arraigned and post bond until Tuesday.

Next, he called the twenty-four-hour hotline for Ventura's Child Protective Services and talked to a social worker there. He fabricated a police agency, saying he was with the Michigan Youth Services Bureau. He told the worker he was pursuing a lead about a runaway, making sure to pepper his request with bureaucratic jargon he knew social workers used. He asked if protective services had taken into protective care one Isabella Rose. He gave her date of birth. That's the way it usually worked. Mom gets popped. Social services picks up the kid.

The social worker said her agency had no record of the girl.

With Bella obviously parked somewhere, Blake figured he had two days before Jackie Rose got out, picked up her daughter, and disappeared again.

In the morning, Blake called Dale Rose. First, he asked, "Why didn't you tell me you showed up at your ex's old address?"

"I was hoping I'd get lucky," Rose said. "Avoid putting everyone through all this trouble."

"You want me to help you," Blake said. "You have to be straight up. Not leave out any details. Even if you don't think they're important."

"Okay," Rose said.

Blake told him he had good news and bad news. He'd located his ex. But he hadn't located his daughter.

"Where is Jackie?" Rose said.

He told him she was an hour away in Ventura County. "She's not going anywhere soon. She's in jail."

"My God."

"But your daughter, she's not in the system. Your ex probably left her with a friend or had someone pick her up. So, your best bet is to visit her at the correctional facility. Ask her where your daughter is."

Rose sounded frustrated. "No. No. No. She'll never tell me." The line was quiet for a moment. "Detective Blake, isn't there some way you can find out?"

Blake told him he'd get back to him.

After the call Blake popped one of Dr. George's pink pills and walked to the pool. Not to swim but to just sit. The tremor in his hand was gone. But he still felt agitated. Blake's first thought was to demand a day fee from Jason Perry. He figured he could be grinding away on the Rose matter for days. While he was at it, tell JP he could *give back* by throwing some bones to that poor bastard Dale Rose. But his second thought went to JP's associate producer offer. If that came through, the Writer's Guild scale was twenty thousand dollars a month. Sure, maybe he could squeeze a couple grand out of JP for the skip trace. But then JP might have second thoughts about hiring him for the TV series.

The math was a no brainer.

That's when Blake decided to take Carla to dinner. If he got her okay, he could finish the job in a couple of days. Not only take care of Dale Rose but show Jason Perry what he paid for when he hired somebody with law enforcement experience, someone who had some real moves.

Over the first few courses at Valentino, he told Carla all about Jason Perry and his promise of an above-the-line job. He told her about Dale and Jackie Rose and the missing daughter Bella. He told her about Jackie being in the Ventura County lockup until Tuesday.

Over dessert, he asked her how she liked the chocolate cheesecake.

"Fabulous. Want a bite?"

"Maybe later."

He eased into his proposal. "What I'm thinking, Carla, I'm

thinking I could wrap this thing up pretty fast if one of your girls got involved."

"They not girls, they're women."

"You know what I mean."

"No, you haven't defined *involved*."

"Look, I know you're protective of your pigeons. That one gal of yours, the one always asking me to hook her up with a job in Detroit. The fired former LAPD undercover cop."

"Veronica."

"Yeah, Veronica. I'm thinking she could go undercover into the jail. Get Jackie's confidence. You know, as a woman. Find out where her daughter is."

Carla said, "You mean visit her?"

Blake shook his head. "You'd have to be on her visitor list. Plus, this Jackie gal is going to be sketched out. A total stranger from the outside? She'll think the narcotics unit sent her."

Carla tilted her head. "I'm not following you."

Blake leaned forward, talking in a lower voice. "One time, when I was in homicide, we were getting nowhere on a drive-by. But we knew this inmate in the county lockup ran with the shooter. So, we had one of the undercover guys from vice arrested on a fabricated charge and he went to work on the dude inside. Became his pal. Found out what we needed."

Carla squinted. "Eddie, what are you trying to tell me?"

"I'm thinking Veronica and I hit some low rent bar up in Ventura. We argue, like a couple. She throws a shit fit. Hits me with a couple of things. Bar calls the cops. They arrest her. Domestic violence charge. And she's in. They can't arraign her until Tuesday. She gets a couple of days to get close to Jackie. Find out where the kid is. And then I go to the police and say I don't want to press charges." Blake held out his hands, palms up. "And just like that, your pigeon Veronica is out."

Carla took a bite of the chocolate cheesecake and then dabbed her lips with a linen napkin. She leaned back and said, "Eddie, even coming from you, that's the craziest idea I've ever heard."

Blake leaned forward again. "Trust me, Carla. It'll work. Veronica has the required skill set. After all, she keeps saying she wants to get back in police work. Every time I've seen her."

"You're not the police, Eddie. And Veronica is working on her first year."

"Meaning?'"

"Her sobriety comes first. She could get triggered in that environment."

"You even said it, Carla. You said jail wasn't so bad."

She laughed. "You're out of your mind. And I'm not saying I'm not nuts myself. The difference is: I know it. And if it were any other place than Ventura County, I might even consider it—for a minute."

"I don't get it."

She lowered her voice. "Eddie, that jail. That's where I did my time."

"Good. Then you can fill Veronica in."

"Yes, I could. But she's *not* going to get arrested. I'll handle it."

Blake winced. "An arrest? I would never put that kind of weight on you."

Carla smirked. "Nobody is getting arrested."

Blake leaned back in his chair. "Now *you* aren't making any sense," he said. He grabbed his napkin off his lap and tossed it on the table.

She rolled her eyes, then said, "Eddie, there's a great women's AA meeting in Ventura on Sunday afternoon. And it's always packed."

Blake frowned. "What the hell does AA have to do with any of this?"

She gave him a coy smile, took a fork full of cheesecake and held it out across the table, offering him a bite.

"Relax, Eddie," she said. "I'm saying I can walk right into the Ventura County jail—no questions asked."

Warren Poole parked on Pico Boulevard, across the street from Valentino, passing the time listening to a local talk radio guy. The host was asking callers whether they considered *geographic desirability* when they decided to date someone in Los Angeles. At first Poole thought the host was talking about hooking up with someone who had money and a nice home. Then he realized the host meant distance alone. One caller said he never took a girl out who lived further than three miles away because at the wrong time of day that could be more than a one-hour drive just to get laid.

Poole wondered how the hell anyone lived in this part of town. He never saw kids playing on the sidewalks, let alone in the streets. He never saw a white man mowing his own lawn. He figured the Mexicans had the lawn market cornered because the white man spent half his day behind a steering wheel with a cell phone to his ear. The outdoor cafes that looked so quaint in the movies were bombarded with fire truck sirens, honking horns, and traffic noise. You could lose a half hour just trying to find a place to take a piss. He rarely saw a fast-food joint or a gas station with bathrooms. Earlier that day, he'd pulled over on Wilshire in Beverly Hills looking for a john. He parked at a meter, tried two office buildings and found the bathrooms locked. So, he walked into a vegan restaurant and asked the maitre d' for the location of the head. The maitre d' said bathrooms were for customers only. Poole told him he had a choice. He could step aside. Or he could relieve himself in front of customers on his loud goddamn patio while they munched on their organic kale. When the guy hesitated, he pushed him aside.

Even parking, sitting on Valentino, waiting for the guy named Blake, was a major hassle. Parked at a meter, he had to move his car to another spot after an hour. When the time expired, he discovered the meter ate his quarters without registering more minutes. When he complained to a guy in a Prius who parked behind him, he told Poole the meters had electronic sensors. It wouldn't register time until he pulled out and another car pulled into that space.

A nearby sign indicated parking was free after 8 p.m. Poole looked at his watch. His time on the meter would expire in a minute, four minutes short of the free time. Earlier he'd spotted an Asian parking cop working Pico in her small, electric three-wheeled vehicle with the yellow flashers on top. Poole reached for the ignition, preparing to move. He glanced at Valentino.

And saw the guy Blake. Coming out with the gal he'd seen him enter the restaurant with almost two hours ago. Poole decided not to start the engine. He liked the Camry right where it was, dimly lit halfway between two streetlights.

Poole had more on the guy now: Edwin Blake, age fifty-two. Former Detroit cop. Trying to make a big score running with the Hollywood crowd. But he didn't have a name for the woman. She looked good. Nice hair. Nice posture. Nice black dress. Perhaps a little tall for his taste, he thought, but doable.

Poole watched Blake hand a call ticket to the restaurant's parking valet. Blake and the woman talking now, waiting for their car. Poole could tell by the way they held hands that they'd been together for a while.

Poole was thinking he should find out more about her.

Until he saw yellow flashers in his rearview mirror and the Asian parking cop behind him. She was standing next to her three-wheeler.

And writing him a ticket one minute before 8 p.m.

12

BLAKE BLASTED THE AC IN the Ram pickup as it idled in the parking lot of the Pre-trial Detention Facility, the jail for Ventura County located in Santa Paula. Twelve miles inland, the temperature was twenty-five degrees higher than at the coast and climbing into the high nineties. Earlier, he'd accompanied Carla into the visitors' waiting room, took one look around and said, "I'll wait in the truck." No way was he going sweat in the heat for two hours on a hard chair among the loved ones of felons and their unruly kids.

He wasn't sure Carla's plan would work. She'd explained that every Sunday there was an Alcoholics Anonymous meeting inside the jail for inmates. The sheriff allowed outside AA people attend to help the prisoners get straight. The department took a week to clear outsiders with background checks. But Carla already had a standing clearance. "I've been going there for years," she'd said. "It's a good reminder where I'll end up again if I relapse."

Blake had checked out the jail's website before they made the hour drive up the coast. The facility had four stories of cells, housing nearly nine hundred inmates. Only a fraction of them women segregated into their own cell block. Still, he seriously doubted Carla was going to connect with inmate Jacqueline Rose. But he had nothing to lose. If Carla wasn't successful, he planned to show up in the courthouse on Tuesday and then tail Jackie if she made bail.

Fifteen minutes into Carla's visit, Blake dozed off in the truck, the white noise of the engine and the air conditioning transporting him into a vivid dream. He found himself in the office of Dr. George, this time the shrink dressed in a Detroit Police uniform. Telling him he had to find his car. Telling him the car had his .45, his Chief's Special. Telling him if meds were ineffective, the pistol was an option. Giving him directions on a prescription pad, recommending he hold the pistol to his temple, not under his chin. Blake told him he already knew that. He'd investigated gun suicides. A shot under the chin only blew off a victim's face. Failing to get the job done.

The passenger door snapped open, startling Blake awake.

Carla entered, excited. "What a great meeting." She slid into the seat.

Blake rubbed his eyes. He was breathing heavily.

Carla said, "You okay?"

Blake nodded. He felt like he needed a cigarette, though he'd quit smoking a year after moving to California.

"You sure?" she said.

"Just a dream."

Carla looked at him for a few moments, then switched gears. She began gesturing wildly. "There was a girl in there who took a nine-month chip. She was sentenced to serve 364 days for embezzling to feed her habit. But get this, she was grateful she had a couple months left. She wanted to stay so she could sponsor newcomers she was helping on the inside."

Blake gripped the steering wheel, steadying his left hand. He put truck in gear with his right. "So, I guess you came up short."

Carla reached into her handbag and handed Blake a pamphlet with the title: Is AA For You?

"Take this," she said.

"All these meetings, now you think *I* have a problem."

She rolled her eyes. "Inside, Eddie. The last page."

He kept his foot on the brake and looked. The last page had a place for phone numbers. He saw an address in Sherman Oaks scrawled on the dotted lines.

Carla had a cocky look. "I memorized it. I wrote it down after I got out of the control center. They don't allow you to take a pen inside. That, Eddie Blake, is where her daughter is."

"Jackie Rose was in the meeting?"

"No, Eddie, I'm going to hang a neon sign in my window and turn a few bucks as a psychic. Yes, and in bad shape. Detoxing. She only came to get out of her cell. Lot of women do that. But after hearing people share, she got the gift of desperation."

"Gift?"

"That's what we call it. It's what brings people into the rooms."

Blake didn't know what excited Carla more. Scoring the address. Or Jackie Rose wanting to get clean. He let her go on for a couple of minutes. Then he probed her for details.

"We talked for a good fifteen minutes after the meeting," Carla said. "She really opened up. I didn't even have to ask. She wondered if I could get a message to her daughter. Let her know that she was in jail."

"She didn't know you get a phone call?"

"She thought the jail phones might be bugged."

"She's right."

"Eddie, she left her daughter with her dealer. That's his house in Sherman Oaks."

"Great maternal instincts," Blake said.

Carla gripped his arm. "Eddie, don't take the coast. Go back on the 101. We can swing by that address on our way back. Her kid must be frantic."

Blake turned onto Todd Road, heading toward the Santa Paula Freeway. He had no plans to merge onto the 101.

He said, "She say how she got popped?"

"The dealer was going to cut her in if she picked up a thousand tabs of oxy from his supplier up here."

Blake nodded. "Why risk the run when you have a mule with lipstick."

"Then, of course, she taps her cut before she drives back. Gets wasted and gets pulled over by a traffic cop for going too slow on the freeway. He found the stash in her car."

"Did the narc unit flip her?"

"They tried. But I guess she kept her mouth shut. She was worried they'd take her daughter from her."

"They'll do that anyway. As soon as they find out her dealer was moonlighting as her sitter."

"But I told her if she made some smart choices, her problems could go away. I told her to ask her public defender to request drug court. A judge will order her into treatment. She'll get probation. If she stays clean, she'll end up with no record and eventually her daughter. I told her I'd be there for her in court on Tuesday."

"Next you're going to tell me you're going to post her bail." Blake thought, that was Carla. Agree to a request, complicate it, and turn it into a mission. He knew he had to be careful about the way he told her what he was planning. He said, "We can swing by the dealer's house, Carla. But that presents a problem."

"It will only take a minute."

"Think about it. This dealer doesn't know who the hell you are. Neither does her kid. And you have no idea what you could be walking into. We hit a lot of dope houses on Squad Seven. These people are inherently paranoid. In my experience, they cover their windows with newspapers and keep track of the world outside through a peephole."

"You could go in with me."

"Not unless I have a crew with a ram."

She crossed her arms and looked at him. He kept his eyes on the road. "Eddie, I gave Jackie my word."

"In a way, you'll be keeping it."

"How?"

"Her father will tell the kid."

"You're going to let him get her?"

"That's what I was hired to do."

"Then what?"

"Like you were saying, the court will work it out. She'll be safe with her dad. The guy is as square as they come. When Jackie gets on the straight and narrow she'll get her daughter back."

Blake saw the entrance to the 101 ahead. When he stopped at the light he looked over. "Carla, think about it. She left her kid in a dope house."

"You know I never did like cops. You guys have all the answers, don't you?"

"Ex-cop. But go figure."

Still, she wouldn't let it go. Blake was hoping he could find a compromise.

"We'll do a dry run," he said.

Forty minutes later, they turned onto an oak-lined residential street in Sherman Oaks that ran parallel to Ventura Boulevard. As Blake slowly drove by the dealer's house, they saw a grey, redwood-sided ranch home, its lawn well kept. Not a tagged, dilapidated crack house on a barren lot like the ones Blake was used to seeing as Detroit drug dens. They saw a family neighborhood with SUVs and minivans parked in driveways and along the curb.

"The guy has a white-collar thing going," Blake said as he turned back onto Ventura Boulevard. "A lot of pill pushers have middle-class buyers, Carla. Makes sense he was supplying Jackie."

"All the more reason we knock on the door," she said.

"Still not a good idea," he said.

She was silent as they drove to her house in Studio City. Blake wanted to drop Carla off at her sober living. He wanted to call Dale Rose and give him the address. Then he wanted to call Jason Perry and tell him mission accomplished.

He pulled up to Carla's house and parked.

"No, Eddie," she said. "I'm keeping my word. We have to go back."

He clenched his jaw. His first thought: smack her in the face. Tell her to get with the program—*his* program. He was surprised that came up as an option. He didn't know if it was the antidepressant or the fact Carla was being such a pain in the ass— or a combination of the two

He'd never laid a hand on a woman.

He took a couple of deep breaths, his hands gripping the steering wheel. "Look, Carla. I appreciate everything you've done. And I know your word means a lot. It's what I love about you." His second thought finally came. "So, I've got an idea. We can go back. But this truck is going to draw eyes. We'll need to take your car."

A half hour later, they were back in the neighborhood in Sherman Oaks. Blake parked Carla's Mini Cooper at the curb down the street from the dealer's house. During the drive over he'd called Dale Rose and told him he had an address, adding that his ex-wife had left his daughter with her dealer and he ought to pick her up as soon as possible.

"I'm on my way," Rose said.

Fifteen minutes passed, Carla watching the house for a while, seemingly satisfied she would soon see the girl picked up by her dad. She began fielding texts from one of her pigeons. Blake was quiet, still rattled about his impulse to smack Carla. Any more thoughts like that he planned to call Dr. George and tell him the antidepressant wasn't for him.

Blake reached for the truck's radio. KJZZ had a blues program on Sundays. Before he could adjust the volume, he spotted Dale Rose.

On foot and alone. Turning the corner on the sidewalk from the next cross street.

Blake switched off the radio. "Carla, check it out."

They both watched Rose walk the half block to the door of the ranch house. He pushed a doorbell, his weight shifting from foot to foot as he waited. Then he knocked.

Nobody answered.

Rose turned around, glancing up and down the street. He never focused on the Mini Cooper, which Blake had tucked in behind an SUV. Finally, he walked across the front lawn and disappeared in a pathway on the side of the house.

Ten minutes passed.

Carla said, "Eddie, this is taking too goddamn long. You need to go in and see what's going on."

Blake's first thought was she was right. But his second thought was that still was ill advised. What was he going to do, anyway? He had no authority. And if things went sideways, he didn't even have his sidearm anymore.

Blake was about to explain his reasons when he saw the front door open and Dale Rose emerge with the girl he recognized as Isabella Rose. She was dressed in black jeans and a sleeveless black T-shirt, the same kind of punk garb he'd seen in her photo. When they reached the sidewalk, Dale Rose gently placed his hand on her shoulder, guiding her in the direction from which he'd come.

Thirty seconds later, they disappeared around the corner.

Blake put the Mini Cooper in gear. "See? All good. We're all done here."

Carla looked at him. "No, we are not. You're going to Ventura with me Tuesday to pick up Jackie. The county impounded her car."

Blake didn't want to do that. He wanted to be done with Dale and Jacqueline Rose.

"Give me one good reason," Blake said.

"Cause you're the guy with all the answers."

"I didn't know there was a question."

"A big one, Eddie. Maybe you can tell me how I'm going to explain all this to Jackie."

"Explain what?"

"How her ex happened to show up and snatch her kid."

13

SUNDAY NIGHT HE SWAM FIFTY lengths of the pool in the dark. The temperature had dropped to the low fifties. The eighty-two-degree pool felt like bathwater. He liked swimming toward the pool light. It gave him the feeling he was in a different dimension. Away from the hassles on dry land.

Blake decided not to call Jason Perry. He figured Dale Rose would probably call JP anyway. Let Rose deliver the news and give JP the opportunity to call Blake and say job well done. Not look so eager to prove himself to the producer.

He spent Monday alone. He watched the original *48 Hrs.* and jotted down some script ideas. He didn't take another swim. Instead, he walked the hiking trail up Temescal Canyon. At the top was a place for a small waterfall. But the winter had been arid. The creek bed was dry.

JP never called.

He picked Carla up on Tuesday morning. He'd worked out what she should say. "You keep it simple. Say we went to the house. But the girl must have called her father. Because he was there picking her up. End of story. You start going into any detail, you'll get tripped up."

During the drive to Ventura, Blake noticed his hand had stopped twitching. He no longer felt agitated, even after they parked the courthouse and Carla said, "I don't like being dishonest, Eddie."

"What's dishonest?"

"What I'm leaving out."

Blake glanced over. "Look, I just asked you to try to get some information. The rest of this is on you. Okay, I get it. You want to help this gal. But just how do you think you're going to do that, how this is all going to go over, if you lay out what really went down? That you had a role in turning her kid over. Her daughter is in much better shape with her dad than being shuttled off to foster care."

Carla said nothing. Blake hoped she got the message.

The woman who stood before a Superior Court judge looked quite a bit different from the suburban mom Blake had seen in Dale Rose's snapshot. She was slimmer, with the exception of breast implants that were visible even in her baggy orange jumpsuit. Her hair no longer was light brown, but a bright, beachy blonde. She appeared dazed. Her eyes remained mostly on the floor as she shuffled handcuffed to the front of the bench from the jury box where a half dozen other defendants in their jumpsuits waited for arraignment.

Her public defender asked that in lieu of a plea she be referred to the drug court.

When the magistrate asked Jackie Rose if she had anything to say, she asked in a barely audible voice if she could have her car and cell phone back. The assistant DA stood up and said the phone was evidence and the car had been impounded under the narcotics seizure law.

The magistrate sided with the prosecutor. Then he released Jacqueline Rose on personal bond and set her drug court hearing in three weeks. The bailiff led her to the back of the room where she disappeared through a door.

An hour later, Blake and Carla were back at the jail in Santa Paula, waiting in the parking lot. Soon, Carla spotted Jackie walking out of the main entrance. She was dressed in heels, skintight black slacks, and a sheer white blouse. She was carrying a brown paper bag.

"Poor thing," Carla said. "They must have seized her purse."

Blake knew if they'd found the drugs in her handbag, police were likely holding it as evidence as well. Blake figured the paper bag contained her ID, her jewelry, and probably a toothbrush the turnkeys gave her for her jail stay.

Blake drove the Dodge Ram to the curb. Carla stepped out and met Jackie fifty feet away on the sidewalk. He watched them talk for a few moments. Then Carla grabbed Jackie's hand and pulled her quickly toward the truck. Blake didn't like the panic he saw in Carla's step.

The two women piled into the truck.

"Hello," Blake said to Jackie as she slid in next to him on the bench seat.

Carla said, "Tell him, Jackie. Tell Eddie what you just told me."

Blake looked over at Jackie Rose. She seemed out of it, staring straight ahead. He could smell the jail in her hair: a mix of body odor, cooking grease, and cleaning fluids.

When Jackie didn't answer, Carla said, "Eddie, whoever picked up her daughter wasn't her husband."

"You mean her ex-husband," Blake said.

"He wasn't her *ex-husband*, either."

"How do you know that?"

Jackie blinked and said in a quiet voice, "My husband was killed four years ago in Afghanistan."

Blake had to resist speeding on the 101 to Sherman Oaks. He didn't need to be convinced to go to the dealer's house. He had more questions than the women did.

While Carla kept reassuring Jackie everything was going to be okay, Blake dialed the cell phone number of the man who claimed to be Dale Rose. The number was no longer in service. He wanted to get JP on the phone. Ask a lot of questions. But he knew he would have to do that later, out of earshot of Jackie and even Carla. At this point, Carla was too involved. Instead, he channeled his anxiety into questions for the woman sitting between them.

"Is there anyone who would want to abduct your daughter?"

Jackie shook her head.

"How about a neighbor? A friend?"

She shook her head again.

"*Anyone* you know?"

When she shook her head again, he said, "Did they cut out your tongue in jail?"

"No."

"Anyone you owe money?"

"No."

Carla, disregarding Blake's advice to keep things simple, revealed she and Blake had seen the man walk Bella to his car. She told Jackie that her daughter didn't seem to be leaving against her will. Carla described the man.

Blake asked, "Do you know anyone who matches that description?"

"No."

Blake wasn't sure if Jackie was in shock, still detoxing, or just being evasive. He looked over at Carla.

Carla said, "We get to the house, you've got to go in with her."

Blake nodded.

Carla squeezed Jackie's hand. "Eddie used to be a detective. He'll help you get to the bottom of this."

Blake wanted to slap duct tape on Carla's mouth. He expected a flurry of questions from Jackie he wasn't prepared to answer.

Instead, Jackie said in a soft voice, "Okay."

Blake shot Carla a look. She finally shut up.

They rode largely in silence for the next half hour, Jackie softly crying a couple of times, Carla handing her tissues and rubbing her back. The stillness made the drive seem longer. Blake wanted to turn on the radio, listen to anything that would turn off his thoughts. But that seemed inappropriate considering the traumatized mother sitting next to him. After he considered all the possibilities, he decided he'd go to the ranch house and see if there was some plausible explanation. If there wasn't, this woman Jackie Rose could go to LAPD. Let those big city dicks figure it all out.

Either way, he was done with this job.

When he turned the corner on the residential street in Sherman Oaks, Blake noticed a few people standing around on the sidewalk. He saw neighbors talking to each other in front of their homes. An approaching SUV blocked his view of the dealer's house ahead. After the SUV passed, Blake saw two LAPD black-and-whites parked along the curb. Closer, he also saw a parked Crown Vic, silver with half-moon hubcaps—a detective's car.

"Eddie, something's going on," Carla said.

Blake glanced at Jackie. She was emotionless now, staring straight ahead.

As he drove closer, Blake was thinking a narcotics crew had probably popped the dealer. He thought that until he was a couple houses away and saw a white van with a blue stripe across the length of its side panel. It was parked in the grey ranch house's driveway. As they passed Blake saw the Los Angeles County seal and blue letters on the van's back door:

CORONER

"Why do you think the police are here, Eddie?" Carla asked, urgency in her voice.

"Somebody is dead," he said.

He felt his hand tremble on the steering wheel. He didn't think it was from the medication.

14

ON ONE HAND, WARREN POOLE was pleased, deciding his impersonation of frantic father Dale Rose went off without a hitch. But the job hadn't gone entirely as he expected. The kid was traumatized when he found her. She'd been practically catatonic. Wouldn't eat. Wouldn't talk. Wouldn't even question why he had her. She spent the night with the covers pulled over her head.

But now she was glaring at him, asking questions, her arms crossed, sitting in a chair at the opposite end of his hotel room in Studio City.

He came up with a story.

Poole said, "Like I tried to tell you yesterday, all I know is your mom was arrested. She's in jail. I don't know when she's getting out."

"Why don't you know?"

This is where the story came in. "The agency calls me. I do what they tell me. They told me to pick you up. Take care of business. Do whatever it takes to assure you're safe. The other details, that's not my area. But I have to say, if you were my daughter, you'd have never been in that situation. You're lucky I showed up when I did."

He took a good look at her as she thought about his words. He decided she had the potential to be an exceptionally cute thirteen-year-old blooming in puberty. But the kid was doing her level best to hide it with the color black. Especially that spiky black hair with its distractive purple streak in the front.

The kid finally said, "So, what, you're some kind of private investigator?"

He half smiled. "I'm just the guy they call when people need something done."

"My mom called the agency?"

"Or she called her attorney. And the attorney called the agency. Like I said, I don't get those details."

The kid's eyes were piercing. "Did the agency tell you to take me to your hotel room?"

Poole waved his hands in front of him. "Hold on now. Have I touched you? It's not like that. I'm waiting for a call. Waiting to find out where I'm supposed to take you."

The kid named Bella stood up. "I want to go home."

"Where's home?"

"Our apartment. It's not far. I want to change."

She turned toward the door.

"You walking?"

"No. You're going to take me. But first I gotta pee."

The kid, he decided, was going to be a problem. No surprise, considering her mother, considering the situation in the ranch house in Sherman Oaks. Her attitude reminded Poole of when he was sixteen, how he'd spent a month in the Cook County Temporary Juvenile Detention Center for taking a new Corvette off a Chevy lot for a joyride. He remembered how the ward officer used to control juveniles incarcerated for everything from rolling rock to murder. He remembered how the officer always gave a defiant kid a choice.

Poole remembered how well that worked.

When the kid came out of the bathroom, Poole said, "So, you want to go to your place?"

She stood just inside the doorway, the purple lock of her hair hanging in front of her left eye. Looking at him like he didn't know shit about anything. "That's what I said, didn't I?"

Poole shrugged. "Sure. We can do that. You can pick up some clothes. Or even stay there if you want. But considering the charges against your mom, the place will probably be under surveillance. You show up? You'll be taken downtown. They'll put you in a tiny room and ask you a lot of questions." He let that sink in for a moment. "Next thing you know, you'll be in the system. They ship you off to a juvenile facility. Or temporary foster care where you bunk with a bunch of smelly poor kids you really don't want to know."

She took a couple of steps away from the door.

He shrugged again. "Or you can stay here. Get something to eat from room service. Use the whirlpool downstairs. Chill out. Meanwhile, I'll wait for my call."

Poole got up and snatched his car keys off a small desk, like he was ready to drive her home. "Makes no difference to me. It's your choice, kiddo."

She didn't want to go to her mother's apartment, a place called the Oakwood Apartments on Barham Boulevard near Warner Brothers Studios. Poole was familiar with the temporary housing chain where you rented a month at a time. There was an Oakwood in Las Vegas. Neither did the kid didn't want to get room service or use the whirlpool.

She wanted to go to In-N-Out Burger on Ventura, only a mile or so from the hotel.

She ordered a double cheese, with a strawberry shake and fries. Poole ordered a double as well with a Coke. They had In-N-Out in Vegas, too. He told the cashier he wanted his "animal style" where they grill the mustard right into the patty and add extra pickles.

"Gross," the kid said. But at least she was talking.

After they picked up their order they sat down in a booth where somebody had left a *Hollywood Reporter*.

Halfway through the double, Poole opened the entertainment trade magazine.

"That's rude," the kid said.

"What?"

"Reading when you've taken someone to lunch."

"I didn't take you to lunch. I got you something to eat."

Poole folded the publication and slid it into his windbreaker. "You need to talk? About your mom? About what happened?"

"Do you?"

"I'm just the guy who got you out of there." He took another bite out of his burger and said, "Why don't you tell me a little about yourself."

She looked at him through the lock of hair. "What, that my life has been declared a disaster zone? That's obvious, isn't it?"

Poole wasn't sure what to say. He noticed a silver chain that disappeared under her T-shirt. "What's that? Around your neck."

"It's my medallion."

"Can I see it?"

She lifted it out from under her shirt. The medallion was black and tarnished silver, depicting what looked like an octopus with wings. "A friend of mine bought it for me in Venice. It's a creature that's supposedly sleeps at the bottom of the sea. It's supposed to awaken at the end of the world."

"Never heard of it."

"My friend read about it in a story. By H. P. Lovecraft."

"Never heard of him, either." He took the last bite of his hamburger, nodding. "But it fits. It's you."

She half-smiled. The first smile he'd seen from the kid. He got to thinking, remembering what Dagney and the Napoleon Hill book she gave him said. About the invisible medallion. On one side was a negative mental attitude, the other side, positive. He decided to try that. Display a positive mental attitude to the kid and see if it worked. See if it resulted in a positive response.

He pushed his tray aside. "Look, as for your situation? Trust me. Nothing looks good for a while. I had my share of problems when I was young." That was true; the next part, not so much. "But what's great? There's plenty of time left. Everything changes with time. I had some rough years. But in time life got good. Yours will, too."

She picked up one of her fries, twirling it between her fingers, her eyes on the table. "I want you to know I tried to get out of there. That guy. He was okay for the first day. But then it got weird. He locked me in the bedroom."

Poole picked at his teeth. "He was a loser. Like I was saying, you're going to be okay."

Her eyes remained on the table.

Poole wiped his lips. "Look, I'm sure your mom really cares about you."

"You don't know that."

"If she didn't, her people would have never sent me."

"She thinks I don't know. But I do. She said he was just a friend, some guy she met online. She said she was going for a job interview. But that was a lie. I wanted her to get some help. I tried to call her sister back in Chicago. But she found out and took my phone."

Poole was feeling good how this was all going. Maybe there was something to this invisible medallion thing. He decided to play it out.

"You're from Chicago?" he asked.

"Near there."

"I left when I turned eighteen."

"Chicago?"

"Near South Side. Came out here and found work in Las Vegas."

"In a casino?"

"Driver at first. I drove a lot of important people around."

"Movie stars?"

"Sometimes. Rock stars, too. Mainly businessmen."

She looked dejected. "I kept asking to go there. After I found out it wasn't that far. But my mom always had other plans."

"Your age, they're not going to let you gamble."

"I wanted to see the Cirque du Soleil. My dad took me when it came to Chicago. But I was little. I heard it was a different show in Las Vegas."

"You'll get there someday. Maybe soon."

"You sound sure."

"In time, like I was saying."

"But my mom."

Poole gathered their empty cups and paper containers, stacking them on his tray and sliding the kid's tray under his. He stood up.

"I'm betting she'll get some help."

"What makes you say that?"

"Jail. Sometimes that's the best thing that can happen."

The kid looked up, frowning. "Seriously?"

"You bet," Poole said, "It's a wakeup call."

On their way back to the hotel they stopped at a Ross Dress for Less on Ventura Boulevard. She picked out underwear, a pair of black jeans, two black tops and a black hoodie, plus a black backpack to put it all in. Poole considered the 120 bucks and change a good deal. The In-N-Out. Their talk. The new clothes. He liked that she was pacified and cooperative.

Back at the BLVD hotel he sat in a chair near the window, listening to her run the shower. He wasn't waiting for a call, as he'd told her. He was supposed to *make* a call. Tell the guy who hired him he had the kid. All that was left to do now was to deliver her, pick up ten thousand, plus another thousand or so in expenses. He'd put in five days. Two thousand a day. That was his rate for a clean job.

But the job was no longer clean.

His deal didn't include leaving a body. He wasn't sure he had all his bases covered. And he wasn't entirely sure about the kid. She could complicate things down the road, long after he left town. He was thinking, minimally, he'd double his rate. To get it, he decided to make the guy who hired him wait a while. That way, in his experience, he'd be relieved when he finally called. Be excited and more likely to pony up.

He had time. He had the kid under control. She wasn't going anywhere.

Poole plopped on the bed and opened the *Hollywood Reporter* from the In-N-Out. He read about movies that were doing well and a couple big budget films that debuted as box office bombs. He read about movies that were planned, a good number of them remakes of old films, others based on comic book characters. He wondered if Hollywood ever was going to make anything that was worth a damn anymore. He liked the old films on Turner Classic Movies he watched while killing time in hotel rooms. Edward G. Robinson crime films like *Little Caesar* and *Key Largo*. Or Bogart, the way he lit a cigarette, and even better, the way he'd always toss a smoke away on the pavement. They were men who wouldn't be caught dead in a superhero costume or playing lead in yet another Hollywood remake.

Poole turned the page to the section about the television business. He saw the headline:

Jason Perry Inks Multi-Million Deal with Warner's TV

The story said the producer was turning the film *48 Hrs.* into a TV series. The studio had also optioned several of his most popular past films so they also could be adapted. Poole shook his head. Another producer adding to the pile of remakes. But that's not what got his full attention.

The news that the deal was worth $10 million did.

Poole heard the shower turn off, the kid getting herself together in the bathroom. He glanced out the window, the cars bumper to bumper on Ventura Boulevard.

Poole began thinking how it was going to go when it came time to collect. He remembered how the guy who hired him detailed his elaborate plan. He remembered him complaining that he had limited funds. He remembered thinking that that didn't square with the guy's crib.

It wasn't a clean job.

He was thinking about that when he remembered the line in the book:

Within every adversity is the seed of an equal or greater benefit.

Ten million bucks.

Warren Poole tossed the *Hollywood Reporter* aside. He decided he needed to put a new plan together. When he had it all worked out, he'd make the call to the guy who hired him—the producer with the big studio score. The producer with the stainless steel gate and the large house on top of the hill.

The 10-million-dollar man who liked to be called JP.

15

AFTER HE SAW THE CORONER's van, Blake started thinking like a working cop. His first thought was to turn around and park. Tell Jackie Rose to go inside. Have her tell the detectives that she'd left her daughter there five days ago. Tell them that a stranger picked up her daughter and now she was missing.

Blake spoke a few of those directions, but Jackie didn't respond. She was doubled over with stomach cramps, moaning and shaking her head, her eyes turned inward as if she were trapped deep inside herself.

Blake said, "Look, I'll go in with you."

She kept shaking her head.

Blake turned to Carla. "If this is any kind of violent crime, a neighborhood like this, police will want to solve this quickly before residents and the local city councilmen are all over their asses. They'll start pulling threads. Trust me, she's better reaching out to them now before they figure out a kid was there and start hunting for her mother."

Hunt for all of us, Blake thought. But he didn't say it.

Blake was about to drive back around the block and approach the detectives himself when Carla reached across Jackie and grabbed his hand.

"Eddie, look at her. She's kicking. She's an addict. Addicts have broken brains."

"You think?"

"What I'm saying, when I got clean, I couldn't even put on lipstick straight for a week."

"She's a potential material witness, Carla. She needs to sit down with a detective. Figure out if this is connected to the guy who picked up her kid."

Carla came back at him in a stern, motherly tone. "Eddie, I told Jackie I'd be there for her. She's in no shape to make an important decision right now. You always check in with your sponsor first."

"So now you're her goddamn AA sponsor?"

"If she'll have me."

Jackie doubled over again and grabbed Carla's arm, squeezing it.

"That's a yes, Eddie. And you don't know what went down in there. It's a dope house. Maybe the guy OD'd. You ever consider that?"

He hadn't. But Blake was pretty sure it wasn't an overdose, or even a suicide, when he saw an *Eyewitness News* truck swing around the corner from Ventura Boulevard.

He kept driving. But he wished he'd turned around.

Not two hours later, they were sitting in the living room at Carla's sober living house in front of what she called her "community TV," Carla next to him on the couch, Jackie rocking and shivering in a straight back chair. Two of Carla's pigeons slouched on a nearby love seat, one complaining that they don't watch the six o'clock version of *Eyewitness News*. They watch the *Real Housewives of New York City* every day on Bravo.

Blake tried to tune out their chatter. He'd been introduced to Carla's newest pigeons weeks ago but hadn't bothered to memorize their names. The woman complaining about the TV was in her late forties with a face pulled by a cosmetic surgeon who'd also enlarged her lips with filler. She was one of Carla's specialties—a wife traded in by a wealthy husband for a new model. She'd probably dealt with the rejection with Xanax or prescription opioid, landed in a luxury Malibu rehab, and then graduated to live in Carla's sober house for a year.

Carla told the woman to stop complaining and to accept life on life's terms. And if she couldn't, Carla suggested that she go to her room and write her thoughts down to deepen her understanding of one of the steps.

"And what step is that?" the woman said.

"The Rolling Stones step," Carla said calmly. "The one that says you can't always get what you fucking want."

The woman walked out to the back patio, taking the other new pigeon with her, a black girl in her twenties. Blake could see them out there lighting cigarettes and bitching. It was exactly the kind of drama that made Blake avoid Carla's house.

A couple moments later, another pigeon strutted in on a pair of well-shaped legs in tiny running pants, a Red Bull cradled in her hand. Veronica always carried herself in a way guaranteed to turn a man's head. She stopped in the middle of the room, looked at Jackie, and then plopped down next to Blake, her thigh pressed against his on the couch.

"Fresh meat, Carla?" Veronica said. "She looks like she belongs in detox."

"Her name is Jackie," Carla said. "She'll be fine. Leave her alone."

Veronica took a healthy sip of the Red Bull and turned to Blake. He knew what was coming.

"Eddie," she said, "You hook me up with your Detroit people yet?"

Blake looked at his watch. Another five minutes before the news came on. "Haven't gotten around to it," he said.

Veronica said, "C'mon, Eddie, you know my rep is too trashed to go back to LAPD."

He kept his eyes on the TV. Maybe then she wouldn't go through her credentials again like the last time he was at the house. Saying how she'd posed as a high-priced escort. Saying how good she was on the job until she got hooked on coke establishing her street cred in the high-end Hollywood party circuit.

Carla jumped in. "You're not ready to go back to work, Veronica."

"Well how the fuck am I supposed to know when I'm ready?"

"When you stop bugging Eddie."

They continued bickering.

Blake was relieved when the news came on—but anxious about what it might report. He picked up the remote, ready to switch channels if nothing showed up on Channel 7.

It was the lead story. Blake watched a Chyron appear at the bottom of the screen:

KILLING IN SHERMAN OAKS

A blond female reporter spouted all the hackneyed lines. Homeowner in peaceful neighborhood found dead with multiple gunshot wounds. Police don't believe it to be a suicide. Obligatory interviews with shocked neighbors. A mother said she now feared for her safety. A woman next door said the slain homeowner kept to himself.

Veronica laughed. "Shocker! The guy no doubt was into some shit. It's like a serial killer with stiffs in his crawl space. You'd keep to your fucking self, too, bitch."

Other than that, the reporter said police only would say that it was a homicide under investigation. No suspects. No background on the victim. No estimates of when the killing occurred.

Blake switched through the other channels, picking up pieces of essentially the same story. When he'd exhausted all the reports, he whispered to Carla, asking her to send Veronica out of the room.

"Veronica," Carla said. "Why don't you join the others? I need to spend some private time with Eddie and Jackie."

Veronica stood, rolled her eyes and walked to the patio.

Blake turned to Jackie. "How do you know this guy?"

She didn't answer.

Blake got up, walked across the room and squatted a couple feet in front of her so he was at eye level. "Jackie, look at me. I said, how do you know this guy?"

She had anger in her eyes. "I told you, I don't know who took my daughter."

Blake shook his head. "Not him, the guy in the house, the dealer who sent you to score. In case you missed the evening news, he's goddamn dead."

"He was just a friend."

"Does that upset you? That your friend is dead?"

She half nodded.

"How much was your *friend* holding?"

"Holding?"

"Yeah *holding*. Drugs. Or cash. In the house." Blake was thinking a rip-off. Customer shows up with a gun and wants all the money and dope. The dealer makes a stand. Gets shot.

She clutched her abdomen, looking down. "I don't know his business."

Blake was getting pissed. "Okay, let's try it this way. Carla told me you picked up a load of oxy. Did you do that a lot? You his mule?"

Jackie looked to Carla, as if she was seeking her permission to answer.

Carla nodded. "You can trust Eddie," she said.

Jackie looked back down at her feet. "It was the first time."

"Where did you first meet this guy?"

"A bar on Ventura."

"How long did you know him?"

"Just a few months."

"And your daughter. You were comfortable leaving her there?"

"Bella liked him. He'd been over to my place. He wasn't what you think."

Blake chuckled. "And just exactly where is the flaw in my thinking when it comes to the character of your basic dope dealer, Jackie?"

Carla interjected. "Eddie, go easy."

Jackie looked up, "He worked at CBS. The studio lot on Radford. He drove around movie stars."

"You mean he drove around his customers." He looked at Carla. "Sounds like a Teamster."

His eyes went back to Jackie, her eyes on the floor again. "Jackie, listen to me. First thing, you need to file a missing persons report."

She looked up. "I can't."

"You can't?" In his peripheral vision Blake sensed the two pigeons returning to the living room.

"I'm already in enough trouble."

Blake's voice rose. "Oh, I get it. Your daughter is missing. You don't know who took her. God knows where she is or what she's doing—or what somebody has her doing. And your top priority is to cover your own ass."

"Eddie," Carla said, shouting it in her motherly tone.

Blake stood up. He wanted to walk out. He could feel his temples pounding. He took a couple steps toward the door.

He heard Jackie say behind him, "She said you were going to help me."

He turned around. Jackie was looking at Carla.

"She told you that?" Blake said.

Jackie nodded.

Blake walked over to Carla, standing over her. "You told her I was going to find her daughter?"

She didn't say yes. She didn't say no. She had a look he'd seen from her before when people around her became agitated, Carla going into armchair therapist mode. "Eddie, breathe," she said.

"I'm breathing just goddamn fine."

Two pigeons now plopped on the couch, looking like they were enjoying the conflict. Carla rose and walked to the kitchen, motioning Blake to follow. He found her leaning against the refrigerator, her arms crossed but no anger in her eyes.

Carla said in calm voice, "Give me some time with her, Eddie. Like I said, she's got a broken brain."

He stopped a couple feet away. "Yeah, a lot of goddamn broken parts that don't fit together. I'm not buying that she doesn't know who took her."

Carla lowered her voice but shook her finger. "This was *your* job, Eddie. I agreed to help you. And now I'm involved. But you have a responsibility here."

"And what responsibility is that?"

She poked his chest. "You gave the guy the kid. And you're the only one who can set this right."

He knew where he had to start as he walked out the door.

16

THE NIGHT DAGNEY MET WARREN Poole she'd just finished her shift on the pole at Cheetahs, the Las Vegas topless club where United Artists filmed the erotic box office bomb *Showgirls*. She was walking to her car when a regular who had dropped a grand in tips on her in less than a month approached and insisted it was time for her to deliver more than a lap dance. When she told him to fuck off, that she was no whore, he slammed her against her Honda Civic and grabbed a handful of her hair extensions. Three seconds later the regular was on the ground, gasping for air. Behind him stood Warren, silhouetted by the distant lights of the Stardust Hotel. He was on his way into the club when he saw her assaulted. She invited him over for a drink and asked him where he'd learned that choke hold takedown. He said he was a Marine. Not quite true, she later learned. But that was Warren: full of shit but also capable of the occasional righteous act as long as it served his purposes.

They saw each other for a few years. Nothing too serious. Just convenient.

They might still be hanging out in Vegas had it not been for the featured dancers that Cheetahs began booking on the week-ends—triple X adult film stars. They came in from LA, their names advertised on the club's marquee. They were like royalty, showing up with bodyguards and three suitcases of costumes. Bills flew at them on the pole. But they made more cash signing glossy photos and videos. Dagney befriended one, a star of more than sixty films, asking her what it took to break into the adult film game. The star gave her the name of an agent in Chatsworth. Told her to take it slow. Do some magazine pictorials first. Then work her way up to hard core. And make sure her first sex scene was on a bed so she was comfortable on camera. "Cause, honey," she said, "after that you're going to be fucking on every surface imaginable." Dagney moved to LA and worked under the stage name Deidra Lynn. She followed the featured star's suggestions. Her beauty and style took care of the rest. Her contracts guaranteed that she had to be pictured on all her VHS and DVD box covers, which established her as a top performer. She grew a big fan base and was featured in *Penthouse* and *Hustler*, including a Q&A in the latter.

Though she was a free spirit when it came to sex, she prided herself on maintaining boundaries. Her contracts specified that her shoots had to be drug free. And Dagney had rules when it came to scenes. She told her agent, "No anal. No slapping or choke outs. No golden showers."

A director took exception once.

Dagney said, "Deidra Lynn is the nice girl next door who happens to have a big rack. I have a wholesome image to maintain."

Her attitude cost her a few jobs. But it gave her a long career.

Ten years into it, the productions with nice costumes, elaborate locations and big crews became rare. Digital cameras replaced film and tape. Porn took to the internet. But Dagney kept in shape, hitting the gym five times a week. She helped create the new MILF genre, playing the horny mom next door who typically happens upon some young guy. Soon, producers wanted to do that kind of scene as a threesome, adding a young girl who was supposed to be her daughter and the guy her boyfriend. She'd have to go down on the daughter. Incest? Exploiting kids? That's where Dagney drew the line.

A year ago, her agency dropped her when she turned forty-eight.

That's when Dagney found the Napoleon Hill book and decided she had to take charge of her own porn destiny. Some top actresses were banking ten to twenty thousand a month with pay websites under their names. She'd spent nearly all her savings securing the rights to her scenes in her best films. But when she went to register DeidraLynn.com it was already taken. A domain farmer had registered it and every conceivable variation. He wanted $50,000 for the transfer. She chiseled him down to $20,000, but she was still short.

She began Tuesday afternoon by checking out crowdfunding sites to see if she could put up a proposal for her website. She found no prohibitions. But mostly she saw pitches to combat pornography. She was contemplating what she was going to write when the phone rang.

"I need a favor," he said. "I've got a girl that's in trouble that needs a place to stay while I attend to some business."

"Warren," she began.

"Look I'm on my way. Just follow my lead when we get there."

And he hung up.

She tried to call back, but he didn't pick up.

Thirty minutes later she was ready to give him holy hell—until she saw the teenage girl dressed in black standing next to him at her door.

They stepped inside. "Dagney, this is Bella," Warren said. "Her mom has run into some legal trouble. The agency said you were available."

"The *agency?*" Dagney said. "The *agency* told you that?"

She looked at the girl again, the purple streak of hair hanging in her face as she rocked back and forth on her heels. She read in one of her books that people who rocked on their heels were often trauma victims.

Dagney said, "Hi, hon," letting the girl see her smile. She turned away to Warren and gave him a penetrating look.

Warren walked past her with the girl. Dagney watched him park the kid on the couch in front of her TV. He handed her the remote. "Find something to watch, kiddo," he said. "I need to fill Dagney in, okay? We're *so lucky* to have her."

He turned to Dagney. "Let's take care of the details in your office."

Before she could respond, Warren walked to the small bedroom where she had a desk, her laptop, and a futon couch. Seconds later, she stood with her arms folded listening to him, Warren saying in a low voice that the girl's mother was in the Ventura County jail, and he needed someplace to park the kid until she got out and he could reunite them.

Dagney said, "What, you're a social worker now?"

"She's part of what I'm doing in LA. And I can't be dragging her around with me while I finish it."

"I told you not to bring your crap here."

"The kid look like crap to you?" Warren said. He sat on the futon couch, spreading his arms, a confident look on his face. "Dagney, it's totally legit."

"Like the agency? What *agency*?"

"I don't know. It's just what I told her. It's just for a day. Maybe two. Till I finish the job. The kid is okay with it."

"I thought you were meeting with some people."

"I did. But I'm not done."

"Met with who?"

"A high-end Hollywood guy."

Dagney spotted the smirk on Warren's face. The last time she saw him like this was when he showed up with a step van loaded with tax-free cartons of Newports and Marlboro Lights. He wanted to park the van in her driveway until he could arrange to distribute the load to Korean convenience stores in South Central.

Dagney said, "A little above your pay grade, aren't you?"

He held out his hands, palms up. "Hey, I'm following your lead. Had a little setback. But that book, how it says when something goes wrong it's really an opportunity. That's what I'm doing. I got a big opportunity. Like I said, it's all on the up and up."

"How far up?"

He spread his arms back on the couch, leaning back. "It's got to be confidential."

"There's confidential. And there's the up and up. It's one or the other."

"I just need to get the girl's mom. Reunite her with the kid."

"You said she was in jail."

"I'm waiting for her to get out."

"Then what?"

"Hook them both up with the Hollywood guy."

"For what purpose?"

"Help them, I guess. The mom has a drug problem. He hired me because I know the street. Anything more, he told me it was a personal matter."

Dagney studied his face, his eyes blinking, like that was the extent of his story and she was supposed to just buy it.

She reached for the door. "Out, Warren. And little miss sunshine, too."

He leaned forward. "Look, Dagney, this is going to pay off. Everything goes the way I've got worked out I'll take care of you."

Dagney laughed. "Take care of me? Last time you parked a van in my driveway for a week and you bought me dinner. This time you tossing in a movie, too?"

She cracked open the door. He rose and closed it. "Dagney, just do it. The kid has had a tough couple of days. I'll give you some walk around money. Take her to the beach or something. Do some girl stuff."

"She doesn't look too girly."

"You'll figure it out. And when it's over, I'm talking a serious payday for you."

"How serious?"

He paused with a painful look. "Ten thousand. Cash."

Dagney studied his face. She wondered why she put up with him, the way he'd disappear for months, even years at a time, and then just show up. Or call from some number she didn't recognize. Always acting like they were still good friends with benefits. Always wanting a favor. God only knows what he was into this time.

She drew a number on his chest with her finger. "Make it twenty," she said.

17

IT WAS DARK BY THE time he arrived in Malibu. There was a security camera at the second entrance gate reserved for Jason Perry's help. A woman with a heavy Spanish accent answered on the intercom. The housekeeper, Blake guessed. He leaned back in the seat of the Dodge Ram, his face obscured for the CCTV.

"Parts for the pool heater," Blake said.

The gate swung open.

Blake's shit detector was pegged in the red. Jason Perry had embroiled him in what seemed like a script for a B-movie. He decided on the drive over he was going to handle JP the way he did interviews on Squad Seven. No phone call. No appointment. No warning. Show up unannounced with a lot of questions. Get them answered face to face so he could look for the tells he'd learned from those old Detroit homicide dicks: behaviors that disclosed a subject was lying.

Blake parked the truck on a gravel pad by a gardener's shed and walked up a hill that led to the back of the house. He planned to find an unlocked door. If not, knock until someone answered. But as he neared the swimming pool, he could hear JP's voice. He walked around the six-foot privacy fence and peeked through the gate. The pool looked like a natural grotto cut into the hillside—rock formations, foliage, and palms surrounding it. It looked more like a natural hot spring than something a contractor had built. Water glowed from submerged lights. The temperature in the hills had plunged to the low forties, generating a blanket of fog over the heated water.

All of it surrounding JP.

He was on a raft chair in the middle, seemingly floating in the vapor as if he were suspended in a cloud. He had a cell phone to his ear, engrossed in what sounded like a contentious call.

Blake quietly opened the gate and walked in.

"You ever drop that phone into the pool?"

JP looked up.

Blake stood with his legs spread and his arms crossed at the foot of the shallow end.

JP didn't answer. He ended the call.

Blake said, "That ever happens, they say you put it in a container of rice overnight. It will dry it out. I tried it once. Didn't work. Some things you can't fix so easily."

"It's waterproof," JP said. He paused. "This is a surprise. Who let you in?"

"Your housekeeper."

"You should have called first."

Blake lied. "I tried."

"I'm hardly presentable."

"Certainly not like the last time I was here."

JP pointed to the pool house. "Throw me a towel, will you?"

Blake fetched a plush white terry cloth from a neat stack on a chrome rack and tossed it across the water to the producer. The fog parted as he caught it, revealing that JP was naked. He covered his groin with the towel but stayed on the recliner.

JP said, "Edward, you must have good news for me."

"Yeah, I found the girl. But the news isn't so good."

JP stared for a moment, then paddled forward with his hands. "Meaning?"

The distance closed between them. "Your friend in Chicago? You might want to give him a shout on your waterproof phone."

"He's on a week-long retreat at Brando's place."

"Marlon Brando?"

JP nodded, his hands still paddling forward.

"Brando is dead, JP."

JP nodded. "All three-hundred-plus pounds of him. I mean the island Marlon bought after *Mutiny on the Bounty*. Tetiaroa. It's a resort now. They have a men's retreat there. Did it once myself. Nice weather. Nice beach. Went there on one of those goddamn self-realization things. Explore your inner being and all that crap. I left after three days. It was boring as all hell."

Blake didn't respond.

JP stopped paddling a few feet from the pool's edge. "I'm not sure what you're trying to tell me, Edward."

Blake looked down at him, getting his eyes. "The name is Edwin, JP. Or, Eddie. But you can call me Blake. Maybe you'll find that easier to remember."

JP's fingers went to his lips, thinking, as if Blake had said something profound that required an astute response.

Before he could speak, Blake said, "I met the guy you wanted me to meet. The ex. The *concerned* dad. Guy even had their divorce papers with him. So, I found the kid. Called the guy. He picked her up."

JP nodded rapidly. "Good. How about his ex? Was she in bad shape, like he said?"

He decided not to tell JP she'd just been released. Hold back some details. See how JP reacted. "She's in jail in Ventura with a court date. But that's not the bad news. The guy Rose? The *ex-husband?* The father of the girl?" Blake paused. "He's neither."

JP looked bewildered. "I don't understand."

"I have a connection. Somebody in the jail. After the 'dad' picks up her daughter, the ex-wife tells my connection her husband died in combat five years ago."

JP's brow furrowed. "Then who was the guy?"

"I was hoping your pal in Chicago might be able to answer that."

"Jesus Christ."

JP paddled the last couple of feet to the pool's steps and climbed out, wrapping the towel around his waist. He said, "Can I have my girl bring you something to drink?"

Blake shook his head, saying, "There's more."

JP didn't appear to hear him. He walked over to the chrome rack, grabbed another towel and wiped off his chest and neck. He casually walked back and stopped a couple feet away, slinging the terry cloth over his neck and gripping each end with his hands.

"Does the mother know what happened?" JP asked.

"I don't know," Blake said, concealing again. "But if I was the mother, when she bonds out this week, I'd probably go to the police. I'd want my daughter back."

"*You* haven't gone to the police, have you—*Blake?*"

Blake shook his head. "The police showed up all on their own."

JP's brow furrowed again.

Blake continued, "Where the phony ex picked up the girl? It was a house in the Valley. Belonged to the mother's dealer. She left her daughter with the dealer and drove to Oxnard to score for the guy. But she was arrested on her way back."

"Well, at least that part is true. She's obviously an unfit mother. Where do the police come in?"

"The dealer's house is homicide scene."

"Homicide?"

"Like I was saying, there's more. Somebody took her dealer out. Could be the guy who picked up the kid. But the cops aren't saying anything yet."

"How do you know all this?"

"I used to work surveillance. But you don't need me. It's all over the local news."

JP walked over to the pool house, discarded the towel around his waist and put on the same brown terry cloth robe he was wearing when he gave Blake the job. He cinched the robe, walked over to a rustic bench and sat down, rubbing his eyes.

Blake closed the distance between them, standing over him now.

JP looked up. "Blake, please. Have a seat."

Blake straddled the bench, facing him.

JP looked over. "You remember what happened to me ten years ago when I took over one of the biggest production houses in town? It was all over the trades."

"I don't read the trades."

JP hunched, resting his elbows on his knees, staring out at the pool. "Fucking place was in trouble after Chinese investors bought the outfit. They didn't know shit about the picture business. Friend of mine, an executive there, came to me. He said, JP, you can set this place right. So, I went to work. Did it as a favor. One year in, I had three films in production, another in post. And next thing I know I was out. The Chicoms claimed I wrote off personal expenses to the company. Well, fuck yeah. Who doesn't? But *they* didn't know that. But you know who handed them the goods? The friend I was trying to help out." JP looked over. "It's not show friendship, Blake. It's show business. Always remember that."

Blake said, "I'm not sure what you're trying to tell me."

"I'm telling you that you do a favor for somebody and what

happens? You put yourself in a position to get fucked in the ass." He hunched over again, eyes on the ground, shaking his head.

A couple seconds later he looked again. "You can help me, Blake."

"And just how can I do that?"

"Find out what happened. On the murder."

Blake said nothing.

"Better yet, maybe you can also get to the mother. Get to her when she gets out and finds out her kid is gone. Offer to help her find her. Make sure we don't have any public exposure here."

"*We?* I found somebody, that's all."

JP caught his eyes. "You've got a stake in this, too, Blake."

Blake nodded slowly. "I feel bad about losing track of the kid." He felt worse that he'd been duped over a French dip. If JP was being truthful, and Blake wasn't sure he was, then Blake had no one to blame but himself for not seeing through the phony dad.

Hendo was right. He was slipping. But he didn't tell JP that.

JP rose to his feet, cinching the robe belt tighter, standing over him now. "Your remorse is thoughtful. But that's not what I meant. I just closed with Warners. I can't have something like this fucking up that deal. Police get involved. Somebody calls a reporter. It won't matter that we were both sucked into this thing. My name will be in every story. The Warners' execs won't tolerate that sort of exposure."

JP stepped closer, so that Blake's face was only a couple feet from the knot in his robe. "What I'm saying, the studio drops me, they drop *48 Hrs.*"

Blake looked up. JP's face was dark, backlit by the pool lights. JP rested his hand on Blake's shoulder, gripping it.

"And, *Blake*," he said. "That means they drop you, too."

18

AFTER HE LEFT DAGNEY'S, HE stopped at a bait shop on Pacific Coast Highway just as the clerk was putting up the closed sign. He talked his way in, bought a used fishing pole and a couple of lead sinkers. He didn't buy hooks or bait.

Warren Poole was getting the feel of how you secured someone's attention in LA.

It was all about appearances, Poole figured. Even if you didn't have anything going for you, you could get over with bullshit. This came to him after he stopped at a deli on Ventura Boulevard for a corned beef on rye and saw a dozen headshots of movie stars on the wall. When he paid up, he asked the cashier how often those actors ate there. The cashier leaned close and said, "They don't. But it brings customers in."

That's where the fishing rig came in. He wanted to present a certain *appearance* for his late-night meeting with Jason Perry. The producer loaded up his cell with messages for two days before he hurled the burner into the Pacific. He finally called him back with a new flip phone he bought at Ralph's grocery. He told Mr. Perry—that's what he liked to call him—they couldn't talk on the phone. He told him he'd see him at 10 p.m. at the end of the Malibu pier.

Poole found himself reminiscing as he drove the coastline. Tony "The Ant" introduced him to the pier many years ago, when Poole was nineteen, a year after his uncle hooked him up with Tony's crew. Tony liked him. Treated him like blood. The Ant was the Chicago Outfit's enforcer in the casinos. But Tony also had his hand in the film business, trading on the mob's clout with movie industry unions. That day, they drove all the way from Nevada so The Ant could tell a theater exhibitor he had to up his tribute if he wanted to avoid problems with the projectionists' union. Afterwards, they walked to a restaurant called Alice's at the end of the pier. Tony bought rounds and they spent a couple hours watching surfers catching waves in front of the lifeguard station.

It was a good memory.

Poole missed those days before Vegas pushed the wise guys out and turned the town into a family-friendly theme park. He knew he'd never be made. But just being on a crew came with perks: Hot girls. Tickets to shows. Drinks and meals on the house. He could walk into someplace and everyone knew his name. Now, restaurants couldn't even get his order right.

Since coming to LA, Warren Poole had started taking stock. He'd started because he was reading *Success Through a Positive Mental Attitude*. No longer spot reading. He was absorbing entire chapters. He'd realized he was going to turn fifty-five in a few months. He had no substantial savings. All his earnings were off the books. Hell, he couldn't even qualify for social security.

Dagney was right. It was time to try some different moves.

For the meeting with Mr. Perry he figured it came down to how he would wear that invisible talisman. He decided he would display a PMA, the book's acronym for a Positive Mental Attitude. A PMA certainly had worked with the kid. And for Mr. Perry, the fishing pole would be a nice touch, presenting the appearance of a man with no worries and plenty of time.

The Napoleon Hill book. The LA way. Now Dagney helping him. Good feelings about the pier. He could feel it all coming together. He didn't need to buy bait.

He already had it. Safe and sound at Dagney's house.

Twenty minutes later, Poole stationed himself on the pier's west railing. The only people around were a couple of Latinos fishing together about twenty-five yards away, their cooler filled with bait and Coronas. It was dark and quiet, except for the rumble of a swell when it hit the pylons below. He dropped his line into the Pacific.

It was a good spot. He wanted Mr. Jason Perry out of his element—and alone.

Ten minutes later, Poole spotted Mr. Perry walking toward him, the white stripes on his running suit glowing as he passed mariner lamps spaced along the rails of the two-hundred-yard-long pier. As the producer approached, Poole pretended not to see him. He kept his eyes on the monofilament line strung into the water two stories below.

Mr. Perry didn't say hello. He said, "With what I'm paying, I expect you to return my calls and have a working phone. Your number is out of service."

Poole kept his eyes on his line. He bobbed the pole's tip up and down, as if to entice a bite. "You'll have to get used to that, Mr. Perry. I suppose I could go down to AT&T, get one of those promotional deals and a nice smartphone. All in my name. Then you'd have me twenty-four-seven. But something happens we don't expect? There's going to be a record."

Mr. Perry said, "Where's the girl?"

"The kid's in good hands," Poole said.

Poole jerked the pole, like he had a bite.

Mr. Perry said, "What the fuck are you doing?"

"I'm fishing, Mr. Perry. Don't get to do that much in the desert."

"I mean what the fuck are *you* doing?"

"I'm working out a couple of kinks," Poole said. "You wanted the mother, too, as I recall." He turned and looked at the café at the end of the pier. "Looks like they fixed the place up since back in the day."

Poole could see Mr. Perry was getting annoyed now as he glanced at the two Latinos fishing nearby. "Do I look like the kind of guy who spends a lot of time here?"

Poole stayed with his plan, the attitude he wanted to present. He motioned toward the small white building where he and Tony ate years ago. "Last time I was here that was called Alice's. I read up on it. Some people say the place inspired the song 'Alice's Restaurant.' But actually, it's the reverse. The restaurant was inspired by the song."

The producer began pacing. Poole saw him do that the day he hired him: The man pacing in a circle in his big house, saying he had what he called a "brilliant idea," a way to find the mother and the kid. But this was a different kind of pacing. Mr. Perry said, "I don't know what kind of fucking game you're playing, Poole. But it's tedious. I don't need a goddamn history lesson."

Poole shrugged, his eyes going back to his fishing line. "Just thought you'd appreciate it, that's all. Made me think of the last time I was here with one of your backers back in the day. Tony. You remember The Ant, don't you?"

JP stopped. He looked at Poole. "Do I look like I give a shit? Everyone has moved on. Or they're dead."

Poole bobbed the pole again and said, "Not exactly."

JP stepped close, trying to be a tough guy now. "You insinuating that should mean something? You're in the wrong decade. And this isn't Las Vegas. You're in *my* town now."

Poole shrugged again. "I don't know. Tony got wacked, of course. But you call one of your old connections. Say you need a guy who can get something done. That's old-school Vegas. There's a few of us still kicking." Poole turned, letting Mr. Perry see him smile, and said, "So you got me."

JP took a step back and looked around to see if anyone was in earshot.

"Relax, Mr. Perry."

"Relax?"

"Look at the high side. Embrace a positive mental attitude. Considering how this has all has gotten kind of complicated, you're actually lucky to have me."

Perry stepped close again, his voice low, but threatening. "Poole, I hired you to get the goddamn mother and the kid. I didn't hire you to take someone out."

Poole bobbed the pole. "So, you know about that. What makes you think I did?"

"It's all over the goddamn news."

Poole shrugged again. "I had no part in that. The kid was in a dope house. It wouldn't be the first time one got hit."

"That wasn't you?"

"Would you want me to tell you if it was? Would you want someone that fucking stupid doing a job for you? The mother was in jail. You said go get the kid. As far as anyone is concerned, I got the kid out of a bad situation."

"You were supposed to get the mother, too. I'm told she's in jail. The ex-cop says he's got somebody on this inside. Maybe you should start there."

"What, call him? Meet him over a coffee?" Poole set the pole in a fishing rod holder on the railing and faced Mr. Perry. "Like I told you in the beginning. I could have handled this whole thing. But you said you wanted to *get creative*. Like it was a movie. Wanted me to play a role. Divide the job up. That way the left hand didn't know what the right hand was doing. I think that's the way you put it. And while I was at it, tail the ex-cop. I have to say, Mr. Perry, for a guy who works in the land of make believe, you are awfully fucking paranoid."

"I'm not hearing a solution."

"Look, I had to get the kid squared away. Get her confidence so she didn't bolt. I'll find the mom. But I didn't think it was a good idea to bring the kid here while we discussed details."

"What kind of *details?*"

"As you were saying, there *was* a problem at that house. High-profile guy like you? You wouldn't want to be connected to that in any way."

"I didn't murder anyone. And neither did you. Or so you say."

"I'm just saying it wouldn't take much for someone to tip off the cops. They start nosing around. Your name comes up, that you were looking for this mother and her kid. Like what's this big-time producer doing slumming? You'd be all over the news."

"Spare me the PR lesson."

Poole gave him a half-smile.

It took a couple moments, but JP finally got it. "You threatening blackmail, Poole? The only one who could make that call right now is you."

Poole shrugged. "Not necessarily. Lots of moving parts here, Mr. Perry. Your pal, the ex-cop Blake. Or the Jackie broad, once she figures what's up. Even the kid. Frankly, that's another reason why I didn't bring her. I'm trying to limit your exposure."

Perry said nothing.

Poole said, "You might also want to look at it this way. The cops find out I was at that house they're going to sweat me hard. I'd like to think I wouldn't give you up. Especially if the money you were paying me was right."

Mr. Perry was still staring but getting the whole picture now.

Poole continued, "So what I'm saying is, you need me to button everything down. Hold on to the kid until I find the mother. Before she goes to the cops. But ten grand, that's hardly a down payment. It could get sticky with the ex-cop."

"Blake won't be a problem," Mr. Perry said.

"What makes you say that?"

"He needs the work."

Mr. Perry looked out at the lifeguard's station. Finally, he said, "So, what are we talking here?"

"A million works for me."

Mr. Perry turned, his voice rising. "You're goddamn insane."

Poole remained calm. "Like I said, I didn't kill anybody. But for a mil, I deliver the girl and the mom. And I keep my mouth shut, no matter what."

"And if I don't pay?"

Poole turned and took the fishing pole out of its holder. He leaned against the railing, bobbing it. "Then you take your chances."

JP folded his hands, tapping them against his chin. Thinking. Poole didn't know if JP was thinking about his bank balance or searching for a way not to pay up. It didn't matter, Poole decided. As far as he was concerned, he had all the leverage.

Finally, Perry stepped close and said, "The girl, Bella. You keep your goddamn hands off of her, you understand?"

Poole kept his eye on the fishing line. "What, like I've got short eyes? Like I said, the kid is in good hands." He bobbed the pole again and then turned to the producer. "Mr. Perry, if you don't mind me asking, what's so important about you hooking up with this broad and her kid, anyway?"

He ignored the question. Instead, he said, "Get Jackie. Then we'll talk business."

Poole nodded, still working the line.

"And answer your goddamn phone," Mr. Perry said over his shoulder as he walked away.

19

BLAKE KEPT WAKING UP. THE initial side effects from the antidepressant were gone. But they were replaced by insomnia. That and the pressure that he had three people needing something from him now. JP wanted more about the homicide. Jackie and Carla wanted him to find the kid. Both requests had something in common.

He had little to go on.

Blake stared at the dark ceiling and wrestled with not reporting Isabella Rose's disappearance to authorities and its potential connection to the homicide. Legally, he knew only a prosecutor could be jailed for withholding material evidence. He also knew he wasn't an accessory, which would require him to incite or *knowingly* assist in a crime. Legally, he believed he was in the clear. But that didn't mean he was comfortable.

There was too much he didn't know.

Blake rolled out of bed in the predawn, slumped at his desk and decided to see what more he could learn about Jason Perry. The internet was loaded mainly with stories about his films and his love life. He also found a *Variety* report about his firing by the Chinese production company. JP had left out a few pertinent details. A lawsuit accused JP of spending millions in company funds to buy a house in

Telluride and a condo in St. Moritz. The company also furnished the homes. The suit was settled without going to trial.

Also, before he left JP's last evening, Blake insisted on getting the name of the friend in Chicago who had referred the imposter claiming to be Dale Rose. His name was Jimmy Vittorio. JP claimed Vittorio didn't directly make the referral. "The ex-husband called me on my personal cell," he said. "Few people have that. The way he talked about knowing Jimmy, there was no reason to doubt him."

Blake began working with the name on his laptop. He found Vittorio used to own a suburban Chicago car dealership where he was known for smacking watermelons with a baseball bat in his TV spots to demonstrate he was smashing prices. Blake found a listing for something called Vittorio Enterprises, Ltd. He also found a 1984 *Chicago Tribune* story about a reputed capo in the Chicago Outfit found dead in a loaner from Vittorio's dealership. Jimmy Vittorio was quoted saying, "I have thousands of happy customers. I don't ask what they do. And everyone gets the same great deal."

Blake remembered hearing gossip in the writer's room during his first job on JP's cop series. A writer said there were rumors that Chicago organized crime had financed a couple of JP's early films. Blake couldn't find anything on that. He did find stories on organized crime involvement in the film industry all the way back to Bugsy Siegel extorting studios by engineering labor union strikes. He saw a story about the Gambino family shaking down an action star, even telling him what kind of movies to make. He saw a more recent report about mobsters in Sicily who had invested in a string of B films to launder drug profits using Hollywood's notorious book-keeping practices.

By sunrise, Blake was wondering if some ambitious wise guys had set JP up. Counting on JP's fear of bad publicity, maybe they'd lured him into a scandal they could use as leverage. The industry generated enormous amounts of money. Everybody was feeding off the pile, from the agents taking their 15 percent down to the illegal alien housekeepers and gardeners they paid in cash to maintain their homes. Blake read the Chicago Cosa Nostra had lost its foothold in Hollywood in recent years. He saw that as another reason the remnants of the Outfit might make a move on the producer—somebody the syndicate had done business with before.

Blackmail was a working theory, Blake decided. Nothing else made much sense.

Blake closed the laptop and began his morning routine. In the shower he thought about Jackie Rose. He'd start with her. Sit her down alone, away from Carla. Extract all the details of her life in LA. Find out who she knew in Chicago as well. Did she know Jimmy Vittorio or anyone associated with the car dealership? Did she know any organized crime figures? He didn't think she was directly culpable. But he thought she might be a patsy, a drug addict easily manipulated into position to connect JP to a murder case.

An hour later Blake walked into Carla's living room, looking for her and Jackie. The pigeon with the plastic surgery and the former narcotics cop Veronica were sitting in front of the TV, watching something called *Cupcake Wars* on the Food Channel, the volume cranked.

Blake walked into the kitchen.

He came back out, asking, "Where's Carla?"

"She left," said the pigeon with the plastic surgery. She was wrapped in a silky robe, her eyes glued to the screen.

"Left where?"

Veronica looked up and said, "The new girl. She tried to check out."

"She bolted?"

Veronica looked back at the TV, seemingly hypnotized by two

teams of bakers racing to fill a cupcake order in a commercial kitchen. "No," she said. "Like, really check out—as in permanently."

Blake pried out the details over the loud TV and between the bakers slathering on frosting. Carla found Jackie unconscious in the bathtub at dawn, they said, with empty bottle of Advil PM nearby on the floor.

"LAFD took her to emergency," Veronica said. "Carla followed the meat wagon in her car."

"Which ER?" Blake asked.

"Cedars probably," the woman in the robe said. "That's where I went."

"No way," Veronica said. "That girl doesn't have shit to her name. My bet, they took her to the county."

Blake walked out to the patio, pulled out his phone and called Carla's cell. She didn't pick up. He checked his cell for messages or texts. Nothing. As he headed back inside, he called his home voice mail to see if she'd left a message there.

He stopped before he stepped back into the living room with the blaring TV. There was a message, but it wasn't from Carla.

It was from the Los Angeles Police Department.

20

LAPD's Van Nuys Community Police Station was located in a large outdoor complex of government buildings on the far end of a commons that had the feel of an outdoor bazaar. Government workers sat on benches and munched on lunch from a nearby food truck. Merchants did business under a line of canopies. They were selling clothes, jewelry, Avon products, energy efficient windows and even burial plots at a local cemetery, a sign advertising:

Lawn Crypt for Two, 10 & Five Percent Down.

Edwin Blake could see the station fifty yards ahead, three stories of windows framed by modern white pillars. Above the stairway to the entrance was a large sign:

Lock it. Hide it. Keep it.
Don't Be A Victim.

Blake didn't feel like a victim. He felt the call from LAPD was a lucky break. The Van Nuys station covered much of the Valley, including Sherman Oaks.

Fifteen minutes later, Blake took a seat in front of a detective named Jack Margolis who was stationed behind a desk piled high with two stacks of paperwork. Margolis, fifty-something, looked like he was on autopilot. Blake guessed he'd probably been showing up for years in the same white, short-sleeve dress shirt and a variety of clip-on ties. His sport coat hung over the back of his chair.

The detective thumbed through one of the stacks for a good minute, saying nothing. Finally, he pulled several sheets out of the pile and positioned them below his eyes. He reached for a coffee mug on this corner of his desk, took a sip, his eyes scanning the paperwork.

"Okay," he said. "First things first. Can I see some ID?"

Blake pushed his license across the desk. Margolis picked it up, looked at its photo and then up at Blake. His eyes went back down to the paperwork as he scrawled something on one of the sheets of paper.

Blake leaned forward. "Do you know how they recovered my Dodge, detective? Was it abandoned?"

Margolis didn't answer right away. He was checking boxes on another sheet. He finally set his pen down and perused what appeared to be the arrest report. "This was my case, actually. Black-and-white made a routine stop on Ventura. The car had no plate. Just one of those dealership placards. But no temporary registration to go with it. They ran the VIN. And bingo."

"The guy in custody?"

"Wasn't a guy."

"Not a guy with a lot of tattoos?"

"Yeah, we've got a line on him, too. We'll pick him up. Soon as we find him."

"So, who was driving it?"

"His girlfriend. Twenty-two-years-old and clueless. With a baby in the back. I guess he gave her the car. Told her he'd bought it for her as a gift. She gave him up."

"Any priors?" Blake asked.

The detective blinked a couple times, as if he didn't commonly hear that phrase from crime victims. "He was released a couple months ago from Tehachapi. Early release program by the governor so he doesn't have to build more prisons. We'll be glad to send him back, presuming you're willing to testify."

"Done," Blake said.

"The DA will be contacting you on that," Margolis said.

The detective pushed a sheet of paper across the desk, saying Blake had to sign and date at the bottom, verifying he was the owner of the impounded vehicle and was responsible for picking it up within five business days or he'd be charged at the rate of $100 a day.

Margolis looked down at another sheet of paper. "It says here it's drivable. If you want, you can pick it up after we're done. The tow yard will have the keys. You'll have to get a new set of plates, but this paperwork will cover you until then."

As Blake signed, Margolis said, "Challenger, huh? One of the quick ones?"

"SRT," Blake said. "Special edition."

Margolis nodded. "Surprised this asshole gave it to the girl."

Blake said, "When I was on patrol, a girl driving a muscle car, I would have taken a second look."

Margolis grinned. "I thought you might be a cop—or an attorney."

Blake nodded. "Used to be. Detroit PD. Twenty-five and out."

Margolis looked up and said, "All twenty-five in a car?"

Blake now knew he had the detective's full attention. He shook his head. "Just eight years. Then the narcotics section. A few years in surveillance. Last ten, detective sergeant in homicide. On a crew called Squad Seven."

"And you decided to come to LA and blow your pension on rent?"

Blake said, "A director brought me out here to work with TV and movie people. You know, help them keep it real."

"Do they listen?"

"Sometimes."

Margolis smirked. "As long as their goddamn checks don't bounce, right?"

"You got it," Blake said.

Margolis leaned back in his chair, his hands clasped behind his head, ready to shoot the shit with another guy this side of the thin blue line. "Valley Bureau Homicide is in this station. I thought about putting in for it. But I decided I could live without the stiffs."

"It's not for everyone," Blake said. He paused. "Speaking of, I saw on the news you had one Monday. Kind of rare around here, isn't it?"

Margolis nodded. "Depends on the neighborhood. But yeah. That part of Sherman Oaks. Pretty unusual."

"Something like that, your robbery unit get involved?"

"Sometimes. Deputy chief is big on community policing. We put out feelers to the locals, reliable snitches."

Blake figured he could ask what he needed to know now—but not directly. "Gal I've been seeing lives in Studio City. She saw it on the news. Couple days after my car got ripped. Ever since, she's been insisting I spend the night at her place. I guess that's okay. But it's a real crawl on the 405 over the hill from the coast."

Margolis nodded. "You know why they call it the 405, don't you? It takes four or five hours to get anywhere on the goddamn thing." Margolis leaned forward. "Tell her not to worry. Looks like a drug hit."

Blake nodded. "That was my old squad's thing. Drug-related homicides."

"Then you know it had to be somebody the guy knew. Like I said, tell her not to worry."

Margolis looked back at his desk. Signed another form and handed it to Blake, saying it authorized him to pick up the car. The address of the impound yard was at the bottom of the form. Blake was surprised the detective had said nothing about his Smith & Wesson.

Blake leaned forward. "You know, I've got a conceal carry. In your report, you should see that I also reported my sidearm was in the car. Anything there about that?"

Margolis shuffled through several sheets, then turned one over. "Noted here. But I don't see it was retrieved."

Blake folded the impound paperwork and slipped it into his shirt pocket. "Any suspects?" Blake asked.

"The guy who took your car probably has your sidearm. We retrieve it, I'll get in touch."

Blake stood up and said, "I mean the homicide."

"Nothing yet. I guess the vic worked on the Radford lot. Amateur hour. If you're going to deal dope, you ought to develop the proper skill set. Learn to protect yourself in a jam."

Blake took a couple steps toward the door, stopped, turned around and said, "What makes you say that?"

Margolis said, "The dumbass was killed with his own gun."

21

BLAKE DROVE STRAIGHT TO THE impound lot after he called Enterprise and a representative said the company would pick up his rented Dodge Challenger there. A police auction was underway as Blake rolled onto the property and parked. An auctioneer with slicked-back hair and a small portable public address system stood in front of a crowd of several dozen people, spitting out bids on a tricked-out '86 Monte Carlo with three bullet holes in the driver's door. Blake lingered for a minute with the crowd and then went to the office, where the yard clerk handed him his keys in exchange for his paperwork.

Blake found the Challenger parked in the far corner of the yard. Buds and tree sap from a tree hanging over the fence line stained its gunmetal finish. Blake popped the locks. He opened the door to the hot smell of urine, fast food, and baby shit. McDonald bags and candy wrappers trashed the interior. Several used diapers were discarded in the back seat, baking in the hot Valley sun. He made several trips to a dumpster behind the tow office. But the car still stunk. Blake then opened all the doors, leaned against the front fender, and tried Carla again.

She still wasn't picking up.

Blake slid in behind the wheel, started the engine and turned on the air, hoping that would kill the smell. He returned to the shade and found himself wondering if he should have probed deeper with the LAPD property crimes detective. He wanted to ask for a time of death. Determine how close it was to the imposter ex-husband picking up the girl. Was it later that day? Or the next day? That might tell him if the guy who claimed to be Dale Rose was the killer. He could picture that scenario. The phony dad shows up. The kid doesn't know him. The dealer makes a stand. And the phony Rose snatches his gun and takes him out. The detective may have known the time of death. Or maybe not. Either way, Blake concluded that asking him would have been pushing it. Time of death, that was too specific. His shit detector would have gone off. Why does this guy picking up his car, ex-cop or not, want to know so goddamn much?

Christ, Blake thought, LAPD had a murder on a street full of worried families—and no suspect. Maybe he should end it all right here. Pick up the phone and call Valley Bureau Homicide. Point those dicks in the right direction. Tell detectives he was coming in. Tell them everything he knew. Tell them about Jackie's daughter. Then call JP and tell him he was done. If that meant losing *48 Hrs.*, so be it.

There would be other jobs.

As he slid again behind the wheel in the cooled interior of the Challenger, the odor still lingering, he remembered what his agent told him about *being difficult*. He remembered what happened to the head makeup artist on the last TV show he'd worked. She'd been in demand for two decades. But then she came out as a Republican during a presidential election. Liberal actors complained. The show-runner replaced her the next day. Blake bumped into her a year ago. She was giving makeup demonstrations in the Macy's cosmetic department.

She hadn't worked in the industry since.

That's the way it was when you were "below the line," a film accounting term used to denote hourly workers low in the pecking order. Word traveled quickly when someone gave you a bad rap. Jason Perry knew everyone. And everyone knew JP. If JP got caught up in a scandal, he'd put the word out that it was Blake who screwed up. JP wouldn't need to provide details or context. JP would eventually reinvent himself once he secured another hot creative property and development money. By contrast, Blake would have no way to tell his side of the story. He'd have no one to tell it to. At that point, nobody would take a meeting with him.

Blake would be just another Hollywood washout. And for good.

Blake thought, then what? Go back to Detroit? Nothing there but a city on its ass. Or what? Find a gig with some security agency in LA? He did that after his first TV show was canceled. Worked security for a pop singer for a couple months. That's how he got the conceal carry. A couple months ago he tried it again, working a premiere in Santa Monica. He hated being one of those stiffs with shades and an ear bud.

Carla once asked him if he ever saw any action.

"One night, we were working the red carpet when a stalker from Wisconsin jumped the rope," Blake told her. "The psycho was convinced the film's female lead was his soul mate. A uniformed SMPD sergeant and I had to wrestle him to the pavement."

Blake had drinks with the cop afterwards. The sergeant said he was thinking about not booking any more premieres. "Movie before this? A rapper in the film showed up in a Black Lives Matter T-shirt. You know, that protest outfit. He asked me to pose with him for the paps— only to flip me off as their cameras clicked away. It went viral. The money isn't worth it."

Blake decided there was only one solution. When it came to JP's job, he had to stop thinking like a cop sworn to uphold justice. He needed to start thinking like a private investigator in the employ of one Jason Perry, even though he wasn't being paid. That's where his allegiance belonged. And as far as he could tell, his client had not committed a crime.

First things first, Blake thought. That's what Carla was always saying, one of her AA slogans. Don't get caught up in the future. You're only guessing anyway. The first thing, he decided, was to somehow find a way to determine the time of death of the homicide. Then talk to Jackie. That should tell him if his theory about the Chicago mob was credible. It might also give him some leads on the location of her kid.

Blake revved the Challenger's engine a couple of times. He liked the way the car sounded. He especially liked the way its Hemi engine rumbled in studio parking structures, its throaty exhaust bouncing off the concrete, drawing stares from Prius drivers.

The auctioneer was still at it as Blake pulled out of the lot.

Ten minutes later he pulled into a car wash on Ventura Boulevard. He asked the attendant to do whatever it took to get the sap off the hood.

"And air freshener," Blake said. "Lots of it."

The guy said, "Lemon. Cherry. Or new car smell."

"New car," Blake said.

The attendant handed him his call slip and walked on to the next car in line. As he took his foot off the brake, Blake spotted the end of a Taco Bell bag jammed under his seat. He reached down to remove it, his hand digging deep into the cavity.

Beyond the bag his fingertips touched steel.

Moments later he was holding his .45 caliber Smith & Wesson, his Chief's Special. It was still in its waistband holster. He pulled the pistol out, removed the magazine, and racked the slide. An unspent round ejected across the car's interior, bouncing off the passenger window. He looked at the magazine, its hollow-point rounds stacked in the mag's feeder. Blake decided he was making progress.

He had his car, his Smith, and seven rounds of ammunition.

He was searching for the ejected round on the floor when the idea hit him. Soon he would be doing research for the creator of the new *48 Hrs.* series.

That would give him entry—at the very place where he could determine a time of death and a whole lot more.

22

WARREN POOLE THOUGHT HE HAD Edwin Blake figured out. Retired cop, getting up in his years, trying to pick up a few bucks, extending minimal effort. But now he wasn't so sure. Blake found the mother in two days. Then nailed the kid's location in Sherman Oaks. Poole wondered how he pulled that off with the mother's ass parked in a jail. Mr. Perry told him the ex-cop had someone on the inside. But who? Like he had a snitch in the lockup? If Blake was a retired Ventura cop that might make sense. But Blake was from Detroit.

Poole decided Blake knew his way around. First thing in the morning, Poole had called the Ventura County jail and discovered that Jackie Rose had bonded out two days ago. Blake wasn't telling JP everything he knew. Poole couldn't hold that against him.

Neither was he.

He was eating the complimentary continental breakfast at the BLVD Hotel & Spa when it dawned on him. Maybe Blake saw through the phony ex-husband move. Figured out who really wanted the mom and her kid. Maybe Blake was shooting a move on Mr. Perry, trying to score a payoff. Poole couldn't blame him for that, either. That didn't make him a bad guy.

That made him a competitor.

After breakfast, Poole drove to the Pacific Palisades to sit on Blake's apartment. He parked along the curb on Sunset a couple hundred feet from the cul de sac. He didn't see the white truck parked out front. So, he waited. He read more of *Success Through a Positive Mental Attitude* but found himself getting too caught up in the book and his eyes off the job. He looked for some talk radio on the AM dial but found only political shows and Spanish-speaking stations. He decided to pass the time just checking out the cars passing on Sunset, the rush hour traffic heading down to the coastal highway or cars coming the other way from Malibu. He didn't see many American models. Just a few Ford and Chevy trucks with Mexicans behind the wheel. Mainly he saw BMWs, Mercedes, and a lot of Jap models, most of them high-end brands like Lexus and Infiniti. Every few minutes he'd spot something special. Over a period of a half hour he counted four Teslas, three red Ferraris, two black Bentleys, and a white Rolls Royce Phantom with a big chrome grill.

Poole thought about the Bentley he saw in Mr. Perry's driveway. The guy sitting fat and happy in his big glassy house, a housekeeper and an assistant anticipating his every request. He remembered the time Tony the Ant asked him to take care of a big TV star when the actor came to Vegas back in the day. He drove the asshole around for three days. The actor paid for nothing. Shows. Restaurants. All on the house, including the two whores the actor wanted sent to his room in the Stardust. That's the way it worked. The rich and the famous—the people who could afford everything—got everything for free. For the people who couldn't afford squat, it was full price. It all seemed half-ass backwards.

He wondered if Dagney's positive thinking book had anything to say about that. He called her. She didn't want to talk about the book. She wanted to talk about the kid.

"We're getting to know each other," Dagney said. "Just in time for you to pick her up."

"Not yet."

"When?"

"I'm not sure."

"Warren, all she does is sit in front of the TV."

"That makes it easy."

"I can't get any work done. I don't want to leave her alone. But she's not exactly conversational."

"You're a woman. She's a girl. That should count for something."

"Warren, I only played a mother in my movies."

Poole saw a late model Dodge Challenger rumble by, slow down and then turn into the cul de sac. He watched the car park at the curb.

And saw Blake get out.

He hung up on Dagney.

Blake disappeared into the building.

Poole drove into the cul de sac to get a better look at the Dodge. Dark metallic grey. Nice black rims. Waxed and detailed. And instead of California plates, it had the name of a Dodge dealership. He thought, ex-cop traded up. Dumped his truck for a muscle ride.

He glanced up at the big window that belonged to Blake's apartment. Blake wasn't at the window. But he didn't want to take any chances. He swung the Camry around and headed back to his parking spot on Sunset. He decided to continue waiting. See if Blake was going to go somewhere with his new ride.

Poole found himself speculating. He wondered if Mr. Perry had forked over a down payment to Blake to deliver the mom, the money already burning a hole in the ex-cop's pocket. Mr. Perry double dealing, cutting into Poole's score. And if Blake was so quick to spend, that meant he had a direct line on Jackie Rose and could deliver.

And probably soon.

He could picture how it would all go: Mr. Perry calling him. Saying never mind about the mother. Blake found her. Poole only had the kid, half the package, but knew it wouldn't stop there. The negotiation would begin. The man didn't make all those movies without knowing how to chisel on a deal.

Blake, the clever ex-cop, and the fancy Mr. Perry, the cheap movie producer, shooting some moves.

Poole decided it was time to up his game. Shoot a few new moves of his own.

23

JUST BEFORE HE LEFT FOR downtown, he finally heard from Carla. She texted that she couldn't talk on the phone. Doctors had pumped Jackie's stomach. Now Carla was at the UCLA emergency psych ward getting Jackie squared away on a 5150. Blake knew that meant the hospital would evaluate Jackie's state of mind on a seventy-two-hour hold. Carla suggested they meet at her house that evening.

As expected, the mid-afternoon traffic was at a near standstill on the eastbound I-10, the Santa Monica freeway. LA traffic flowed the opposite way of most cities. In the morning the freeway was slammed from downtown to the coast. In the afternoon it was the reverse. He once read that more than a million people headed to Santa Monica each day to work or play.

Blake got off the freeway and took Olympic Boulevard, cutting through West Los Angeles, the flats of Beverly Hills, and Korea Town. Near USC, he returned to the freeway. Even using his best shortcuts, it had taken an hour to go ten miles. He wondered how many people died in ambulances on their way to an ER. He hoped if he ever had a medical emergency, it was after midnight when everyone could speed.

Blake found himself thinking about his health. He'd taken pretty good care of himself, cutting back on the fried food, easy to do with the menu choices in Southern California. He swam laps. But he'd also spent the first year in LA smoking cigarettes. He'd quit when he was in Detroit, but he picked it up again, simply because there was so much anti-smoking fever in LA. When he was a kid, his father was always on his case. Not for smoking. For his general attitude, claiming he had what he called "a rebellious streak."

Considering that, it was ironic Blake became a cop. He enrolled in Wayne State University, rejecting the grease and grime in his father's tool and die shop. But by the end of his junior year, he really had no career plan. He worked a part-time student job for a university department called Space Inventory. He measured classrooms to see if the square footage matched the blueprints the university had on file. He didn't mind going out on campus to measure. But most of his day was spent in a cubicle looking at blueprints. One day, he was sent to Public Safety, the university's police department. As he stretched a tape across a squad room, he complained about his job to a curious patrol sergeant. The sergeant said if he wanted to do something meaningful, he should take some criminal justice classes and apply to the department before he finished his degree. "I suppose I like helping people," Blake said. The sergeant said, "If you want to help people, join the fire department. But I guarantee, as a cop you won't be bored." The following year Blake didn't even show up at his graduation ceremony. He was in the police academy. He spent a year on the university force and then hired into Detroit PD for better pay and benefits.

Twenty-five years on the job, Blake thought. Twenty-five years of eating at all those greasy spoons and soul food restaurants his partner Hendo loved. Blake liked the fried chicken and ham hocks with mustard greens. And he liked the cigs. But he was glad he'd left that all behind. He wanted to feel good about his health, not worry about death.

Especially today. He was headed to the LA county morgue.

The public information representative there was named Bob Sutter. Blake had worked with him on a pilot a couple years ago. The coroner's office sent Sutter to oversee the props the art department had created for a crime scene. LAPD and other county agencies generally cooperated with productions. If you were going to portray their units on film, the bureaucrats wanted their seals, uniforms, and equipment depicted accurately.

Blake mostly avoided the morgue in Detroit. He rarely showed up for victim autopsies. He used to tell TV writers that the boiler-plate scene with a detective attending an autopsy was a Hollywood cliché. Many detectives didn't subject themselves to the smell and head games the pathologists often played. Making bad jokes. Munching on a pastry between organ removals. Why attend? You could get everything you needed from their written reports.

That's exactly what Blake had in mind as he turned into the complex off North Mission known as the office of the Los Angeles County Medical Examiner-Coroner.

Blake parked on the side of a two-story, red brick building that looked like it had been built in the thirties or forties. Inside, he found a receptionist behind a glass enclosure, framed in aging varnished cherry. The place had the feel of Detroit police headquarters at 1300 Beaubien: marble walls, a worn mosaic tile floor, pebble glass doors with varnished framing.

Blake approached the receptionist, a middle-aged woman who looked as if she never smiled. "My name is Edwin Blake," he said. "I'm here to see Bob Sutter. He's expecting me."

She suggested he take a seat, adding, "I'll notify his office you're here."

But all the seats were taken. A couple of families, pained looks on their faces, were sitting in the two chairs and a mission-style couch in the center of the small lobby. In one, an older woman was crying as her daughter comforted her, handing her tissues. Blake saw lettering on the pebble glass doors off the lobby. One was PERSONAL PROPERTY RELEASE. Another, IDENTIFICATION SECTION. Those seated were waiting to identify dead loved ones or pick up their belongings.

Another closed door was labeled:

SKELETONS IN THE CLOSET.

Blake walked back to the receptionist and asked what was behind that door.

"Our gift shop," she said.

At first, he thought he misheard her, her voice muffled by the glass. He asked again.

"A *gift shop*," she said, louder. "Have a look. Mr. Sutter will be about five minutes."

Seconds later, Blake entered an environment dramatically different than the scene just a few feet outside its door. "Welcome to Skeletons in the Closet," said the young woman in a medical examiner's uniform. She was smiling, arranging some sales slips near her cash drawer.

Blake nodded and looked around. The room was about the size of any tiny gift shop you'd find in a small town. Everything was for sale: T-shirts. Beach towels. Coffee mugs. Crime scene tape. Plastic human skeletons. Most of the merchandise had the coroner's official logo—the chalk outline of a body. A lot of the items were humor based.

Blake asked the woman behind the register, "Who comes in here? Buys this stuff?"

She looked up from her sales slips. "People from all over the world. Tourists. Local people. Around Halloween we get really busy. The stars like it, too. They come in after they've shot scenes on the grounds."

She pointed out their photos on the walls. Signed headshots. Others snapped in the gift shop. Some were labeled just so people knew who they were. Others were obvious. Matt Damon. Gary Cole. Adrienne Barbeau. Emily Deschanel from the TV series *Bones*.

Blake spotted a snapshot of Dustin Hoffman. "He was in here?"

She nodded enthusiastically, saying, "He bought a load of stuff for his kids."

"Whose idea was this?" Blake asked.

"Mr. Hoffman's."

"I mean the gift shop."

She explained a former medical examiner several years back had some T-shirts made up for his staff as a joke. Other people saw the shirts and wanted them.

"It took off from there," she said. She reached into a box and held up a T-shirt, unfolding it so he could see it. "We just got a new one in."

It had the coroner's logo and read:

OUR BODIES OF WORK SPEAK FOR THEMSELVES.

"Don't you just love it?" she said.

24

Bob Sutter was waiting for Blake behind a desk in a small office. He didn't look much different than when they worked together. Fifty something. A mustache. Dressed in a collared shirt, no tie.

Sutter said, "So you got an idea for a TV show. You and about a thousand other people."

Blake said, "Yeah, but I think this one is going to go. Jason Perry, a big producer, is behind it. We're redoing *48 Hrs.* as a series."

"Do I know the writer?"

Blake didn't even know who the writer was. But he knew how writers talked. He knew the same industry buzzwords that made someone sound legit.

"They're still deciding. But the EP has me doing research. He wants a case ripped from the headlines. You know, a Dick Wolf *Law & Order* kind of thing but spread out over ten episodes on one case. I'm looking for a good autopsy so they can feed the writer an accurate crime scene."

Sutter pointed to a four-foot-wide bottom drawer in a cabinet against an opposite wall.

"That whole drawer, that's all celebrities: Whitney Houston. Patrick Swayze. The Phil Spector case. You name it. I'm getting requests every week from autopsy shows on cable. Anything like that interest you?"

Blake shook his head. "We're thinking low key. Something that seems like an ordinary homicide, but once you start pulling on the strings it gets complicated."

Blake paused. He opened a small folio notebook he brought with him, looking down and saying, "There was murder in Sherman Oaks last week. I saw it on the news. Detective at the Van Nuys station told me the victim was a drug dealer. I'm thinking that's in the ballpark. What do you have on that?"

Sutter reached for his mouse. He moved and clicked it a couple of times, his eyes scanning his monitor. "Here. Decedent, Lawrence James Rossi. Investigator's narrative and autopsy report were just filed last night."

Blake nodded. "That'll work."

Sutter's brow furrowed. "A homicide, a new one like this? Unsolved? Usually there's a hold." Sutter scrolled through the document on his screen, then said, "Huh. I don't see one here." He looked at Blake. "Did you know there's still a hold on the OJ? How many years has it been? And I get requests for that one every goddamn week."

Sutter's eyes shifted to his phone. "I better check with the Valley Bureau."

Blake leaned forward. "Bob, it's fiction."

"What?"

"No real names or locations. I just want a basis for the writer. I wouldn't even need a report if we were shooting in Detroit. I could do it from memory. But the LA protocol is different. And I want to get it right."

Sutter gripped his phone but didn't pick it up. "There's a reason I've lasted twenty years here, Eddie. It's called cover my ass."

Blake said, "There's no hold on it at this moment, right?"

Blake saw Sutter's hand relax a little.

Blake held up two fingers like a boy scout. "I'll shred the god-damn thing when I'm done."

Their eyes locked for a moment. Then Sutter's hand went back to the mouse. He clicked it a couple of times, looking at the screen. "Better hope our printer is working. It was down yesterday."

Sutter left the room. When he returned, he plopped down in his chair and pushed a quarter-inch thick stack of paper across the desk.

Blake said, "How much do I owe the county for the copies? Go easy on me, Bob. I want to hit the gift shop on my way out."

Sutter leaned back in his chair, clasping his hands behind his head. "I liked *48 Hrs.* I liked the way Nick Nolte kept punching Eddie Murphy in the jaw when he pissed him off. You people need to keep that."

Blake stood up. "I'll pass that along." He pulled out his money clip. "So how much?"

Sutter looked up and said, "Just make sure I get invited to the wrap party."

After Warren Poole saw Blake emerge from the red brick building, get in his Dodge, and pull out of the coroner's lot, he decided to call Mr. Perry. He'd tailed the Challenger all the way from the Palisades. Now Blake was on the move again.

Poole was thinking that a lot of shit Blake was doing just didn't make sense.

He called Mr. Perry's phone. The producer didn't pick up. He called again and still got his voice mail. He didn't leave a message. Poole was couple car lengths behind the Challenger on the I-10 now. He guessed Blake was heading back to the coast.

Poole called Mr. Perry again. It rang only once.

Poole didn't say hello. He said, "Your boy, the ex-cop, he still working for you?"

"Poole? Jesus, you find Jackie?"

"I'm working on it. But what about the ex-cop?"

"He's mostly done with his part."

"You sure about that?"

"I've hired him for a cop show I'm doing, but that's not your concern." Mr. Perry's voice got louder. "Get to your point."

"Your boy just came out of the county morgue with a big smile on his face. Came out wearing an official morgue hat. Place like that hires a lot of ex-cops."

"He's probably doing research for my series. But what about Jackie? You should be focusing on that."

"Why do you think I'm following the man? You said he might know something."

"Don't let him see you."

"That only happens in one of your movies, Mr. Perry."

Poole watched the Challenger pass the I-10 to the coast and then merge onto the entrance of the 101, heading toward Hollywood and the Valley. Traffic was backing up. Poole blasted his horn at the car next to him, motioning that he needed to merge. The driver, a woman wearing large sunglasses in a Volvo SUV, just closed the gap. But the driver behind him, a Mexican gardener in a white truck, let him in.

Poole flashed a thumbs-up sign to the pickup and talked into the phone again. "Mr. Perry, you need to really think long and hard before deciding to *get creative*."

"What the hell are you talking about?"

"Oh, I don't know. Your boy hardly had a pot to piss in. Lives in a little crib. You say he needs a job. But now he seems to have come into a lot of cash. Got himself a new car. A whole new look."

"Get to your goddamn point, Poole."

Poole raised his voice. "You deal with me—and only me—on the mother and the kid. You follow? No side deals. No game show. No bitch in a tight dress, spinning a big wheel. Best contestant wins the prize."

Mr. Perry sounded agitated. "I'm a busy man, Poole. I don't have time for people below the line. My line producer handles the money. I don't know what Blake is getting paid, so I can't help you with that. And just because the guy has a new hat means nothing. Maybe he picked up some swag."

Poole saw the Challenger ahead swing into the middle lane and accelerate. That Dodge could really move.

Shit, he was losing him.

Poole swung into the right lane, cutting off the woman in the large sunglasses. He caught up to the Challenger. He wanted to yell, but he kept his voice steady. "Mr. Perry, I need you to listen to me. You try anything cute. You try to short me—"

"Just find Jackie," the producer said, interrupting.

Poole half chuckled. "Well, that's on you, isn't it, *Mr. Perry*? 'Cuz if you fuck me, you—or anyone else—will never see that kid again. You follow?"

Poole ended the call before the producer could respond.

25

PEOPLE WERE COMING AND GOING at Carla's, guys picking up her pigeons for dates or giving them rides to AA meetings.

Blake watched the former narcotics cop Veronica in a heated dispute with the boyfriend, a car salesman named Kurt she'd met in rehab. He'd seen the two argue before. Kurt's latest thing was his transformation into a biker in black leather and a two-inch beard. He'd shown up at Carla's on his new Harley Softail with an extra helmet for her. But Veronica told him there was no way she was putting her fine ass in a short black dress on that Hog. If he wanted to take her to dinner, he needed to take her in a car.

Kurt stormed out the door.

After that, Blake couldn't get Carla's full attention. She was counseling Veronica on the couch, saying the argument was perfect evidence that it wasn't a good idea to get into a serious relationship in the first year of sobriety.

Blake took the report from coroner's office to the back patio, sliding the glass door closed behind him. He sat at the table under a string of twinkle lights hanging from the canopy. He had just enough light to read.

He began with the pages titled INVESTIGATOR'S NARRATIVE.

They reminded him of the reports he'd read from the Wayne County medical examiner in Detroit. The narrative stated Valley Bureau homicide summoned the coroner to the scene. Looking at the date, Blake could see it was the day after the man who claimed to be Dale Rose picked up Isabella. The location was described as a 2,300-square-foot home in a residential area in Sherman Oaks. The names of patrolmen and detectives on the scene were noted. Blake immediately recognized one of them, the detective he'd consulted with two years ago on his last film.

Paul Ricardo had caught the case.

"According to Det. Ricardo," the coroner's investigator stated, "a 9-1-1 call was received at 0510 hours from a domestic worker who had access to the dwelling and arrived to clean the house. Patrol from the Van Nuys station was first dispatched to the location and relayed what appeared to be a firearm homicide to detectives in the division. The decedent was identified by the housekeeper as Lawrence Rossi, who she stated was the owner of the home. She stated Mr. Rossi lived there alone."

Blake read that evidence technicians and photographers were called to the scene. The narrative became interesting when he delved into a section titled SCENE DESCRIPTION:

"The decedent's body is in the living room of the residence, located on the west side of the single-floor home. The decedent is sitting with his legs extended in front of him in an easy chair on the north side of the room. Both arms of the decedent hang over the sides of the chair. A half-eaten hot dog and a half-full can of Budweiser are within arm's reach of the decedent. The chair faces a flat screen television. Patrol informed the writer that upon their entry they found the TV tuned to the Hustler adult film channel. Between the decedent and the television, a .38 caliber Colt Cobra revolver was on the floor, five feet from the decedent. The weapon, upon inspection by Det. Ricardo, showed three live rounds and three expended rounds of Winchester ammunition."

Blake turned the page to a section titled BODY EXAMINATION. He read that the victim was barefoot and wearing a pair of cargo shorts and a tan short sleeve shirt with a CBS logo on its breast. The investigator noted that the belt on his cargo shorts was unbuckled and his shirt had three blood-soaked areas that corresponded to holes in its fabric. One was in the right shoulder. Another in the lower abdomen. And another in the left breast.

The next sentence piqued Blake's interest. "Rigor mortis is not present. There is the presence of extensive livor mortis in the bottom of the thighs, ankles and feet." Blake knew rigor mortis was usually present only in the first eighteen hours after death. By contrast, he knew *livor* mortis, the pooling of blood in the lowest part of the body, starts after the first two hours, continues and remains with the corpse.

Rossi had been dead in that chair for at least a day.

Blake worked his way through the twenty-five-page autopsy report that followed the investigator's section. He speed-read through the descriptions of organs and the victim's general health. A full toxicology report was pending, but a preliminary test had shown the presence of alcohol, opioids, and cocaine.

Blake heard a phone ring inside. He turned toward the glass patio doors and saw Carla talking on her cell in the dining room.

Blake's eyes went back to the report, a section titled DESCRIPTION OF GUN SHOT WOUNDS. He read that of the three gunshots, the one to the chest was the fatal injury. It severed Rossi's aorta from the upper chamber of the heart. All three bullets entered at a downward angle, front to back. This suggested to Blake the victim was sitting in the chair when he was killed.

Several paragraphs later Blake found what he was looking for.

The deputy medical examiner made his determination based on the lack of rigor mortis, the presence of livor mortis, and the contents of the victim's stomach. Hot dog remains found there were not digested.

The ME fixed the time of death was between 2 p.m. and 3 p.m. Blake was pretty sure that was around the time they watched Isabella Rose get picked up. But it also could have been after.

Blake heard piano chords and a breathy flute play on the outdoor patio speakers. He knew Carla turned on the New Age music when she needed to unwind. Seconds later the door slid open. Carla set her cell phone and two cups of tea on the table.

She sat. "She'll be okay."

Blake said, "Every time I'm here Veronica is either hitting me up for a job or fighting with her boyfriend."

"No, Jackie," Carla said. "She called from the psych ward. They told her if her stay went well, she'd be released Saturday afternoon."

Blake looked up from the paperwork. "That's more than two goddamn days. They allow visitors?"

Carla nodded.

"I need to talk to her," Blake said. "The sooner the better."

"Eddie, let the shrinks do their thing. You go in there, upset her, they'll put another hold on her. Then what are you going to do?"

Her cell phone chimed. A text coming in. She picked it up, read a text and typed something back.

Blake found her text habit annoying. But this time it generated an idea. "Carla, do you still have your texts from the day we watched the phony dad pick up the girl? It was sometime after lunch."

"Maybe," she said. She tapped her finger on his paperwork. "What are you reading anyway?

"A medical examiner's report. About the homicide."

"How did you get that?"

Blake rubbed his temples. He was tired, his brain foggy from lack of sleep. "I'll explain later. What time did the goddamn guy pick up the kid?"

"I don't know, Eddie. I try to live in the moment."

He pointed at her cell. "I mean the texts. You were burning that phone up that day." He reached for her cell. "It will have a time stamp."

She pulled it away. "My messages are confidential between sponsor and sponsee."

Carla took a minute scrolling. "Here it is," she finally said. "That was Veronica. Her last text to me was at 2:42 p.m. Right before the guy went in." Carla set the phone down. "So, what's this all about?"

Blake's first thought was to tell her nothing. She'd already complicated the entire Jackie situation. But his second thought was she deserved to know. He'd recruited her into the job.

Blake said, "The homicide victim, it fits right in that timeline."

"What timeline?"

Blake tapped the autopsy report with his index finger. "The guy who picked up the girl likely murdered the guy in the dope house. Remember how you were saying, why is he taking so long in there? Looks like that's what he was up to."

Carla's fingers came up to her mouth. "Jesus Christ, Eddie."

He rose out of the patio chair. "Now you know why I need to talk to Jackie. Tonight is as good a time as any."

Carla didn't budge. "Visiting hours are over. And I'm speaking at a meeting tonight." She shook her finger at him. "'Till then, I'm not goddamn moving until you tell me what you're into with all this. And I mean *everything*."

He took five minutes to lay it all out, Carla listening, not even sipping her tea. He told her how her he'd used pretense to get information. He told her what they both knew could be crucially important to police. They weren't in legal jeopardy, but they perhaps had an issue ethically.

"*Perhaps?*" Carla said.

But here were other things to consider, he said. He felt an obligation to Jason Perry. JP didn't want him contacting the police. He'd agreed to do a job for the man, he said. He planned on keeping his word. At least until he figured out what the hell was going on. "Otherwise," he said. "I'm no different than half the people I've worked with in this town."

"Eddie, I told you these Hollywood people are batshit crazy," she said. "You should never have gotten involved."

"Carla, I've been involved since the day I showed up in LA."

"So that's it, isn't it? You're still banking on that *48 Hrs.* thing."

"Damn right," Blake said. "And this blows up? The guy with the most to lose is goddamn me."

Blake let that sink in and then leaned forward. "Carla, Jackie is holding out. Mother loses her kid and hardly has anything to say? Something doesn't fit."

"You are dead right, Eddie," she said sarcastically. "She doesn't talk. People usually don't talk right before they kill themselves."

"With Advil? Maybe she knows the kid is okay. Maybe she's part of all this."

"To what end?"

"To set Jason Perry up. He's got old connections with some heavies from Chicago. And where is Jackie from?"

Carla thought about it. Maybe she was getting the picture. "What if you're wrong, Eddie?" she finally said.

"It's all I have to go on right now."

Carla picked up the autopsy report. Leafed through it. Then slid it back across the table. "She wouldn't be the first addict to be up to her ass in something," she said. "But if she's just a victim, I still want to help her get clean and sober. It's the only way I can think of to make amends."

"Amends for what?"

"If it wasn't for me, she wouldn't be missing a daughter."

Blake took her hand and said, "It all starts with Jackie, Carla. Like I said, I need to talk to her. *Alone.*"

"What if she doesn't want to talk?"

"I'll get what I need from her. One way or the other."

Carla took away her hand. "What you gonna do, Eddie? Beat it out of her with a rubber hose?"

26

POOLE WAS PRETTY SURE WHAT he was looking at as he watched the house in Studio City after Blake went inside. Men picking up nicely dressed girls one at a time. Probably their drivers. A biker showing up. Inside for only a few minutes and then leaving quickly. The guy fetching the cash drop, Poole guessed. He'd picked up for a few operations like that himself in the past. Escort services located in good neighborhoods. A half dozen girls sharing a home or large apartment, catering to both in-call and out-call.

Blake was visiting your basic LA whorehouse, Poole decided, the man no doubt spending more of his big earnings.

Poole checked his watch. He'd been tailing Blake all day. He considered calling it a night. Go back to the hotel. Get a couple drinks at the bar. Maybe hit the whirlpool. Call Dagney to see how the kid was doing. Hopefully, Dagney wouldn't be a pain in the ass and demand he pick up the kid again.

But as the sun fell below the hills, Poole decided to move in for a closer look. He pulled the Beretta Tomcat from its ankle holster and slipped it into his windbreaker. He like the pistol because it was so concealable, one of the smallest .32 caliber semi-autos ever made. It carried seven rounds. But there was no need to rack the slide to chamber a shell. The barrel popped up so you could place in a single bullet. On certain jobs, Poole never fired more than one bullet. If you needed more than one, you weren't qualified for that type of work.

The property was perched under a slope surrounded by a thick tree line. Poole quietly opened and closed the door on the Camry. He crossed the street so he could hug a fence line. It was getting dark now. His plan was to approach the house and peek through the windows. But as he got closer, he heard music coming from the back. He carefully worked his way through a thick stand of young eucalyptus trees. He was only fifty feet away when he saw the patio lined with tiny lights.

Blake, sitting there. Not talking. Listening to a woman sitting across from him. She was talking and gesturing a lot. He couldn't make out what she was saying. He couldn't see her face.

But Blake didn't look pleased. If he'd shown up for a friendly in-call, he was getting none of that. He looked like a guy taking a lecture from his mother or a pissed off girlfriend. Finally, the woman stood up and snatched a cup off the table, turned around and walked into the house.

Now Poole recognized her. Not all decked out like she was at the restaurant. This time she was wearing tight jeans and a blouse. He thought, former detective hooking up with a whore, or more likely, the brothel's madam. He'd seen that kind of thing with cops on the take in Vegas.

Ex-cop Edwin Blake, he decided, was no fucking choirboy.

Ten to one Jackie Rose was in the house—he perfect place to stash her. But he couldn't get any closer with Blake sitting outside reading something on the table in front of him. Then the ex-cop leaned back in his chair, looking around at nothing in particular. He sat there like that for a good while.

Poole retreated through the tree stand and decided to wait Blake out in his car. He slumped down in the seat and turned on talk radio. The host, a black guy, was running a contest for listeners called "phone a bro." Callers had to guess voices in sound bites of public figures he played. If they got all the names right, they won a pair of concert tickets. When they couldn't come up with an answer, they could ask for a hint from the host's brother who was on standby on a phone line. A gal won the contest, getting the names right for Jesse Jackson, Nancy Reagan, and legendary anchor Walter Cronkite. She needed to phone a bro for the last two. It reminded him of a section he read in the Napoleon Hill success book. If you can't figure something out for yourself, ask someone who knows.

Poole bet Blake's girlfriend knew about Jackie Rose.

A few minutes later he watched the ex-cop emerge from the house, get in his Challenger and speed off, its pipes reverberating off the ranch homes up the street. It was very dark now in the hills above the San Fernando Valley. There were only a couple dim streetlights. Poole cracked open his car door. Night had brought a chill to the still air. He felt for the Berretta in his windbreaker.

One way or the other he was going to find out who was in that house.

27

HE'D PEEPED THROUGH THE WINDOWS into three bedrooms. Two single beds in each, the beds nicely made. He saw a woman reclining on one, reading, but she wasn't Jackie Rose. He didn't see any mood lighting. He didn't see any nightstands with tissue boxes or condoms or massage oils, standard fair for any in-call brothel.

Poole concealed himself behind a hedge to peer into the final window. What he saw was Blake's girlfriend getting undressed next to a king-size bed. She disrobed down to her bra and panties, then disappeared into a bathroom.

He waited.

She eventually emerged, her hair and makeup nicely done. He was hoping she'd put on a garter belt and pull on some nylons. Instead, she put on a white blouse, a black skirt, and some low heels. She looked dressed for a business meeting. He walked back to his car and waited. If she was going anywhere, he planned to find out where.

Now, an hour later, Poole wasn't sure what he was looking as he watched the crowd outside the log cabin–like building on a narrow street in West Hollywood. He watched from across the street, his head covered with a Cubs ball cap. People were standing around shooting the shit and smoking cigarettes. The sign in the gable over the door read WEST HOLLYWOOD LION'S CLUB. But the collection of hipsters and young women in skintight jeans outside didn't look like the types who raised money for the blind.

Blake's girlfriend was chatting with people at the edge of the crowd.

As if on cue, everyone began filing into the building. Poole pulled the cap low over his forehead and crossed the street. At the door a guy in ripped black jeans, a leather jacket and silver bracelets stuck out his hand and said, "Welcome to the Saturday Night Special."

Poole ignored him and walked in. Inside, he saw a lectern and people sitting in a dozen rows of chairs. His eyes found Blake's girlfriend as she took a seat in the front row. The room smelled of fresh brewed coffee. Poole took a chair along the back wall near two five-gallon coffee urns, one of them labeled decaf.

A line began to form for the coffee, people anxiously filling their cups like it was in short supply. The guy in the black jeans and silver bracelets from the front door stepped into the coffee line. When he arrived at the urn, he stuck out his hand again.

"I'm Delmar," he said. "You new? Or an out of towner?"

Poole shook it this time. "Something like that."

"What's your name?"

"Frank," he said. He'd used that name before. He liked it. Wished his parents had named him that. He'd always liked Sinatra after he saw him with Basie's band at Bally's in Reno in '89. He was only twenty-three. But that show destroyed any notion he had that Sinatra was only his parents' music.

The guy said, "Well, welcome, Frank. I hope you stick around."

Poole decided to find another seat. He saw one vacant in a back corner. He sat down there. A few seconds later, a heavy black woman in a muumuu sat next to him. She introduced herself.

Poole only nodded.

She smiled. "It's okay. I can see you're new, hon. I've been there."

Poole surveyed the room, nearly full now, most of the people seemingly jacked up on coffee. Talking. Hugging. Laughing.

Everyone sat quickly sat down and grew quiet when a woman in a miniskirt and leather jacket took the lectern. "Good evening," she said. "Welcome to the Saturday Night Special meeting of Alcoholics Anonymous. I'm Judy, your alcoholic secretary."

The whole room answered, "Hi, Judy."

Poole thought, so this was what an AA meeting looked like. In Vegas he worked with a wise guy, Tommy Donofrio, who developed a drinking problem, quit, and went to meetings. He invited Poole a couple of times, but he passed. Pretty soon Tommy said he had to quit their crew because he said he couldn't keep jacking trucks and stay sober. But he had to give the guy his due. After he left the outfit, cops tried to flip him. He told the cops to fuck off and moved to Vietnam. Tommy was always trying to get Poole to visit, saying he had a nice big crib, a house girl, and a house boy. He was living large off a strip club be opened in Saigon with a pile of American cash he'd shipped from Vegas. But Poole had an arrest record and didn't think he could get a visa. He also had no desire to spend twenty hours crammed into a goddamn airplane.

For the first five minutes, Poole had no idea where the meeting was going. Somebody read something called "How It Works," which detailed the Twelve Steps. It was followed by applause. Then baskets were passed, most people dropping in a dollar. Poole slid in a single. Then a woman got up and did something she called "chips." She called off days and months—thirty days, sixty days, ninety days, six months, nine months—and people came up in each category to get a poker chip, hug the woman, and say their first names, followed by "I'm an alcoholic." People applauded all of them. Then she asked if there were any sober birthdays, but there were no takers.

Finally, the secretary took the lectern again and asked everyone to welcome the speaker for the evening. Poole's thoughts raced as he watched Blake's girlfriend get up from her chair as the room applauded. She hugged the secretary and settled in behind the lectern.

"Hello everyone," she said. "My name is Carla and I'm an alcoholic."

"Hi, Carla," people answered back, enthusiastically.

Poole said it enthusiastically, too.

What happened next, she began telling her story. Later, he would think he could not have extracted that much information from her with a scorching hot curling iron.

Carla said she was raised in Santa Monica where her father was a high-end entertainment attorney. She spent her summers roller skating in Venice and winters attending an uptight private high school—until she happened upon the women's roller derby circuit being carried on ESPN as filler between traditional sports events. The month she was supposed to show up for her first year at Pepperdine University she made the Thunderbirds, skating with them their last season as a jammer.

"My dad never came to a match," she told the meeting. "My mother had been checked out for years on Xanax and Chardonnay. It only made me want to skate and kick those bitches' asses more and then party my brains out afterward."

She told everyone about a move she called the "can opener" where she sent her opponents airborne. Poole could see it in his mind's eye: young roller girl in those short shorts and knee and elbow pads. Hair flying behind her. Laying somebody out.

Everyone laughed. He thought it was hot.

The laughing stopped when she talked about the pain pill habit she developed skating in Houston. She called pills "alcohol in the solid form." First Tylenol 3. Then Norco. Then Percocet. She skated loaded into her early thirties, bouncing from team to team.

"Until I couldn't anymore," she said. "I spent the next couple of years back here living on handouts from my dad," Carla said, "If you're an alcoholic or an addict you're headed to one of four places: jail, a psychiatric institution, an early grave, or recovery. I didn't mind the psych ward. It had a lot of good dope. What got my attention was the jail in Ventura."

Carla said she regularly went back to the jail where she bottomed out to help other addicts and drunks. She said she sponsored a lot of women and ran a sober living house where some of them stayed.

"I'm sponsoring a woman I just met in that jail meeting," she said. "She's in the hospital right now. I'm going to take her in when she gets out in a couple of days. She isn't going to be easy. But that's how we give back."

Carla didn't say which hospital. That was okay. Carla wasn't running a whorehouse, either. That also didn't matter. Poole could see the entire picture coming together.

He knew where Jackie Rose was going to land.

Poole listened to another ten minutes of catchy phrases about sobriety, gratitude, and serving others. Carla talked a lot about maintaining a positive attitude. Poole thought Dagney ought to check out an AA meeting. She'd fit right in.

The talk finished. Everyone clapped. The secretary made a couple announcements, thanking people who helped put the meeting on. Then it ended with a short prayer, everyone holding hands.

After he let go of the hand of the soul sister in the muumuu, Poole noticed most people weren't leaving right away. They formed a line in front of the lectern, one by one thanking Carla. Some shaking her hand. Others hugging her.

Poole stepped into the line. It took a good five minutes before he finally got close. He heard the guy in front of him say, "Thank you for your share."

Poole said it, too, when he approached her.

She smiled. "What's your name?"

"Frank," he said. "Loved what you had to say."

She tilted her head. "Are you new?"

"I guess."

"Well, welcome, Frank. Keep coming back."

He spread his arms, deciding he should hug her. She hesitated, but then she embraced him. He liked the feeling of her soft breasts against his chest.

Picking up on the lingo in the room, Poole said, "I'm *grateful* I came."

And he was. But that had nothing to do with sobriety.

28

As far back as he could remember, Blake was into cars. Most Detroit boys were. But Blake had an edge in his uncle Daryl who worked at Detroit-Hamtramck Assembly. Uncle Daryl was a throwback, a veteran of the Sixties muscle car cruises on Woodward Avenue. Daryl used to rattle off the specs of his car: *'63 Chevy Impala Super Sport, big block 409, balanced and blue printed, tri-power, Doug headers with a Hurst four-on-the-floor.* Blake used to hang out in his garage in Ferndale, Uncle Daryl with the hood up, a cigarette dangling from his lips as he tweaked its three carbs. For Blake's eighth birthday his uncle took him to see the car compete in the quarter at the Detroit Dragway. He'll never forget the Impala coming off the line, those Doug headers roaring, its street-legal cheater slicks engulfed in blue smoke.

Blake credited his uncle for his appreciation of American horsepower and his ability to spot an automobile's make, year, and model. As a kid that gave him serious cred. Five years in a squad car only sharpened the skill. Even with models that hardly changed, Blake could spot small alterations in trim or wheel cover designs that revealed the year. Working surveillance, he would regularly impress partners with his ability to ID a suspect's car.

On the junction to the 405 Blake was thinking about the car he saw with a Nevada plate: a 2006 silver Toyota Camry parked near the turn fifty yards from Carla's. He was familiar with that make and model. He remembered when his partner Al Henderson bought a Camry. He busted Hendo's chops for driving a Jap car in the Motor City. Back then there were still signs in the parking lot for the United Auto Workers Solidarity House that warned if you weren't driving an American car you should park it in Tokyo.

Blake was sure he'd recently noticed a 2006 Camry like that. But he was operating on little sleep and couldn't nail it down. There was a reason he'd asked the psychiatrist Dr. George about memory and depression six days ago. He'd been struggling for months with short-term recall. Sometimes he couldn't remember public figures who were household names. He wrote that off to his smartphone, his mind getting lazy by looking stuff up. But forgetting what he'd had for dinner or where he was a week ago, that was a different kind of problem. Those types of memories only clicked in with an association—when he saw something connected to what he was trying to remember.

He was sure he'd seen the Camry. He just couldn't remember where.

As Blake merged onto the 405, he saw traffic was light, rush hour ending hours ago. Blake floored the Challenger and roared up the Sepulveda pass, hitting one hundred in just a few seconds. "Blowing the carbon out," Uncle Daryl used to call the move. A couple minutes later he exited at Sunset Boulevard and switched the car into sport mode, a feature that stiffened the suspension so it could hug the numerous turns as Sunset snaked through Brentwood.

Ten minutes later he arrived in the Palisades village, a collection of grocery stores and small businesses along Sunset. Ahead he saw traffic squeezing from two lanes into one. A DPW truck was parked in the right lane, workers attending to a malfunctioning traffic signal. Blake rolled to a stop, waiting for a worker to signal waiting cars through the intersection. A bar of caution lights on the truck pulsed, painting a line of parking meters yellow.

The pulsing amber generated a memory: Saturday at Valentino. He remembered waiting for the valet after dinner with Carla. He remembered the way flashing caution lights on a Santa Monica Police tricycle drew his attention as it rolled up across Pico. He remembered a female parking enforcement officer getting out.

He remembered she wrote a ticket—to a 2006 silver Toyota Camry.

Carla knocked on Blake's door just before midnight. He wouldn't call her hysterical. Carla rarely was hysterical. She was angry, which is the way she acted when she was afraid. She walked into the apartment and remained on her feet as she told him about the man who approached her in the speaker line.

Blake said, "You sure it was the same guy?"

"He was dressed differently," she said. "But I'm pretty damn sure it was him. I first saw him sitting in the back when I was speaking. But I really didn't think much about it then. But after that, I got a closer look. Real close."

Blake reminded her the imposter who claimed to be Dale Rose was fifty yards away when she saw him pick up the kid.

"Up close did you see a bald spot?" Blake asked. "On the crown of his head?"

She said he was wearing a ball cap, a blue one with a red C on it.

"Chicago Cubs," Blake said.

"He said he was a newcomer. He creeped me out. When he hugged me. One of those long hugs. And he smelled."

"You mean body odor?"

She shook her head. "No, citrus. Lime maybe."

"Aftershave?" Royall Lyme, Blake thought.

"Or cologne. Lots of it."

Blake suggested she take a seat. But she remained standing. He decided not to tell her about the silver Toyota Camry. He'd save that. She'd only become more frightened. He walked over to his window, spreading apart its blinds slightly. He saw her Mini Cooper parked on the cul de sac. He didn't see the Camry.

Blake sat in his office chair and said, "Sounds like the guy."

"And just how does he manage to show up at my meeting?"

"I think he's been following me."

Carla walked closer and stood over him. "Goddamn it, Eddie, he followed *me*."

Blake looked up. "I can understand why you're upset."

"Why would he do that?"

"He's probably looking for Jackie." Blake had heard Carla speak before at meetings, the way she told stories. "You didn't say anything, did you, Carla? Mention Jackie in your talk?"

"It's Alcoholics *Anonymous,* Eddie. We don't advertise names of new people. Break their anonymity." Saying it with authority. Then a troubled look came over her face. She plopped down on the edge of his bed. "Jesus, Eddie. I said I met a newcomer in the Ventura jail. That she was in the hospital. And she was coming to live with me when she got out."

"Did you say which hospital?"

Carla shook her head.

"Did you say when?"

"I think I said a couple of days."

Blake walked over and sat down on the bed next to her. He stroked her hair and then held her close. "Stay here tonight. After that, you need to land somewhere else for a few days."

"What about my pigeons?"

"He's only interested in Jackie. When she's released, we'll get her squared away, too."

Carla came out of his embrace, looking at him. "You say that like you have a plan."

Blake nodded. "A couple of them, in fact."

29

DAGNEY COULDN'T WAIT TO GIVE Warren a piece of her mind. It was Thursday, the start of her third day watching the kid named Bella. No call. His number no longer good. She wondered if she'd ever see that twenty grand. Money or no money, she thought, the shifty sonovabitch was just plain inconsiderate.

On the first night, Dagney removed from her office the three posters of her best adult films and made up the futon for the girl. She also signed off her laptop. She didn't want a thirteen-year-old discovering the large cache of Diedre Gibson's best XXX-rated scenes kept there as video files. The next morning, Bella parked herself in front of the TV and spent the day skipping through channels, bouncing between reruns of *I Love Lucy*, the Cartoon Network and metal band concerts. Dagney made her a sandwich for lunch and a chicken pasta dish for dinner. Still, she could only drag one-word answers out of the girl.

Now Bella was back at it, sulking and surfing channels after sleeping in most of the morning.

It was noon.

Washing the dishes, Dagney decided she'd had enough. She

smacked her hand against the kitchen door frame and said, "Put on some shoes. We're going to the beach. We both need some fresh air."

Bella rolled her eyes. "I hate the beach."

"You won't hate this one," Dagney said.

Twenty minutes later, they were on Pacific Coast Highway. Her Honda Civic passed the Malibu pier and Pepperdine University. Ten miles later they passed Zuma, a half mile stretch of flat beach just past Point Dume. Bella pointed at the lifeguard stations. In February, only a few people dotted the sand with chairs and blankets.

"There's a beach," she said.

Dagney kept driving. "Not what I had in mind."

Soon, the PCH elevated along a bluff, the ocean now to their left in the distance. When Dagney saw the sign for El Matador State Beach she turned into its small gravel parking lot. There were less than a half dozen cars parked in the lot that overlooked the ocean a couple hundred feet below.

Bella said, "I don't see a beach."

"Best kept secret in LA," Dagney said. She didn't tell the girl people sometimes used a far end cove there as a nude beach. She didn't tell her she used to get rid of her tan lines there when she was doing four hard-core scenes a week.

They walked down a steep incline to a stairway below the bluff. A stirring vista appeared. El Matador was unlike anything on the LA-area coastline. Tidal pools and two-story-high rock formations dotted the beach. Some were hollowed out with arches and small caves. Lines of cormorants and pelicans perched on top of the rocks,

The musky fragrance of the Pacific filled Dagney's nostrils. "Smell that?" she said. "That's what the ocean smells like when you get away from the city."

Bella eyed the seascape.

"Take off your shoes," Dagney said.

The girl sat down on the last step and began unlacing her black high-top sneakers. Dagney didn't wait. She kicked off her sandals and ran to the water's edge. A wave crashed onto the sand, the Pacific streaming across her ankles. She turned to Bella, still standing by the stairs.

"C'mon, girl," Dagney shouted, waiving her hand.

She was surprised when the girl ran towards her, then past her, stopping as the next wave covered her legs up to her knees.

She let out a scream. "It's cold!"

There was something about this beach, Dagney thought. That's why she brought the girl. That's why she was there as well. It was impossible to stay pissed off at anything at El Matador.

Later, they walked, saying little, exploring the tidal pools. Bella was fascinated by the alien-looking kelp bulbs that had washed up and the starfish that clung to some of the rocks. After they explored west, they turned around and walked southeast of the staircase. No longer a state beach, it was lined with multimillion-dollar modern homes, most of them square structures of glass and stucco with multi-story, ocean-view decks.

Bella stopped and pointed at the ocean. "Look. Sharks."

Dagney saw a fin surface. Then several others. "Those are dolphins. It's a pod."

"A pod?"

"When they travel together. Like a family."

They watched for a minute or two, the pod following the shoreline, then disappearing into deeper waters.

They resumed their walk. "I used to bug my mom to take me to the beach," Dagney said. "But I never saw the ocean until I took a road trip after high school."

"Why didn't she?"

"No beaches in Barstow."

"Where's that?"

"California high desert. Where I grew up."

"My dad used to take us to Lake Michigan," Bella said, her eyes on the sand.

"Your dad? Does he know about your situation?"

She shook her head. "He was killed. Fighting in the war."

"How old were you?"

"Eight." Her eyes were still lowered.

"I'll bet you miss him."

Bella said, "Do you miss yours?"

"What makes you think he wasn't around?"

"He probably would have taken you to the beach."

Dagney nodded. "That's because I don't know who my dad is."

"Seriously?"

"You'd have to know my mother."

"That sucks."

"Yeah. I kept waiting for someone to knock on my door one day. You know like you see in the movies. Some stranger shows up and says he's your dad and he's been looking for you for years. After a while, you just learn to not give a shit."

"You never wanted to look?"

Dagney chuckled. "Like I said, my mother? I wouldn't even know where to start."

They walked a couple hundred feet, saying nothing. A sand-piper scampered in front of them along the tide line. Bella ran after the bird in short sprints, trying to catch it. But it matched her gait, always staying just ahead.

Dagney laughed. So did Bella.

Eventually the sandpiper took off, flying away just above the waves.

Bella frowned. "I didn't mean to scare it off."

"I don't think you did," Dagney said.

Twenty or thirty yards later, Bella looked over, making eye contact. "Sometimes I have this dream. It's always the same one."

"Your dad?"

Bella nodded, staring straight ahead now. "I'm looking out my bedroom window, waiting for friends to come. It's dark and I see a man in a uniform walking up the street. I think it's my dad coming home. Like one of those surprise visits you see soldiers do on the news. *Wrong.*"

"Wrong?"

"It's the guy who tells my mother that he's dead. I hear my mother scream. Then the guy comes into my bedroom and—" She stopped walking.

Dagney stopped, too. She could see a mix of anger and despair in the girl's eyes.

"And?" Dagney said.

Bella said, "I wake up."

A half hour later, they sat down for lunch at Neptune's Net, a seafood shack on the Los Angeles and Ventura county line popular with bikers. Dagney ordered crab cakes, Bella the fish and chips. They took a seat at a table overlooking a dozen motorcycles parked out front and waited for their number to be called to pick up their order.

Bella glanced at the bikes and then back at Dagney. "Do you think they're going to take me away from my mom?" she asked.

Dagney said, "What makes you say that?"

"The guy who dropped me off said I could end up in a foster home."

Dagney squinted. "Warren? He doesn't know that. That's up to a judge. And that depends on what your mother does when she gets out."

"How do you know that?"

"Some people I used to work with got strung out. Some got it together. Others, it didn't turn out so well." Dagney immediately wished she hadn't said the last part.

Bella said, "What kind of work?"

Dagney never liked lying. Lying required too much work. So, she limited her answer. "I used to do some modeling."

Bella persisted. "What kind? You mean like in magazines?"

"Something like that. Swimsuit stuff."

Before Bella could follow up with another question, their order blared over the loudspeaker. Dagney walked thirty feet to the counter and took her place at the end of the pick-up line. When she returned to the table with their tray the girl was gone. She scanned the restaurant and the parking lot. Finally, she spotted Bella talking to a young biker in racing leathers who was sitting sidesaddle on a Yamaha sport bike.

Dagney walked over, saying their food was ready.

The guy stuck out his hand. "My name is Rick. This your daughter?"

Dagney shook her head. "C'mon, Bella, nothing worse than cold seafood."

She hesitated. "He said he'd give me a ride if I wanted."

"I'll bet he did." Dagney shot the guy a look. "She's thirteen."

The guy held up his hands in surrender. "Hey, she asked."

Dagney grabbed her hand and led her back to the table. Bella didn't say anything for a few minutes as she munched on her fish.

Finally, Dagney said, "I'm just looking out for you, Bella. Guy like that, you don't know where you might end up. You understand what I'm saying?"

She shrugged. "He seemed nice."

"But he was a stranger."

"You're a stranger."

Dagney nodded. "You're right. But hopefully we're getting to know each other."

Bella's eyes went back to her food.

"How's your fish?"

Bella nodded and said, "The guy you work with, he said my mom was in jail in Ventura. I saw Ventura on a sign back there. Are we close?"

Dagney took her last bite of crab cake. "It's up PCH. Not too far."

Her eyes brightened. "Let's go visit her."

"I'm not sure that would be a good idea."

"Why not? I want to talk to her."

"And what would you say?"

"I'd ask her to do what the judge says. So I don't end up in a foster home."

"It's too bad you don't have a phone. She could have called you." That was odd, now that Dagney thought about it. "Why don't you have a phone? Most girls your age do."

Bella looked down. "She took it away. It's a long story." Then she looked up and brought her palms together prayer-like. "*Please,* Dagney." It was the first time the girl used her name. "How am I ever going to ask her unless we go see her?"

Dagney said. "Finish your fish." She pulled out her phone, hoping Warren's number might be working now. But the number was still out of service. She hung up.

"Can we?" Bella asked again.

Poor kid, Dagney thought, dumped off with no real lifeline. In a way, she was surprised the girl was handling it all as well as she did.

Dagney said, "Hang on."

She searched for Ventura County jail visiting hours on her

phone. Visits at the Ventura County Pretrial Detention Center were from 1:30 until 4:30 p.m. She pasted its Santa Paula address into the phone's map. From their location, it calculated a thirty-five-minute drive up the coast to a direct shot inland on the Santa Paula Freeway. Traffic was sparse on the map. Dagney looked at the current time displayed on her phone.

The trip was doable. It was just past 3 p.m.

30

WARREN POOLE SLEPT IN AND woke up feeling positive. He read a little bit of the Napoleon Hill book on the toilet. Then he went for another massage, this time forgoing the hot rock treatment and lavender but keeping the scalp massage.

He had a destination picked for lunch. The day before he'd spotted a place called Mel's Drive-In on Ventura Boulevard. It reminded him of the movie *American Graffiti*. There was a big neon sign out front. The words HOME STYLE COOKING and an arrow pointing down that read: EAT.

Inside Mel's he found jukebox consoles in every booth. Poole dropped in a quarter and played Chuck Berry's "Little Queenie." He liked the look of his waitress. Early twenties with a pretty face and nice legs. She was wearing a short, pink skirt with a small white apron hanging from her tiny waist.

Poole asked her if she was an actress when she brought his order. He asked her if she was from east. She said no, she was from Reseda and was attending a community college to prepare for nursing school. Poole had to give LA that. The town had a lot of eye candy. He decided it was the gene pool, generations of homecoming queens arriving with dreams of stardom. Few made it but stayed anyway and had kids after hooking up with some rich fuck with a big house and a pool boy.

Poole chowed down on steak and eggs over easy and crisp hash browns the way he liked them. He watched the waitress between bites. The way she bent over at the booths, the short skirt hiking up in the back and exposing a ruffled slip underneath. He smiled at her when she passed his booth a couple times. But she was in a hurry, her eyes elsewhere.

After the waitress brought the check, he tried calling Mr. Perry's cell. He wanted to tell the man to get his money together. Tell him the kid was fine and he had a line on Jackie. He tried three times, but the producer didn't pick up. He had another number and called it. A gal named Lindsay answered, saying she was Mr. Perry's assistant. He'd never met her. He and Mr. Perry had only met alone at his home.

He decided to play the assistant on the down low. He said his name was Frank, that he'd met Mr. Perry in Las Vegas and the producer wanted him to give him a call when he was in town. He had some good news for him. Poole expected Mr. Perry would figure out what the message meant.

"Unfortunately, JP is unavailable," she said. "He's in Vancouver and can't be reached right now."

He asked when he was expected to return.

"That's unclear. You might try back in a couple of days. I'll have an update."

He thanked her and hung up. Her story was bullshit, he decided. Mr. Perry was *unavailable* because he was giving the ex-cop Blake room to operate and deliver Jackie. Now he was sure of it.

Poole called over his waitress and dropped a twenty and a ten on the table over his check. He told her to keep the change and winked when she picked it up.

"Thank you," she said. But she didn't smile.

Driving back to Studio City he noticed the traffic wasn't as thick as it was when he headed to lunch. He was starting to get a feel for how it flowed in LA. Three rush hours: One in the morning starting at 7:00 a.m. Another in the afternoon that began at about 3:30 when the schools got out, setting up the after-work crush. But there was a third lighter one, a lunch rush hour that ran from noon until 2 p.m.

Ten minutes later he turned on Laurel Canyon Boulevard, drove a couple blocks toward the hills and turned onto a residential street. The street started out straight, but then forked to the right, elevating as it snaked through mainly ranch homes on both sides. A quarter mile later he slowed.

He didn't see Blake's Dodge Challenger or Carla's Mini Cooper.

Poole pulled his Camry to the curb, looking the place over this time in the daylight, planning what he wanted to do after Jackie moved in. He figured it was maybe fifty steps from his car to the front door. Do it when Blake wasn't there. Walk right up to the door. Ask for Jackie. Say he had her daughter and she needed her mom. Tell Jackie he was there for a friend who was looking after them both. If she resisted, or the woman Carla got involved, offer a choice, like he did with her daughter.

Tell her they could do it the easy way or the hard way.

31

BLAKE ROSE AT DAWN AFTER another restless night, leaving Carla a note and letting her sleep. He drove to Santa Monica. The night before he'd set up a breakfast meeting with the Santa Monica sergeant who helped him take down the stalker who jumped the rope line on the red carpet.

They met at the Bulletproof Coffee on Main before the sergeant's shift. He was a cop in his early fifties, slightly overweight with a ruddy face and a spotless uniform. Blake bought him a breakfast beef bowl with two eggs and one of the cafe's special coffees made with butter and something the shop called Brain Octane Oil.

The sergeant dug into the breakfast bowl. "So, you said you needed a favor," he said.

Blake nodded. "My girlfriend. She's got a stalker. Some asshole who spotted her at an AA meeting."

"You got a name for me? Maybe a DOB?"

Blake shook his head. "That's the problem. She doesn't have a name. But get this, he's been following her. Parking near her house. She wants to get a RO. As soon as she can get an ID."

"I don't like lurkers," the sergeant said, his mouth full of eggs.

Blake leaned forward. "But I think she might have got lucky.

The other night? She was coming out of Valentino and there he was. Parked across Pico. She said the meter reader was writing him up." Blake paused. "I guess that's where the favor comes in."

The sergeant wiped his lips. "Traffic Services will have that. Valentino. That's the three-thousand block. Do you have a date and time?"

An hour later, Blake answered his cell as he walked into his apartment, finding Carla no longer there. The sergeant had run the Camry's plate. The car was registered to a name and address in Las Vegas.

"Warren James Poole, age forty-eight," he said. "You want to hear his sheet?"

"If that's not a problem."

"Like I said, I don't like lurkers."

Blake noted down more than a half dozen different arrests for Warren James Poole, most of them more than twenty-five to thirty years ago. Extortion. Commercial theft. Loan sharking. Two felonious assaults. Possession of stolen property.

"He's either got one hell of a lawyer, or he's one lucky sonovabitch," the sergeant said. "Not a single conviction."

As Blake was winding up the call, Carla returned carrying a grocery bag. She went straight to his kitchen. He heard her pulling plates out of the cupboard. After he hung up, he turned and saw his table set with bagels, lox, cream cheese, and two glasses of orange juice. She was waiting for him.

He slid the notes he'd been keeping on the job into a file folder, set it on the table and sat down across from her.

"Well?" she said.

"Have you heard from Jackie?"

She nodded. "She's being released tomorrow at noon."

He could see a look in her eyes he knew well. A look of determination. None of the fear he saw last night.

"Have you found a place to stay?"

She pushed his juice closer to his hand. "I'm not leaving my pigeons."

He opened up his folder and laid it out for her: Poole's full name. That he was from Las Vegas. His arrests, pointing out that two of them involved violence. "But no convictions," he said. "No prison time served."

She took a sip of juice. "He's innocent?"

"No, that means he's dangerous."

"How do you figure?"

"These types of arrests? They're typical of someone who was hooked up. And they're at a time when Vegas was mobbed up."

"Typical?"

"I'm thinking he was on a crew. You get bennies like a paid off judge or the best defense money can buy."

"What are you saying, Eddie?"

"His skill set, the way he tailed us. The way he posed as the ex. He's found a new line of work. He's freelancing."

"Doing what?"

Blake took a sip of his juice. "Hired gun."

Carla looked irritated. "What? Like we're in a goddamn western?"

"It's a term. Somebody with some muscle. Somebody working off the books."

She didn't respond. She spread cream cheese on a bagel and pushed it across the table.

He took a couple of bites. He could see her thinking.

Finally, she leaned back in her chair. "One of my old Thunderbirds teammates, Moxie. She married this commercial real estate guy. They have a big boat. They keep it in Marina Del Rey. She told me if I ever wanted to take a break from the Valley I could stay there. I guess the thing never leaves the dock."

"Call her," Blake said.

"Maybe it's time we call the police."

"Your girl Jackie doesn't want that."

"She's not well enough to know what she wants."

"I need to talk to her first. See if I can put some pieces together. If this guy Poole is for hire, the question is who hired him. She might know something."

Carla said, "What, Eddie, so you can keep this producer out of it? Why do you give a damn about this Hollywood asshole?"

"Personally, I don't. But you wouldn't like Michigan. It gets really cold."

"What does Michigan have to do with it?"

"I'd like to stick around. Be able to make a decent buck here."

Her eyebrows raised. "Are you saying if you had to leave LA you'd want me to go with you?"

Blake reached for her hand across the table. "I should have probably blown off this town two years ago. Gone back to Michigan, or Texas, maybe. Someplace that works on a cop's pension instead of paying a couple grand for an apartment the size of a hotel room. You're a giant pain in the ass with those pigeons. But I wanted to stick around. Why do you think I have?"

He didn't have to get specific. Didn't have to come straight out with it. He could see in the warmth of her eyes that she knew what he was saying.

She rose from her chair, came around the table and straddled his lap, facing him. He cupped her face in his hands, looking into her eyes, making sure she knew he was sincere. He kissed her lightly at first. Then deeply, sensing she wanted it that way. As his hands slid into her hair, hers slid under his shirt, then for his belt. He lifted her and stood. He heard something drop off the table, but he didn't look.

She was leading him to his bed.

Unlike the past six months, what was happening didn't feel like work. She had her clothes off before he removed his. He saw a beautiful woman leaning against the headboard, her skin radiant in the warm morning light She reached up and pulled him down. He'd learned over the years that making love was always better if you let the woman take you to bed. Not the other way around, the way he thought when he was a dumb kid.

Afterwards, they held each other for a while, not saying much, watching an offshore wind play with the tips of the palms on the other side of the cul de sac.

Carla finally said, "I think what Dr. George gave you might be kicking in."

"What makes you say that?"

"The fact that we're even like this."

"I don't know," Blake said. "All I know is I can't seem to get a good night's sleep."

She turned on her side, looking at him. "Eddie. I want you to know I'm not going to let Jackie come between us."

He touched her hair. "I know you want to help her."

"That's not really it. It's like what I heard a guy say at a meeting once. But I'm not sure you'd understand."

"Try me."

"He said that he'd sponsored a dozen people since he got into the program. And everyone one of them was a success. Somebody asked him, so they all got sober? And he said, no every one of them drank again. Then he said, but I'm still sober." She waited until she had his eyes. "*I* need to do it, Eddie. Can you understand?"

He nodded and kissed her.

A few minutes later, he slid off the bed and told her he needed a shower.

When he came out of the bathroom, a towel wrapped around his waist, Carla was wearing one of his button-down shirts and standing by the dining table. She had his file folder in her hand.

She saw him and said, "I wasn't snooping."

"It's okay."

"This fell on the floor."

She slid the folder back on the table. But she also had something in her hand. She handed it to him. "Where was this taken? Looks like in the mountains somewhere."

It was the photo of Jacqueline and Isabella Rose that Warren Poole, playing the phony ex, had given him at Philippe. "I'm not sure," Blake said.

He hadn't looked at the photo for seven days. Hadn't looked at the good-looking woman in her late thirties, dressed in a pair of tight jeans and a halter top. Hadn't studied the Goth daughter with the streak of purple in her hair. But he wasn't looking at mother and daughter now. He was looking at what was behind them.

Edwin Blake realized he had seen those boulders before.

32

DAGNEY WASN'T SURE WHAT TO do with the girl when they left the jail yesterday. The teenager's tears flowed as they walked out of the Ventura Pretrial Facility, not a minute after the visitation clerk told them that inmate Jacqueline Margaret Rose had been discharged four days ago. In the parking lot Dagney suggested they try calling her mother. Dagney punched in a number Bella thought was her mom's. The voice mail didn't pick up. They raced to the Hall of Justice to check on her mother's status. They arrived at 4:05. The court clerk's office closed at 4 p.m.

Dagney said, "I'm sure there's some explanation."

She didn't respond. The tears had stopped. She was lost somewhere inside her head.

As they headed back to LA, Dagney was pretty sure what the girl was feeling. She thought, her father dies overseas, now her mother is in the wind, the kid no doubt conjuring up the worst possible scenario. Dagney remembered what her psychotherapist told her when she spent six months on the couch exploring why she liked shooting porn. "It's called fear of abandonment," the therapist said. "It will haunt you for a lifetime unless you deal with it." The therapist pointed out the trauma of her father leaving would recycle at the end of any serious relationship. The therapist said, "Consider that you may like having sex on camera because you are in control. So, you can pick your partners and then say goodbye with no strings attached."

As she thought about it, Dagney decided that probably was why she hooked up with Warren and now, years later, still tolerated his sporadic visits. Warren was familiar. But he was also artificial. Nothing to hook into that could break her heart.

Or maybe it all was just psychobabble. Either way, Dagney considered it too heavy to lay on a traumatized thirteen-year-old. She was searching her mind for another solution when she noticed the sign for the Camarillo Retail Outlets on the 101.

She glanced a Bella. "You know what I do when I'm having a shitty day?"

Bella shook her head.

"Retail therapy."

A few minutes later, Dagney pulled into the complex, a sprawling collection of name-brand factory outlets.

She drove slowly past the storefronts. "Tell me what turns you on," Dagney said.

They rolled by Saks, DKNY, Adidas, Tommy Hilfiger, Guess, and the Disney Outlet. Bella remained silent as they passed a half dozen more stores.

Then Bella pointed. "There."

Dagney braked. She saw a sign for Robert Wayne Footwear. Dagney said, "You know what they say. A girl can't have enough shoes."

As they walked up to the store Bella pointed at a sign in the window advertising the lines the outlet carried, Bella saying, "They have Doc Martens."

Inside, she made a beeline to the section, a collection of lace-up high boots that Dagney always thought looked like black combat boots. She knew they were popular with punk rockers and Goth types.

Dagney sat in a chair. "Take your time, hon."

She watched Bella run her fingers over the display models, picking each one of them up, looking inside, examining their rubber soles. At the end of the rack she turned around and presented Dagney with her choice: a pair called the 14-Eye Vonda boot. It was black leather with red roses embroidered over the toe and uppers that reached to mid-calf. A clerk brought a pair. Bella laced up all fourteen eyelets on both feet and then stood, admiring them in a mirror.

Bella turned around. "What do you think?"

"They're hot," Dagney said. "And you can kick the shit out of anybody who backs you into a corner."

"They're expensive."

Dagney smiled. "Don't worry about it, hon."

They were $175. Dagney used a credit card.

Now, in the morning as Bella slept, Dagney checked her card balance as she sipped coffee at her kitchen table. Another fifty dollars and she would have maxed out her credit line. But she concluded it was money well spent. She'd not only come to like the girl. The teenager was pulling at her heart.

Dagney decided, abandonment be damned. She wanted to help the kid. Maybe that would be good for both of them, especially after their talk well past midnight.

Isabella Rose had really opened up.

33

HE PICKED UP A NEW burner in the morning and then sat on Mr. Perry's house in Malibu. He only had to wait an hour. The Tesla left. He followed it for twenty miles. He could tail the car because Mr. Perry had never seen his Camry. The one time they met at his house Mr. Perry didn't bother to see him to the door.

The ride ended with the Tesla turning into a parking structure in Beverly Hills. Poole drove on, found a meter down the street and then watched from the sidewalk. Mr. Perry looked different when he emerged. No longer dressed like a vagrant. He wore a blue blazer and a dress shirt, his beard trimmed and his hair shorter. Poole watched him walk a half block and then enter through a set of double doors off Dayton Way, the sign overhead reading, THE GRILL ON THE ALLEY.

Poole entered the restaurant a few minutes later.

Inside, the hostess was seating a party. Poole surveyed the room from just inside. A bar. Booths on the wall in dark walnut. A black-and-white tile floor. Framed sketches on the walls. Waiters in white coats. Poole saw customers in suits and women in business attire. Others were dressed down in jeans and T-shirts. He spotted an aging actress he'd seen in films. She was dressed in a jogging suit with black sunglasses covering half her face. Everyone was talking loudly like they were taking care of business.

Only two guys with drinks were sitting at the bar. Poole walked to the rail, not bothering to wait for the hostess. He took the last stool next to the bar setup. He sat sidesaddle at first, which provided a line of sight to a booth along the wall about twenty feet away. A man and a woman sitting there with their backs to him. He couldn't see their faces. But he could see who was sitting across from them.

He could see Mr. Perry.

The producer was talking, gesturing. Poole could make out a few words. It sounded like movie talk. Poole continued facing him and waited. Waited until the man looked up. Just glancing at first, not fully registering. Then looking up again, his brow rising, their eyes locking —seeing Poole smiling. He appreciated the way Mr. Perry was looking at him.

Like *what the fuck are you doing here?*

As Perry looked away, Poole swung his feet toward the bar and flagged the bartender. He ordered a Jack on the rocks. He was only going to have a drink. But the bartender said he could eat at the bar and slid him a menu. Poole considered the twenty-eight-dollar skirt steak, then thought about the jumbo lump crab cakes for thirty-five. But when he overheard the producer ask his waiter for the petite New York steak, he ordered the same with a Caesar to start.

The steak came medium rare, just the way Poole ordered it. He took his time with the meal, washing bites down with a Heineken. He liked the bartender, a young guy in a white shirt and black vest who answered all his questions. Saying the place had just been rated by the *Hollywood Reporter* as one of the top ten power lunch spots in Hollywood. Telling him that one of its early investors was an art collector and the sketches on the walls were from art students at UCLA.

A few minutes after the bartender took away his empty plate, Poole saw Mr. Perry slide out of his booth, walk past him, and disappear up a stairwell at the other end of the bar. Poole picked up a bar napkin and asked to borrow the bartender's pen. Seconds later, he headed for the stairs where he saw a sign stating that the restrooms were on the second floor.

The men's room was small. A marble sink, two urinals and one stall. Mr. Perry was waiting, his arms crossed. Standing there in the kind of power pose like he was posing for the cover of *Forbes* magazine. He glared as Poole came closer.

"Just what in goddamn hell do you think you're doing?"

Poole smiled. "Steak was good, don't you think?" He took a couple steps closer. "How was Vancouver? Me? Never been. Only Toronto."

Mr. Perry didn't answer.

Poole said, "That's what I thought."

He decided it was time to stop fucking around. In one motion he grabbed the man by his lapels and shoved him into the stall, slamming his ass down hard on the toilet seat.

Poole over him now, his hands still gripping his lapels. "Well, look at you now," he said calmly. "Sittin' here on the crapper with a gut full of meat."

Blinking rapidly, Mr. Perry asked, "Okay, okay. What do you want?"

Poole gripped his lapels tighter. "Your boy has been busy. He's got the mom squared away. And if he hasn't told you that, the man is holding out on you. But I'm figuring with you being out of touch on your mystery trip, you—or maybe both of you—are trying to shoot a move on me. Hell, as far as I know, you got him looking for the daughter. Take me completely out of the picture." He shook him a couple of times, his voice rising. "Ain't gonna happen, you follow?"

Mr. Perry looked down at his feet.

Poole slapped his face. Hard. "Look at me."

The man looking really scared now. Used to people kissing his ass. Used to people fetching everything. Poole doubted anyone had ever manhandled him that way.

He bent over close to his face. "No more games. You follow? I deliver the mom and the girl. Like we agreed. Should be any day now. Maybe even tomorrow. No more *trips.*"

Mr. Perry nodded. A short fast nod.

"You got the money together?"

"I'm working on it." He said it in a shaky, quiet voice,

Poole locked onto his eyes again. "No money? Or you pull some shit? I don't leave witnesses, *Mr. Perry.* No girl. No mother. They disappear. Your cop pal, and the roller girl he hangs with? They go, too. Everybody takes a dirt nap. You try to play solid citizen, bring anybody else into this, I mean *anybody*, I'm watching you. You follow?"

Mr. Perry nodded.

"Say it."

"Yes."

Poole slammed him back against the toilet as he let go of his lapels. He stepped back, looking over the man. His sports jacket rumpled. His top shirt button popped. No longer a big deal at his power lunch. He tossed the napkin with his new cell phone number at his feet.

"Call me when you have the money together."

Poole washed his hands and toweled them off. He turned around. The producer was still sitting on the toilet, his head in his hands.

Before he left, he said, "I'd say it's time to shit or get off the pot, *Mr. Perry.*"

34

BLAKE CALLED JASON PERRY AFTER sunset and said he had some news, but they needed to meet face to face. He told JP to meet him at a scenic turnoff that overlooked the valley at the top of Topanga Canyon Road.

"I'll see you in a half hour," Blake said. "Take Mulholland. It will be a nice workout for your Ferrari."

JP started to say something. But Blake hung up.

Forty minutes later, he heard the exhaust of JP's 488 Spider negotiating the curves before he ever saw the Ferrari's headlights. Blake was leaning against the hood of his Challenger, his eyes on the expanse of lights in the San Fernando Valley below. Other than a young couple locked in a romantic embrace at the far end of the turnoff, he was alone.

JP screeched into the parking lot, emerged from his red sports car and walked toward him in an agitated gait. He glanced at the couple, then at Blake, saying, "The way it works, Blake, the guy who pays the goddamn bills picks the location of the meeting."

Blake turned. "So far, JP, you haven't paid me a dime."

JP stepped closer, looking like he was going to say something. Tell Blake he was out of line. But before he could speak, Blake reached into his back pocket and handed JP the report from the coroner's office.

"Read it," he said. He was curious if the illiteracy rumors were true.

JP glanced at the paperwork. "I don't have time to read. What is this?"

"It's an official document. From the Los Angeles County medical examiner's office."

JP handed it back. "Give me the log line."

"The log line reads that you have officially stepped into some deep shit."

JP blinked a couple times.

Blake had a lot more than the catchy sentence producers request to sum up a film or TV show. "Seems like your *friend of a friend* left the stiff in Sherman Oaks. Three gunshots. Time of death coinciding with when he picked up the kid. You know, the girl named Bella, Jackie Rose's daughter. I'm guessing you're already very familiar with their names."

JP started to say something, but Blake cut him off again. "You wanted me to find out about the homicide. Done. But something has been bugging me. Since day one, actually. Guy like you doing a favor for some poor sonovabitch from Chicago. It's not your style, JP. Nobody is going to put your picture in a magazine. This one is not your kind of charity event."

JP took a step closer. "Now you listen to me, Blake."

Blake held up his hand like a cop stopping traffic. "I'm not done." He lowered his hand. "So, the guy who claims he's the kid's dad? He shows me a picture of his ex-wife and the kid. But then I find out the real dad is a dead war hero. And so, I get to thinking, where did the phony dad get that photo?"

Blake pulled out the snapshot and handed it to JP.

JP glanced at it. He handed it back. "How the fuck would I know?"

Blake pushed it back into his hand. "Take a good look. You're in the picture business. You know what makes a good shot. It's not just the actors, the blocking. You need a good set designer. The background should tell the story, too."

JP looked up from the photo.

Blake said, "Just like mother nature, isn't it? Back where I come from, you don't see a pool laid out like that. You don't even see a goddamn pool. People just open a fire hydrant or get one of those plastic blow-ups and fill with a water hose."

JP's eyes blinked rapidly.

Blake said, "So, JP, how much did it cost to haul in all those big boulders from the mountains, anyway?"

JP took a deep breath and exhaled. He walked five feet over to the rail fence that kept visitors from tumbling down a steep incline. He gripped the railing with one hand, turned and said, "What do you want?"

"I want to know what the hell you've gotten me into."

JP looked at the photo again, then dangled it over the railing, staring straight ahead. He didn't say anything for a good thirty seconds. Blake didn't press him. He let silence do it.

Finally, JP said, "Do you have any idea what it's like to be me?"

"I don't have a Ferrari."

"Blake, I really don't have anybody. No kids. No heirs. A couple weeks ago. Two girls came over. In their twenties. Can't even remember where I met them. Couple of models trying to break into pictures. Within an hour the three of us were naked in my whirlpool. The threesome started there." He turned to Blake. "I'm sixty-eight fucking years old. Out of shape. I can barely see my own dick. Now I ask you, do you really think those girls give a rat's ass about me?"

"You really want me to answer that question?"

JP shook his head. "Jackie? She didn't know anything. Not a thing about who I was or what I did."

Blake felt himself getting angry. He'd known all day he had JP nailed with the photo. But now he hated hearing it. He wasn't angry at JP. He was angry at himself for not seeing it from day one.

JP continued, "I met her about a year ago. Thanksgiving. I was dishing out meals at a homeless mission downtown. A lot of us do that. Actors. Hollywood people. But you can only do a one-hour shift because all the celebs want to get in on the action. Have their publicists show everybody we're not a bunch of selfish assholes. Jackie, she was there volunteering on cleanup. All day. She had the girl with her. Bella. We started talking. One thing led to another."

Blake said, "Led where?"

"There was a chemistry. But I wanted to be sure. So, I came up with a plan. We talked a lot on the phone first. I told her I was retired. From the chamber of commerce. She never asked for details. Then dinners. Nothing fancy. None of the industry places. You have to understand, Blake, I can't even walk into a place without some-body trying to shove a fucking script in my hand. I even drove my assistant's BMW. Jackie never had a goddamn clue."

Blake shook his head. "JP, anybody can type your name into decent phone and find out everything about you."

"I used my birth name. It's the same initials."

"You're not Jason Perry?"

"That's the name I registered with SAG when I started as an actor. I kept it. Changed it legally when I started producing."

Blake wanted to ask him what his real name was. Instead, he said, "You can't keep a secret like that secret from a woman very long."

JP glanced over at the couple in the parking lot. They were

making out now. "After about a month, when I was sure what she was feeling for me was real, I asked her and Bella to move in. She saw the house, the cars, the posters, the awards. She was upset I'd lied. But she eventually understood." He looked back at the valley below. "You see, Blake, she didn't fall in love with Jason Perry. She fell in love with Janek Polakowski, just a regular working-class kid from Chicago."

"Russian?"

JP turned to Blake. "Polish. You'd have changed the fucking thing, too if you grew up listening to Polack jokes. Plus, I wasn't a Jew. So, it was no help in the industry. Roman had the Polish film-maker persona cornered by then."

Blake shook his head, thinking what Carla had said. Carnies in nice clothes. Blake rested his elbows on the railing and said, "The writers would say that's quite a backstory, JP. But it doesn't really tell me a lot about how you get from there to here."

JP glanced down at the snapshot. "It's this goddamn town."

Blake waited for him to continue.

JP looked back at the Valley. "Everything was fine for the first few months. Until I threw a dinner party for some folks involved in the Warners deal. Let me tell you something, Blake. Women? They don't look good for guys. They look good for other women. These industry wives and girlfriends? They did a real number on Jackie. You know, she felt—inadequate. Next thing I know, I'm paying for a new set of tits. I can't say I objected. And I should have gotten a goddamn bulk discount from those fucking surgeons on Roxbury for the number of girlfriends I've equipped. But that's where it started."

"You mean the painkillers."

JP nodded. "She wanted some work on her nose. Then lipo. Then a brow lift and more. Six surgeries in all. She had her god-damn snatch trimmed and her asshole bleached. Those 90210 docs?

They're not stingy with the meds. I'm not sure she was even going for the work. I think she was going for the scripts."

JP held up the photo. "The girl, Bella? She began to change. Smart kid, really. She saw what was happening. She'd find her mom nodded out in the bathroom. The kid started acting out. That's what my therapist called it. Dyed her hair. Wore black. Hung out in Venice with a bad crowd. She disappeared a few times, in fact."

Blake wondered out loud if the police had to locate her. If they did, the girl would be in the LAPD system. That could make it easier to find her.

JP shook his head. "She always came back. But like I've been telling you, cops are the last place I'm going to go."

"Yeah, I got that."

"I kept trying to convince Jackie to get off the stuff. She'd say they were doctor's orders. I told her Anna Nicole had doctor's orders, too. In the end we were arguing a lot. Or she'd just mentally check out. Then one day, I came home from the Warners lot and they were both gone. As well as twenty thousand in cash."

"You gave her access to your bank account?"

JP shook his head again. "I keep a quarter mil in my home safe. She must have seen me working the combination. It's my get-out-of-Dodge money. You know, if we get another riot. Or something worse. I guess I'm lucky she didn't fucking take it all."

Blake looked over at JP. He seemed resigned.

Blake said, "So, Midwest single mom comes to LA. Gets caught up in the life. Changes. Becomes a dope fiend and rips you off for 20k. So that begs the question: why in the world would you want her back? Is it the money?"

JP shrugged. "The money means nothing. I want *Jackie* back. The woman I first met. You see, I went about it all wrong. Now I know there are experts, something called an intervention. Get her into one of those Malibu rehabs. Plus, Bella, her life has to be hell at this point. The girl needs some stability." JP turned to Blake. "I know everybody in this town thinks I'm one shallow sonovabitch. But, Blake, when it comes to this, I feel responsible."

Blake was silent for a good minute, digesting the whole story. Finally, he said, "Sad story, JP. But the question I'm asking myself, why in God's name go through all this? Putting two people on the job. This bullshit act with the phony dad."

JP shrugged. "Seemed smart to me."

"Smart?"

JP turned from the railing, gesturing like he was pitching a project. "Don't you see it? It was genius. The kind of stuff that makes a great picture. I produced this political thriller a few years back. It did big business. One of the characters had something the writer called 'plausible deniability.' You know, so the right hand doesn't know what the left is doing. That way, things go bad, nobody knows the entire story. Nobody is totally exposed."

JP paused, his voice taking on a sincere tone. "Actually, if you think about it, I was protecting you, Blake."

Blake stepped closer. "This situation isn't going to protect me or you. Not with a homicide on the books."

JP turned back toward the railing. "Since I'm putting everything on the table here, there's something else you should know. The guy I hired?"

"You mean Warren Poole? Yeah, he's got a sheet. Ties to old Vegas and probably the old Chicago Outfit." Blake paused a second. "Just like you, JP."

JP glanced over again, seemingly surprised Blake had figured it out. "That was a long time ago."

"Wise guys have long memories."

"I guess he was right."

"Poole?"

"He said you've been busy." JP shook his head. "Sonovabitch showed up at my lunch today. Out of nowhere. Roughed me up. The situation has gotten complex."

"How complex?"

"He wants a million dollars for Jackie and the girl."

"He doesn't have Jackie."

"He says you do."

"I know where she is. That's all."

"He says he knows, too. And he says he'll have her soon."

Blake thought about telling him more. But he couldn't trust Jason Perry. At the very least, he couldn't trust him to keep his mouth shut with Warren Poole.

"So, are you going to pay it?"

"I'm not that liquid."

Blake glanced over at the Ferrari, $350,000 out the door. Another quarter million in the Bentley parked at home. A twenty-million-dollar house. The man had his priorities.

Blake said, "So you simplify things."

"How?"

"Tell him no deal. And walk away."

"I can't do that."

"Okay. Then I'll deliver the message. By my count, he's looking at several felonies. And if I'm right on what went down, a murder charge. You've got all the leverage, presuming you're willing to follow through."

"In what way?"

"By convincing him you're willing to go to the authorities."

"We've been over that."

"You've got bigger problems right now than some bad headlines. That's *his* leverage. You're a player, JP. You take his leverage away, you win."

"It's more than that. He told me today if I don't deliver, he won't leave any witnesses. He'll make Jackie and Bella disappear."

"And you believe that?"

JP nodded slowly. "After that murder, I believe him even more." He turned toward Blake. "You've got someone you care about, too, don't you?"

"He told you that?"

"He said both of you were witnesses, too." JP turned back toward the railing, staring at the lights again.

"He left out one."

JP looked over.

"You," Blake said.

JP hadn't thought of that. "I really mucked this up, didn't I? I wouldn't blame you if you told me to go fuck myself." He turned and gripped Blake's shoulders, waiting until he had his eyes. "But if you can find a way to get me out of this goddamn mess, you'll never work below the line again, man. You have my word."

JP let go. Blake turned and leaned back against the railing, no longer looking at the lights of the Valley, his eyes on the black sky overhead. He was thinking how JP had killed his first TV show. Thinking how he'd sucked him into the skip trace job. Thinking how he'd been lying up until a half hour ago.

Maybe he was still lying.

Blake said, "By the way, how the hell did Poole get those divorce papers?"

JP had a look on his face, like he was a clever guy. "That was easy. I had a prop house make them up."

Blake's first thought was to walk. Walk now. It was his second thought.

And his third.

Instead, he said, "You have a way to get in touch with Poole?"

35

THEY TOOK TWO CARS, MEETING Saturday in the parking structure below the Ronald Reagan UCLA Medical Center. Carla told him they could use the valet out front. Blake not only wasn't going to turn his Challenger over to a car jockey, he told her he wanted their cars readily available. He was reaching under his seat in the underground structure when Carla walked up. She watched him slide his holstered Smith onto his waistband, covering it with his shirt.

Carla said, "This is where I'm supposed to say you're scaring me."

"Am I?"

She kissed his cheek. "Thank you for doing this," she said. "You've changed my perception."

"About what?"

"I used to hate cops."

"Ex-cop," Blake said.

They took an elevator up to an expansive lobby where sunlight poured in through large windows over the main entrance. Blake scanned the faces of dozens of visitors and medical personnel coming and going across its stone floor. If Poole was going to pull something stupid, Blake thought, there would be no shortage of witnesses.

But Warren Poole wasn't stupid, Blake decided. Not as long as

Poole thought he could score a big pile of cash. He'd instructed JP to reach out to the hired gun. Tell him he had only a half million for both the mother and the daughter. Tell him Blake had called. That Blake was going to pick up Jackie Rose Saturday at the UCLA psychiatric unit when she was released at noon. Blake used moves like that back in Detroit. You baited a mark with cash, drugs, or an undercover female to lure a criminal out of the shadows. He was sure Poole would show up, if only to get a look at Jackie Rose.

"What are you going to do?" JP asked.

Blake told him, "I'm going to throw you under the bus. He comes back to you about that, just be a dummy. Call on your old acting talent."

Carla checked them in at the information desk. A receptionist handed them passes to the fourth floor, the location of the psych ward. A minute later, they stepped off the elevator into a small common area with a half dozen seats in front of a large window. A lot of light, but dead quiet, the seats empty. Blake spotted an exit stairwell next to the elevator door.

"Give me your car keys," he said. He handed Carla the keys to the Dodge. "Poole shows up, you take Jackie. Don't say anything. Don't wait for the elevator. Use the stairs. Take the car and leave."

"Why your car?"

"More horsepower."

"And go where?"

"Go directly to your friend's boat."

Carla led him through a vestibule to a hallway. It was long and empty except for large black-and-white photographic prints of Yellowstone Park with small placards describing the photos and crediting the photographer. Blake could feel his stomach tensing, a feeling he used to get on the job in unfamiliar surroundings that were dead quiet. He looked at his watch. It was almost noon.

"Where's Jackie?"

"They'll have her waiting inside." Carla pointed to a pair of steel double doors with a sign:

PLEASE CHECK IN WITH GREETER PRIOR TO ENTERING UNIT.

Carla pressed a button under a small speaker panel. A staffer answered. She told him they were there for patient Jacqueline Rose. The double doors buzzed open. Inside there was another set of doors with wire mesh windows. Blake peeked through the glass. He could see a nurses' station. Beyond that, only an empty hall.

A few seconds later, a male nurse in blue scrubs and a man bun emerged from the station. He came to the window and held up his finger, signaling they had to wait. He disappeared down the hall.

Carla said, "This seems like a good place to ask you."

"What?"

"You been following Dr. George's orders?"

"Haven't missed a day. I just wish I could get a decent night's sleep. I'm going to call him if it keeps up. Tell him his love potion isn't for me."

More than five minutes passed. Blake became agitated. He tried the outer door, but it was electronically locked. He didn't like being stuck there, not knowing what was going on in the hallway outside. He kept checking through the mesh windows into the psych ward for any sign of Jackie.

Carla said, "It takes some time to discharge a patient, Eddie."

"After we get her, just remember what I said."

"If we have to go, where will I find you?"

"I'll find you. If you don't hear from me within an hour, go to the Valley Bureau Homicide in Van Nuys and tell them everything you know."

"Now you *are* scaring me."

Before he could respond Blake detected movement in his peripheral vision. He turned to the mesh window and saw Jackie walking toward them, accompanied by the male nurse. She was dressed in the same clothes she wore when they picked her up at the courthouse. This time she was carrying a white plastic bag. He'd dealt with scores of junkies back in Detroit. Most of them were shifty and cared only about their next score. He wanted to think Jackie Rose was different, an innocent Hollywood casualty. And here she was again—everything she had to her name contained in another goddamn sack.

For the first time, Blake felt sorry for her.

The nurse unlocked the inner door. Jackie walked straight to Carla. They hugged. Blake heard the electric lock on the outer door release. He pushed it open a couple inches, peeking outside. The hall was empty. It seemed like the two women embraced for a long time, saying nothing. Blake looked at his watch. It was nearly thirty minutes past noon.

"Carla," Blake said. "Time to go."

Carla released Jackie from their embrace. "Hon, let's get you the hell out of here."

Out the double solid doors now, the hallway still empty. Carla holding Jackie's arm. They turned and walked past a large print of a bison in the snow, hanging in the vestibule leading to the common area and the elevators.

"Jackie, you remember Eddie," Carla said.

Blake turned and smiled.

Jackie said, "Did you find my daughter?"

"No, ma'am, he did not."

Blake turned toward the voice. Warren Poole was sitting in front of the window, a paperback book in his lap.

Poole stood up.

Blake turned to Carla. "Go. *Now*."

36

POOLE TUCKED THE PAPERBACK UNDER his right arm and walked toward Blake casually with a half-smile. Like one of those disingenuous salesmen who approached when you were browsing in a used car lot. He stopped about three feet away, pulled the paperback from his armpit and held it up for a moment in his left hand.

Blake glanced at the word SUCCESS in red print on the cover.

"Good book," Poole said. "A great guide for getting stuff done. Says if you have a positive mental attitude, you can pretty much do anything. But something tells me you're not feeling very positive right now, *Detective Blake.*"

They were face to face now in front of the bison print. Blake stayed with Poole's eyes, his peripheral vision tracking Poole's right hand, where it was in relation to his side pants pocket where he could conceal a weapon.

Blake said, "I'm positive Jason Perry has a big fucking mouth."

Poole tucked the paperback into his left pocket. When his right hand lowered, Blake spun him around and slammed him up against the wall, his face kissing the bison print. Poole didn't resist. He put up his hands without being prompted.

Poole looked back, grinning. "Mr. Blake, is it? Or do you prefer

Edwin? I can't really call you *detective* anymore, can I? But I supposed I should thank you for your service."

Blake pushed Poole's head back into the bison. "Clever guy. Showing up with some court paperwork. Not a bad actor, either. You should go down to the SAG office. Get a card. Maybe land a non-speaking role as a run-of-the-mill sociopath on some bad guy's crew."

Blake squatted and frisked his legs. Felt something hard below the right calf. Seconds later, he was gripping a Barretta. Blake slid the semi-auto into his back pocket. He kept Poole in the position for a couple more seconds then spun him around and stepped back.

Poole wasn't smiling anymore. He ran his hands through his hair, arranging his locks over his bald spot. Then he tucked in his shirt. He appeared more concerned with his appearance than anything he thought Blake might do next.

Settled now, Poole glanced at Blake's waistline, spotting the slight rise in his shirt. He grinned again. "What were we both thinking? We're in a gun-free zone, aren't we, Edwin? You pull that heater. Or I pull mine. Somebody spots a gun. That would be a mess, wouldn't it? They shut the hospital down. The entire campus, too." He made quote marks with his fingers. "'Active shooter.' 'Shelter in place.' All that happy horseshit."

Blake's first thought was he wished he had cuffs. He'd spin Poole around again. Cuff and walk him with his hands held high behind his back so it hurt. March him into LAPD. Swear out a statement. His second thought was to pull his Chief's Special. Put the .45's muzzle to Poole's temple and make the asshole take him to the girl. But Poole was right. Anyone sees a gun all hell would break loose. They'd both be in the twenty-four-hour news cycle before sundown.

Blake went with his third thought, the one he'd worked out the night before. He needed to bring Jason Perry into the picture.

Blake said, "Did you really think you were going to come down here and grab Jackie? Go pick up a million bucks and head back to Vegas?"

Poole's brow furrowed.

"Yeah, that's right. JP filled me in. I don't know who's more delusional. Or who's a bigger goddamn liar. You or him?"

Poole shrugged. "I just wanted to make sure Ms. Jackie was all right."

Blake gave him a smart-ass grin. "I'll pass along your concern."

Poole took a couple of steps to the bench seat and sat down, the window at his back, spreading his legs and arms like he just wanted to relax in the sunlight. "You see, I got to thinking last night, Edwin. There was one way to do this. Take you out of the picture first. Come down here and walk out with what I wanted." He pulled the paperback out of his pocket and waved it. "On the other hand, reading this, I got to thinking. That was negative. Why not take a positive approach? So, I decided to just show up. Tell Ms. Jackie I got her kid. That she's in good hands."

Blake said, "Something tells me there's more."

"Sure. It's simple. I reunite the two. Take them to Mr. Perry. And it's over." Poole leaned back deeper into the chair. "But you had to complicate everything, sending Ms. Jackie down those stairs."

Blake said, "They've been complicated since the mess you left in Sherman Oaks."

Poole held up his hands. "I had nothing to do with that. And the kid? She was in bad shape. Emotionally, I mean. She was lucky I showed up when I did."

Blake chuckled. "Kind of like your sheet. You never cause trouble. You just always happen to be around it."

Blake wanted to press him for more details on the homicide, but he didn't have time to listen to a bullshit story. He needed to get to the business at hand.

He began, "So here's how it is: First, *you* don't get to talk to 'Ms. Jackie' because she isn't yours. I found her. She is—as show biz people say—my work product. Second, you need to rethink some things. Rethink that you're going to find her. Or what you're going to do and who you're going to do it to." He paused. "Like I said, JP has a big mouth. And he's not exactly stable, either. In case you haven't figured that out."

Poole squinted as if he was trying to figure where Blake he was going.

The elevator doors opened. There was an argument underway inside. A guy, maybe fifty, not very good looking, but in a nicely tailored suit, stepped off with an attractive blond in her early thirties. When the woman hesitated, the man grabbed her arm and tried to march her toward the hallway. She didn't budge. "You're hurting me," she said.

Blake saw Poole checking them out, looking like he wanted to get up, maybe intervene. The couple noticed him and resumed walking. Poole's eyes followed them as they disappeared down the hall.

Blake said, "How do you think an asshole lands a gal like that, Poole?"

"Like Mr. Perry. The man must be making bank."

Blake stepped closer, standing over Poole now. "Enough to pay a million? Like I said, you're delusional. JP puts on a good show. But he's got a couple ex-wives tapping his ass. He hasn't done a film that's done big business in years." Blake paused, then added, "You get paid to play daddy dearest, Poole?"

"I don't show up without something up front." Saying it confidently, like it was a company policy.

"Well, I didn't," Blake said. "Point being, the man plays with other people's money. Studio money mainly."

"You got that right. They just gave him ten mil."

Blake laughed, wanting Poole to think he was clueless. "That's just the way they announce it, Poole. It's Hollywood bullshit. They don't fork it all over. He maybe gets some office space on the lot. His production company gets installments, based on the shows he produces. But first he's got to get the shows on the air and hope they have a run. You know how hard that is to do, *Warren*? You got better odds playing the slots. I know. I worked on a half dozen pilots that went fucking nowhere."

Poole looked up. "Look at you. Pleading the man's case."

Blake sat down two seats away, saying in a firm voice, "I'm not pleading jack shit. Like I said, JP's unstable. I want to be done with the man."

Poole leaned back in the seat, his palms up. "Like I said, I can make that easy for you."

Blake pointed at him, his hand in the shape of gun. "You see that's the difference between you and me. You're looking for a shortcut. That's the reason a guy like you has a sheet."

"Now you sound like a cop."

"Old habit."

Poole smirked. "Only one taking a shortcut is Mr. Perry. He thinks he can short me. Because you got Ms. Jackie. And you'll deliver her for free."

"Well, you've got that almost right," Blake said.

"*Almost?*"

"The free part." Blake paused, letting it sink in. "You don't see it, do you?"

"See what?"

"That's way these Hollywood fucks like JP roll. It's their hustle. Lots of promises. Very few deliverables."

"You signed up for that. Not me."

"That was before I got the mom."

"Now you're talking like a *dirty* cop."

"I guess you don't know much about Detroit PD." Blake stood up. "You're not as smart as I thought you were, Warren. JP didn't make thirty motion pictures being a chump. He's playing us both."

"So what?"

"So, we let him keep thinking he's doing it. You'll never get a million. But if you do it my way, you can get half of that."

"Your way?"

"That's right. A half mil to you. In cash. JP trusts me. He'll listen to me."

"And what's in it for you?"

"I give you the mom and you split the 500k with me."

Poole nodded, thinking, the last part getting his attention.

This is where Blake planned to set the hook. He had to make himself vulnerable. Let Poole think he had the upper hand.

He said, "But I have a couple of conditions. First, you'll deliver the mom and the kid. But JP can't know I'm involved. I still need to make a living in this town."

"Okay."

"Second, I have to know the daughter is okay."

"She's in good hands."

"Not good enough."

"Now you're losing me."

Blake sat back down. "Open your eyes, man. We're sitting outside a locked-down psych ward. The woman went suicidal when she found out her daughter was grabbed. Now she's counting on me. I tell her I still don't know if her kid's okay. She decides to take herself out again. Then what are you going to do? Deliver her in a goddamn box?"

"So, you keep an eye on her."

"Or it could go another way. Jackie and Carla? They're gettin' real close. She's going to advocate for her in drug court. Jackie sails through that she's going to be thinking LAPD. Then they'll squeeze me. You think I'm going to hold back? I'm not going down for Jason Perry. And I'm sure as hell not going down for you."

Blake stood up, pacing a little now, Poole's eyes following him. "I need to be able to give your Ms. Jackie something. Let her know I'm making progress. I don't, we both could end up with squat. You need to think things through."

Poole looked down at his paperback, running his thumb along the edges of the pages. He looked at the cover, then the back.

Blake said, "Give me your number."

Poole looked up. "I need to get a new phone."

"Then take mine." Blake pulled out a small spiral notebook, scratched out his number and dropped it in Poole's lap.

Blake continued, "There's a bar on Pico called Barkowski. Meet me there tomorrow when it opens at 5 p.m. Prove to me the daughter is okay. Then we can figure out how to finish the job. It works out, you can even have your heater back."

Poole glanced at the phone number, then back up at Blake. "You don't honestly expect me to show up with the kid?"

Blake walked to the elevator and pressed the call button. "I said proof."

"What kind of proof?"

The elevator chimed and opened. Blake stepped in and turned around.

As the doors closed, he said, "Think positively. You'll figure it out."

37

When Blake arrived at the Marina Del Rey boat slip, a boisterous brunette named Moxie was standing on the deck, telling Carla and Jackie about her boat as if she were selling real estate. Carla's old derby teammate said the yacht was named *The Closer*. It was a Grand Banks Aleutian. Seventy-two feet. The price tag well more than a million.

Blake followed the three women below into an interior of teak and leather upholstery. The galley was larger than most kitchens. Next was the salon. The size of an average living room, it had an L-shaped sofa and swiveling leather recliners. Moxie pushed a button near one of the chairs and motorized curtains closed over the windows.

"You won't even have to get off your ass for a little privacy," she said, winking at Blake.

As they toured, Jackie followed closely behind Carla, her eyes taking in each room. There were three heads. There were three staterooms, flat panel televisions in each. Moxie called the bow cabin the "VIP stateroom." Jackie listened closely, appearing far more present than the woman they'd picked up in Ventura five days ago. She also was no longer in the clothes she'd been wearing since the jail. Carla had taken her shopping and outfitted her in a blouse, black leggings, and running shoes.

After Moxie departed the yacht, they returned to the salon. Blake sat in one of the soft leather chairs, Carla and Jackie on the leather sofa behind a teak coffee table. Earlier, Blake had asked Carla to keep Jackie in the dark, that Blake would explain everything after they got squared away on the boat.

Before Blake had a chance to speak, Jackie asked him if he'd found her daughter.

"I'm working on it," he said.

"Working how?"

"Someone connected to people you may know picked her up." He wondered if she would reveal her relationship with Jason Perry and if it would match up with JP's story.

Jackie said, "That man we saw in the hospital, he has her, doesn't he?"

Blake nodded. "That's what I'm working on."

"How do you know him?"

"I don't."

"He seemed to know *you*."

Blake didn't respond.

Jackie's hands were folded in her lap. He felt like she was scrutinizing him.

Jackie said, "How did he know where I was?"

"He's been following me."

"Why would he do that?"

"Because he was looking for you. He probably saw us pick you up at the jail."

"If he has Bella, how did he find her?"

"Like I said, he must have known some people."

"*Eddie?*" Carla said.

"Yeah," Blake said. He glanced at Carla, his eyes telling her to keep her mouth shut.

Jackie turned and looked out the salon window, watching a sailboat motoring by in the channel. She watched it for a good twenty seconds, her right hand twirling a strand of her hair.

She looked back and said, "Can I call you Eddie?"

Blake nodded.

"Eddie, there's some things you should know."

Blake remained silent.

"There's a man. I think he may be behind this." She paused.

"I'm listening."

"A man I was involved with. Bella and I spent the summer at his house. In Malibu."

"Okay."

She leaned forward. "He's a freak."

Blake saw a flash of anger in her eyes. He leaned forward, mirroring her body language, still letting his silence prompt her.

"He was very nice at first. He was—generous. But then, you know, after we moved in, things began to change. I mean, he changed. And he wanted to change me."

"In what way?"

"It was exciting at first. He hired a personal stylist. Clothes, accessories he said were *me*. Beautiful things from Barney's and Rodeo Drive. Who would complain? But then his plastic surgeon. I mean we all could use an improvement somewhere. I was happy at first. You have a kid. Things drop. But then it was like, let's do something about that nose. Let's do something about those eyes."

"Lot of people go for that here," Blake said.

"But he didn't stop. Then it was what I ate. How I talked to Bella. Where I could go. What I could do. Who I could see. Then, just when he seemed to have me just the way he wanted, he lost interest. You know, sexually. And that was before I got strung out."

Carla said, "Sounds like a control freak."

She turned to Carla with an apologetic look. "That's how I got started. It made the situation tolerable."

Blake said, "You mean your habit?"

Jackie nodded. "I'm not saying I was a saint. But I think he liked me messed up. He'd send out his assistant to pick up my scripts."

"What makes you think he might be involved in taking your daughter?

Jackie looked at Carla. "He told me if I ever left him he'd find me. That he knew people. People who would hunt me down."

"But why snatch your daughter?" Blake asked.

She looked back at Blake. "Because he knows I'll have to see him then. Then he'll make all kinds of promises to get me back. Say he's only trying to help me. He's very persuasive."

"And you would believe him?"

"He has lots of money."

"That makes him persuasive?"

"I was pretty much out of money when I met him. I'm in worse shape now."

Blake rose, walked across the salon and sat in the corner of the couch, a couple feet away from her. "Jackie," he said. "Do you remember when I suggested you go to the authorities about your daughter?"

She nodded.

"Are you ready to do that now?"

Jackie didn't answer.

Blake glanced over at Carla

Carla turned, saying, "What's holding you back, hon?"

Jackie took a breath and said, "I don't want to go to jail."

Blake said, "Seems to me you've already been there, done that."

Jackie turned to Carla. "I stole money. From the guy. Lots of money."

"How much, hon?" Carla asked.

"Twenty thousand." She looked down at her feet. "I could have taken more. But I just wanted enough to start over."

Blake said, "Have you talked to this guy? Since you left?"

She half nodded. "Once, before I changed my number. He said if I did not come back, he'd have me locked up." She looked back at Carla. "So, you see, if I go to the police, so will he, and he'll tell them a story. He's a powerful man. And now I'm the unfit mother with a drug problem. And then what happens to Bella? I lose her no matter what I do."

Carla chimed in. Blake didn't interrupt her. She dispensed recovery advice he'd heard her tell her pigeons before. Saying that she needed to take first things first by staying clean and sober. Saying she wouldn't necessarily lose Bella. And if she did, it would only be temporary. Blake walked to the bridge, leaving them to talk alone. He sat down in the captain's swivel chair in front of a complex panel of controls and monitors. He concluded both Jackie and JP had markedly different portrayals of one another. And neither rang true. He also questioned why Jackie would risk her daughter's safety by refusing to go to the police.

When he heard Carla and Jackie stop talking, he walked back toward the salon, stopping at the top of the four steps that descended from the galley. He had one more question, though he already knew the answer.

"The name," Blake said. "What's the name of the guy in Malibu?

Jackie looked up. "Jason Perry. But everyone calls him JP."

Blake asked Carla to follow him into the master stateroom. He closed the door, reached into his jacket and produced the Beretta Tomcat he'd taken from Warren Poole.

"Can you handle a gun?" he asked.

Carla eyed the weapon for a couple seconds and then nodded. "In Houston, I had this guy. Was at every match. Started following me home. One of the girls told me it was an occupational hazard. She was a Texas girl. She took me to the range. I carried one of hers for a couple months."

Blake gestured with the pistol. "It won't come to this," he said. "But just in case. There's seven in the magazine." He racked the slide. "And now one in the chamber." He pointed above the grip. "That lever? That's the safety. Flip it down and you're good to go."

She raised one eyebrow. "I know what a safety is, Eddie."

He placed the Beretta in the bottom dresser drawer under neatly folded women's lingerie.

Carla said, "So you're not staying."

"I can't be here twenty-four seven."

Carla followed him. He stopped on the aft deck and said, "Jackie tell you anything else? Because this whole goddamn thing isn't making much sense."

Carla shook her head. "Only that she's counting on you, Eddie. That's my fault. I should never have told her you were going to find her daughter."

Blake looked out over the hundreds of boats moored in the slips and beyond that the high-rise apartment buildings and condos that made up Marina Del Rey.

"She's got one thing right," Blake said quietly. "She's an unfit mother. She doesn't deserve to have the kid."

"What are you going to do, Eddie?"

"I've got something in mind. I'm going to do it for the kid. Because I don't know who to believe, her or Jason Perry."

Carla nodded. "She wouldn't be the first dope fiend with a bullshit story."

He looked at Carla. "I'm going to need some help."

"You're going to the cops?"

"An ex-cop," Blake said. "And this time you can't say no."

38

BLAKE TOLD VERONICA, "THIS JOB will require a good cover and some acting talent by you if it's going to work."

Veronica said, "Fuck you, Eddie. What do you think I was doing in the Hollywood Division?"

Kurt was sitting next to her.

"Let me guess," Blake said. "You were a hot number with a bad attitude. I'll bet that worked with those creative types with mother issues. You dish out a shitload of abuse and then ask them where you can get some good blow."

Kurt said, "This explains a lot."

She turned to her boyfriend. "And fuck you, too, Kurt."

They were sitting alone around a table in the courtyard of the 18th Street Coffee House in Santa Monica, the place closing in an hour. A half dozen remaining customers were inside, several of them working on laptops. Blake called Veronica after he left the Marina, telling her he had a job for her and asked her to bring Kurt, too.

"So, where's the job, Eddie?" Veronica asked. "What department?"

"There is no department," Blake said. "Think of this as your tryout. You do well, I'll make some calls. Some suburban Detroit departments I worked with on task forces. I'm sure they'd love to have you."

"A tryout?"

She wasn't happy with the idea. But she listened as he laid out Jackie Rose's situation and what he knew about Warren Poole. The way he explained the job, it was the kind of operation he used with Detroit narcotics once to find a large drug ring's stash house.

Blake said, "We staged a phony street assault on one of our good-looking undercover officers. Just a few feet from our suspect. He played the hero and intervened, hoping to get lucky. They hung out. By the end of the day, she had the location of the stash house and a whole lot more."

"Honey pot," Veronica said. "Old school."

Blake said, "Honey pot with an assault twist."

Blake told them he was sure the move would work on Warren Poole. "I saw a lot of tells at UCLA. He was ogling this gal who taking a lot of grief from her boyfriend. I think he's insecure about his appearance. I'm betting he makes up for that by being the guy who comes in for the rescue."

He told Veronica and Kurt he'd set up a meeting with Poole at Barkowski. "The way it will go, you two show up on your bike. Wear your leathers. And Veronica, something hot, but classy. We're not talking biker trash here."

"More like a RUB," Kurt said.

"What's that?" Veronica said.

"Rich urban biker," Kurt said.

"That's it," Blake said.

Veronica said, "I don't like riding on that goddamn thing. They call them donor cycles at the ER because of all the organs they harvest."

Kurt said, "I'll put on a bitch bar for you."

She turned, giving him the evil eye. "And just what the fuck is that?"

"A back rest so you won't fall off."

Blake laid out the timeline. He was meeting Poole at 5 p.m. They should show up at 5:15 and sit at the bar or a table within earshot of where he and Poole would be sitting.

"But we don't drink," Veronica said.

"Then order something that looks like a drink."

Blake told them they'd get a signal as to when to start the show. "When I get up and go to the john, that's when you start an argument. Play it from a slow burn and then get really serious. But when you get to that point—and Kurt, you have to sell it—make like you're just about to beat the shit out of her."

"You know I don't put up with that crap," Veronica said.

"That's where the acting comes in," Blake said. "You have to play the victim here."

Kurt smirked. "I can smack her?"

"Fuck you, Kurt," Veronica said.

Blake shook his head. "No, you dump her. Walk out. Speed off on the bike. Let him hear those pipes outside on Pico."

Kurt nodded, liking the idea.

Blake said, "If I got this guy figured right. Poole will come over. Want to buy you a drink."

"I'm staying sober, Eddie."

"Tell him you don't need a drink. Tell him you need a ride."

"To where?"

"It doesn't matter. Anywhere but Carla's. This is where you play him. Make a night of it if you need to. Suggest you go to his place. Say you can't go home because you live with the boyfriend. See if he drops any clues. He must have left the kid with somebody. He's had her for nearly a week. That's too long to keep a thirteen-year-old tied up in a hotel room."

"You're telling me I have to fuck him?"

Kurt looked at Blake, not pleased.

"Did I say that? Look, if it gets too heavy, you bolt. That's your call."

Veronica said, "Carla okay this?"

"Reluctantly."

Veronica nodded. "Then I like it."

Kurt said, "And just exactly what are we supposed to be arguing about anyway?"

Blake said. "Seems to me you two have plenty of material. You'll figure it out."

39

WARREN POOLE HAD NO DOUBT he could prove the kid was okay. He'd seen how that was done in a movie. Sunday he could get a copy of the *Los Angeles Times* at a 7-Eleven. Take it over to Dagney's. Have the kid hold up the front page and snap a picture, its date showing. But after he called Dagney he wasn't sure how that would go. She busted his balls for not staying in touch. Saying they needed to talk about the kid. Calling her "poor Bella" and saying that she was concerned about *Bella's* welfare and *Bella's* emotional state.

"I don't have time for this shit," Poole said.

"You're a being a first-rate asshole, Warren," she said.

He hung up.

Later, he began thinking about how he was going to explain to the kid the photo with the newspaper. He also could picture Dagney asking questions, and when he didn't answer, Dagney throwing another fit.

She could fuck everything up.

Now he was sitting in his hotel room, waiting for another idea to come while watching one of his favorite flicks, *Key Largo*, on Turner Classic Movies. Bogart playing the troubled good guy, a soldier back from World War II, his romantic interest a young Lauren Bacall.

Edward G. Robinson portraying the gangster Johnny Rocco, trying to get a boat to Cuba and escape the law, but stuck in the Key Largo hotel waiting for a hurricane to pass. Rocco believing he could solve everything with his gun, so full of himself he couldn't see how Bogart was playing him.

Halfway through the film, Poole found himself thinking about Blake. The ex-cop was a lot like the Bogart character. Yes, Blake demanded a cut, but he also seemed to care about Ms. Jackie and the kid. Something didn't sit right. Dirty cops he dealt with in Vegas, all they cared about was money or tapping some ass in a protected whorehouse.

Poole stayed with the film until the end, the final scene on the boat. Rocco coming out of the stateroom, shouting out to Bogart that he was unarmed but with a revolver in his hand. Bogart hiding somewhere. Then Rocco making a stupid move. Walking onto the deck. Failing to take a good look around. Running his mouth instead of looking up and seeing Bogart on the roof above him. Bogart shooting him through an open hatch. The end always had bothered Poole. Why didn't Rocco scope out his surroundings before pulling the heater, Bogart above him in plain sight.

That was the difference between him and the movie gangster, Poole concluded. He would never make a big move without checking everything out first. He turned off the television and put on his jacket.

An hour later, he parked his car on Pico Boulevard, not worrying about street parking this time. The tiny lights on the meters were off. It was nearly 10 p.m. Fifty feet from his car the sign BARKOWSKI hung over a doorway. On the building facade was a large black-and-white drawing of a guy sitting at table with a typewriter and a can of beer. He thought it was a strange name for a saloon no bigger than a typical dive bar.

Inside, Barkowski was packed. Some good-looking women and younger guys were sitting on a red leather bench behind small tables along the wall. The bar stools in red leather also were all occupied. On the walls Poole saw several large photographs of the same guy in the drawing out front. The guy's hair was greasy, his face pockmarked. One ugly bastard, Poole thought. The saloon looked like a shrine to the guy.

Poole walked up to the end of the bar and ordered a Heineken. When the bartender slid him the bottle, he asked who the guy in the pictures was.

"Due, that's Buk," he said, pronouncing the *u* like *you*. "Charles Bukowski. You know, the author."

"Never heard of him." Poole said.

"Some say he was a beat writer, but he really wasn't associated with that generation."

"Beat?"

"Yeah, you know. Like Kerouac. Ginsberg."

Poole tipped the bartender a buck.

"You see *Barfly* with Mickey Rourke and Faye Dunaway?"

"Missed that one," Poole said.

"Check it out. That's kind of Buk's story."

He picked up his bottle and walked through the crowd, looking around. He found quotes from Charles Bukowski hanging in small frames. He read a couple:

BAD DECISIONS MAKE GOOD STORIES.
FIND WHAT YOU LOVE AND LET IT KILL YOU.

Poole thought, this guy Buk not only looked like a reprobate he sounded like one, too. But he admired his attitude.

Poole walked past a bumper pool table and checked out a second room. It was lined with booths, also in red leather. Poole wasn't focusing on the decor anymore. He was focusing on the room's layout. Not a window in the place. No way to see who was coming in off the street. And the only back exit was around the corner and through the kitchen.

Warren Poole could picture how it would be at 5 p.m. tomorrow when the saloon opened. Hardly anybody there, except maybe a couple of hard drinkers at the rail. Blake would want to sit somewhere where they wouldn't be overheard. They would not sit in the benches with small tables along the wall in the room with the bar rail. That meant they'd be in a booth in the side room Poole was checking out.

Blake would have him right where he wanted him, he concluded, isolated and clueless as to what was happening in the rest of the bar. If he was being set up, he'd never see cops, or maybe some muscle, coming.

And no way to bolt out a door.

Poole returned to the main room, at one point having to squeeze between two hipsters tag teaming a blond in a tight dress. Nearby, he saw more framed words from the author. He walked over and finished off the Heineken as he read it.

IF YOU WANT TO KNOW WHO YOUR FRIENDS ARE,
GET YOURSELF A JAIL SENTENCE.
—CHARLES BUKOWSKI—

He thought, this Buk dude knows the score. Poole found those words true the time he was busted on a heist for Tony the Ant. Tony put the word out and paid the jailers when Poole was awaiting trial in the lockup. Those screws took good care of him in the Clark County Detention Center. Back then he was untouchable.

Those were the good old days. But this was now.

40

Veronica and Kurt argued loudly at the bar rail in Barkowski. Veronica was saying she didn't like the way Kurt took chances on that Hog, splitting lanes between cars, riding the white line. Saying she knew traffic codes.

"Lane splitting is only permissible when traffic is stopped or crawling and must be done in a safe and prudent manner," she said. "Not at fucking seventy miles an hour on the I-10."

"You have trust issues," Kurt said. "And I think it's become as serious threat to our relationship."

The bartender was washing glasses, looking like he was going to intervene if they got any louder.

Blake listened to them go on. The argument would have been a bravo performance, he thought, if only it were an act. They'd showed up on Kurt's Harley at 5:15 p.m. as planned. Blake looked at his watch. It was nearly 5:50 and not even a call from Warren Poole.

He was a no show.

Blake finished his club soda and lime, still sticking with his no drinking protocol. He stood and walked over, saying, "We're all done here, kids."

"Yeah, I'm totally done," Veronica said. "I ain't riding back with this crazy motherfucker."

Kurt swiveled out of the bar stool, slipped on his leather jacket and stormed out. Veronica spun back in the direction of the bar rail and downed the last of what looked like a Shirley Temple. Moments later, Blake heard the Harley start and speed away on Pico.

The bright sun stung Blake's eyes when he and Veronica walked out of the dark saloon a couple minutes later. Veronica lit a Parliament and asked him where his car was. He asked her for a cigarette.

"You don't smoke," she said.

"I do today," he said.

It tasted different than what he remembered a good smoke should taste. He took a couple more drags and then tossed it as they walked along the sidewalk.

"That's a $500 fine in California," Veronica said.

"Fuck 'em," Blake said.

They walked half a block, Blake stopping next to Carla's Mini Cooper. He'd given Carla his Dodge Challenger for the day. She wanted to run errands with Jackie. Ever since Poole had attended her AA meeting, Blake was feeling especially protective of Carla. He felt she was safer in his muscle car.

Blake opened the door for Veronica. "I'll drop you off at Carla's."

She said she didn't want to be taken back to Studio City. She said she wanted him to drop her off at Kurt's.

"After all that?"

She flipped a strand of hair away from her eyes. "Kurt's a good guy. I guess I love him." She paused. "I guess I love him because he doesn't put up with my shit."

Blake took the I-10. It was twenty-five miles to Kurt's house in Los Feliz, west of downtown. Veronica spent the first ten miles telling Blake her role in one of the biggest ecstasy busts in U.S.

history—a half million pills. She told him how she made a buy from a low-level dealer in the rave scene and spent the next seven months working her way up to the main distributor in Monterey Park. It was the first time Blake took the time to listen to her police background. He'd always assumed she worked only the Hollywood parties and clubs on the Strip, busting nickel-and-dime buys.

She obviously had undercover moves.

Blake said, "Veronica, it takes a special talent to fuck up a good service record like that."

She wanted to light a cigarette. He told her Carla would go ballistic if she smelled cigarette smoke in her car.

She held it in her fingers unlit and said, "I want you to know, Eddie. I was booking collars right to the end."

"How did you get started? Chipping, I mean."

"I began taking shortcuts. It made it easier to make buys. Blow mainly. Just now and then at first. Near the end I was basing the shit three or four days a week." She looked over. "You know what Carla says about shortcuts?"

"What's that?"

"You take shortcuts, you end up at the back of the line."

Blake exited the I-10 and took the I-110 that skirted the skyscrapers downtown, heading for the 101.

Veronica looked up at the buildings. "Can you imagine what it's like to work there? Driving downtown every goddamn day to sit in a cubicle. Pushing paper. Making phone calls. Not for me, man. Eddie, you got to help me get back on the fucking street."

Blake glanced over. "So, what took you down?"

"I told you. I was a dope fiend."

"What I'm asking, how did you get popped?"

She buzzed down her window and lit the Parliament. "There was this director up in the hills. He'd throw these big blow parties.

I'd hooked up with his supplier a couple weeks earlier, just a mid-level dealer. I was working him to get to the next level. Thing is, this director, word was he was into teenage boys—runaways, child actors. So, I was trying to keep my distance from the freak. I didn't want anything to do with that scene."

Blake nodded.

"So, I go up there one night to make a buy from his supplier, saying I wanted more where that came from. The director insists we stay and party. I didn't see any kids. We stay a couple hours. Eventually leave." She took a drag on the Parliament and exhaled. "Next morning, the director gets popped as a pedo. Turns out the guy had security cameras everywhere. The assistant DA reviews the footage and recognizes me. Doesn't like seeing me sucking on a crack pipe. He turns me in to internal affairs. And the DA's office scrutinizes all my busts. Those DA's were fucking pissed. Especially after they had to bounce three of my cases that had already gone to pre-trial."

Blake nodded again. "That will do it."

"Technically, I can rejoin the department if I'm clean. American disability act and all that crap. But they'll make me a desk jockey. LAPD's not going to let me near *anything* that's going to end up in court."

She took another hit off the cigarette, thinking. She turned and said, "Hey, Eddie, I got a great idea. No department hires me. You should get a PI license. Do more of this kind of PI stuff for your rich Hollywood pals. We could partner up."

Blake glanced over, but he didn't answer.

He left the freeway at the Rampart exit. A couple blocks later Veronica had him turn on Sunset Boulevard and then a residential street a few blocks east. It was old LA, the street lined with aging bungalows and small two-story houses. Veronica pointed out Kurt's place, a stucco two-story ahead. Blake pulled to the curb just behind his Harley.

He put the Mini in park and looked over, "Thanks for the effort, V. Tell Kurt that, too." He let a moment pass, then said, "I'll make some calls to Detroit. See what I can do."

She leaned over and kissed him on the cheek, then leaned back against the door. "Can I ask you a question?"

"Sure."

"Why are you dicking around with this job?"

"That's the way you see it?"

She nodded. "What you know, what you got, I don't know why you don't walk into homicide. Put a posse on this guy Poole's ass."

"It's complicated."

"It must be really complicated."

She leaned forward. "I want you to know, Eddie. I was never fucking dirty. I didn't take money. And I paid for the dope. I could have skimmed a lot of big hauls. I'm not saying I wasn't tempted. But that's where I drew the line."

Blake looked over again. "And why was that?"

"I may have been a dope fiend. And I did my share of whoring, working some dude to give something up." She rolled the dead Parliament between her fingers. "But some shit just doesn't leave you, Eddie."

"Like what?" he said.

She reached for the door, looked back at him and said, "Even when I was all fucked up, I was still a good goddamn cop."

41

Warren Poole was perched on a stool at the small bar called the Backdrop Lounge in his hotel, *Success Through Positive Mental Attitude* sitting next to his Heineken. He was trying to stay positive. But he was sick of fucking around with big time producer Jason Perry and ex-cop Edwin Blake.

A guy, maybe fifty, sat down next to him. He was wearing a black *Chucky Gets Lucky* movie T-shirt under his sport coat.

The guy spotted his paperback and said, "Good book. Lots of upbeat stuff. But sometimes you have to draw some blood to close a deal." He motioned the bartender over, ordered a Budweiser and turned to Poole. "You in sales?"

Poole shook his head.

The guy didn't ask what work he did. He said, "Jesus Christ, what the fuck is with this town. There's no place to smoke a cigarette, let alone a good cigar."

Poole didn't look over. "It's not Vegas. That's for sure."

"That's where you're from?"

Poole nodded.

"Johnny Seitz." Poole looked at him, the guy's hand extended. Poole hesitated, but then shook it.

Johnny Seitz liked to talk. He said he was from Gary, Indiana, and had just come from some business in the City of Industry east of downtown.

"What's there?" Poole asked.

Seitz took a sip of his beer. "Machinery auction. Plant closing. I buy and sell big steel processing machinery. Slitting lines. Recoilers. Big presses."

Poole knew a little about steel. His uncle worked in one of those plants in Chicago before he hooked up with a crew.

Seitz took another pull off his Bud. "Back home they call me Machine Johnny. Some people call me the Undertaker."

Poole looked over. "What, you bury the stuff?"

He shook his head. "I show up at a plant? Everybody knows it's over. They're going under. Happens a lot in Chicago. Detroit. The whole rust belt. I come in. Grab the iron. Locate buyers. And ship it. Most goes overseas. A lot to the Far East. Sometimes, it ain't pretty. Grabbing the iron, I mean." Seitz leaned closer. "You ever see a grown man weep?"

Poole shook his head. He wasn't going to tell him about the guy in Toronto who saw him coming, dropped to his knees and cried like a baby.

Seitz said, "A month ago. Johnstown, P.A. I watched my riggers unbolt a cut-to-length line from the floor right while some poor sonovabitch was still trying to run it. His last day on the job. Been on that machine for twenty fucking years. He wept when we craned it out the door." He took another drink. "Big money in it, though." He pointed to his T-shirt. "Shit like that, I figured I owed myself a break. Took the tour over at the Universal Studios."

Poole nodded. He really didn't want to engage the guy. But Machine Johnny ordered another Bud and bought him a Heineken.

"Travel much?" Seitz asked.

"Road trip here and there," Poole said. "Don't fly unless I have to. It's a pain in the ass."

"You need to get the TSA PreCheck, my man. You apply. Takes only about an hour. They check you out for a couple weeks. See you're no terrorist. Give you a number. No more security line bullshit. But if you go abroad a lot, make sure you get the international version."

Poole looked over. "You say you do business in the Far East?"

"I find buyers. That's half the game."

"Places like Vietnam?"

"Korea. Thailand. China. Vietnam. You name it. All day long."

"Got an old friend in Saigon. He wants me to visit."

"Expat? Your friend?"

"Something like that."

"Shit, man, go. Saigon? They call it Ho Chi Minh City now. It ain't your uncle's Vietnam."

"So I've heard."

"What's stopping you?"

Poole hesitated, but then decided the guy was okay. "I'd have trouble getting a visa."

"What kind of trouble?"

Poole hesitated again. But he liked the guy's attitude. "Got into a little trouble. When I was younger."

Seitz laughed. "Shit, who hasn't. You know you can get that expunged."

"I wasn't convicted. But the judge wouldn't bond me out while I was awaiting trial. Did a few months in the county jail."

"You ever go to Canada? Any trouble getting in there?"

Poole shook his head.

"You got a passport?"

Poole nodded.

"Then shit, man. You're all set. Those commies wised up. They want those fucking Yankee dollars. I got a multiple entry visa, the business version. Good for a year. No sweat." He leaned closer, saying quietly, "And in my twenties I was convicted for fencing a bunch of stolen shit."

Poole looked over. "But you had it knocked off your record."

"Turns out I didn't need to."

The guy knew his stuff, Poole thought. He asked, "So, what? You go to an embassy, right? Lots of paperwork? I wonder if there's one here in Los Angeles."

"Only four consulates in the U.S. Closest is San Francisco. But that's not a problem. You said you have a passport?"

Poole nodded.

"That's all you need. You apply online. One-month visa. Three-month. One year. Whatever you want. Couple hundred bucks max. They email you back an approval letter in two days. You get on the plane with that. They have your visa waiting for you when get off the plane in Ho Chi Minh City."

Poole took a sip of his Heineken, thinking. Shit, only two days. Finish the job and then go to Nam for a year and wait and see how things played out. Or if he liked it, stay like Tommy Donofrio did. Get permanent residency. *Expat.* He liked the sound of that. He liked the idea of Mr. fucking Perry's American dollars going a long way and a house girl waiting on him night and day.

The idea of it opened some new options.

Poole called the bartender over.

"Two shots of Wild Turkey, if you don't mind," he said. "One for me and one for my friend, Machine Johnny."

"So, what are you thinking?" Seitz asked.

Poole said, "I'm thinking I need to take things to the next level."

42

BLAKE DIDN'T SEE HIS CHALLENGER parked anywhere in the marina lot as he pulled up in Carla's Mini Cooper. The temperature had climbed a good twenty degrees. Santa Ana winds were blowing desert heat to the coast. Blake slung his jacket over his shoulder and walked to *The Closer*'s slip.

On the yacht he found Jackie in a pair of shorts and a lowcut tank top. She was sitting sidesaddle on a bench on the aft deck, her arms around her knees, her eyes on the sky.

She glanced at Blake and said, "Bella? Anything?"

"Still working on it," he said.

She looked back at the sky. "Carla says I need to have faith. To not be in fear. F-E-A-R. She says that stands for False Evidence Appearing Real." She pointed. "Look, you can see the stars out here."

He looked up, then back at her. He was surprised she appeared so relaxed. But he'd seen Carla do that before, counsel someone in crisis into a state of calm.

Blake said, "Where's Carla?"

"She left. We're going to go to a midnight meeting when she gets back."

Blake walked closer, standing over her now. "Where?"

"A meeting out here somewhere."

Blake felt irritation well up. "No, where did she go?"

Jackie looked up. "To her house."

"Why would she do that?"

She shrugged. "The woman from Beverly Hills. They were on the phone a long time. I guess she was having a hard time or something."

"How long has she been gone?

Jackie shrugged again. "Maybe thirty minutes. Maybe an hour. I don't know."

Blake walked to the bow on the slim perimeter deck, dialing as he walked. He reached Carla's voice mail. "Just talked to Jackie." he began. For the rest he tried not to sound agitated. She usually ignored him when he was aggravated.

"Look, Poole never showed," he said. "I don't know where he is or what he's up to. You need to turn around. Come back to the boat."

He followed the voice mail with a similar text.

Blake walked back to the stern. Jackie was no longer on the deck. He found her in the salon in one of the leather chairs, looking like she'd just showered. She twirled a strand of her wet hair as she watched him enter. Blake sat on the couch on the other side of the salon, looking at his phone to see if Carla had texted back.

Nothing.

"You know what I'm thinking," Jackie said.

Blake looked up. In the light of the salon, she looked sleepy.

"I'm thinking my Bella has just run off." She was twirling her hair again. "She's done that before, you know. But she always comes back."

He didn't correct her. But he said, "Bella doesn't know where to come back to, Jackie."

"She'll call."

"You don't have a phone."

"Carla said we're going to get one."

He thought, then what? You send your fucking number with smoke signals? Blake looked down at his phone again.

Jackie said, "Eddie, have you gone to see JP?"

He looked up. "He's not that kind of guy. You don't just knock on his door."

She sat up. "He thinks he's really clever.'

"What makes you say that?"

"When we first met he claimed to be somebody else."

"And where was that?"

"This volunteer thing. Ran this whole story how he was in the chamber of commerce. I mean, *everybody* there knew who he was. I don't just hook up with anybody. You know, I check a guy out. But he kept up his act for weeks." She laughed.

Blake hadn't seen Jackie laugh before.

"And why would JP do that?" Blake asked.

"He thought women were after his money."

"Were you?"

Jackie got up and walked over. "Eddie," she said, drawing out his name. "Why would you say something like that?"

He looked up. "You obviously played along."

"Wouldn't you?" she said. "He was a catch."

"I'm not a switch-hitter."

"You know what I mean."

Blake was tracking the way she was talking. The coy tone in her voice.

She plopped down on the couch right next to him, as if her body was heavy. She reached out and put her hand on his shoulder, rubbing it. "I want you to know how much I appreciate everything you're doing," she said. "And Carla, too."

She was close now. Close enough that he could smell a remnant of ginger shampoo in her wet hair. Her nipples were firm and pushing out the tank top. But it was her breathing that had his full attention. It was slow. Even a little labored.

Blake focused on her eyes. Not the way she was looking at him. Not the way she appeared to be flirting. He focused on her pupils.

They were pinpoints.

Blake stood up, pulling her to her feet as he did. "Where the fuck is it?"

Jackie tried to pull her arm away. "You're hurting me."

He gripped it tighter. "You're hurting yourself. Where did you get the shit?"

When she didn't answer he walked her across the salon to the first head. She stood in the doorway as he opened up its drawers and medicine cabinet. He found hairbrushes and beauty products. He saw pills for allergies and pain, but all were over-the-counter. Blake marched her to the next two bathrooms and repeated the search.

Nothing.

Blake said, "You can tell me where the shit is, or you can watch me take apart this whole goddamn boat."

She remained mute. But he saw her eyes glance toward the VIP stateroom.

When they arrived there, she fell back on the queen-size bed, resting on her elbows, looking up at him. He turned and rummaged through the cabin's teak dresser drawers. He looked behind the books in the shelving above the headboard.

He looked back at Jackie. She was sitting up now, her legs dangling over the side of the bed, her hands gripping the edge of the mattress. Blake approached, squatted and slid his hand under the mattress between her legs.

His fingertips found the bottle. The 40 mg oxy script was written by a doctor in Beverly Hills in Moxie's name. The bottle was half full.

Jackie looked up with pleading eyes. "Please don't tell Carla. She'll put me out on the street."

He was going to tell her Carla wasn't the point. But before he could, she stood and came close, her breasts almost touching his chest.

Jackie touched his cheek. "Eddie, I know you were a cop," she said in a sensual voice. "But that doesn't mean you have to be a snitch."

Jacqueline Rose was fucked up, Blake decided. She was fucked up whether she was high or not. He remembered Carla told him once, "You know what you get when you sober up a horse thief? You get a sober horse thief."

Blake pushed Jackie back, watching her fall flat on her back on the king size bed. She gave him a coy smile, looking at him like he'd tossed her there so he could take her. She was breathing deeply now.

He tossed the bottle of oxy onto her heaving breasts.

"Knock yourself fucking out," he said.

Blake wasn't sure how long he'd been standing on the aft deck. He was looking across the channel at an apartment building the reflected in the water. Half the windows glowed from lights inside, the others dark in no particular pattern, the collection of squares of looking like a mixed-up Rubik's cube. It occurred to him that he'd tossed Jackie the pills because that would solve everything. She ODs and he's done with the entire fucked-up scenario.

Then he thought about the girl. Bella. An innocent kid with no dad and a wacked-out mom. And he'd delivered her right into Poole's hands. He'd made lots of mistakes, he told himself. Ignored red flags. He should have spotted JP's *friend of a friend* scam. He should have scrutinized Poole's phony divorce decree. He should have accompanied Poole into the house in Sherman Oaks. Blake concluded that he'd handled the entire job like an old washed-up dick.

He'd done it willingly, numbing his instincts with the promise of a Hollywood job.

Blake remembered his disturbing dream. Dr. George prescribing instructions for a proper suicide. He remembered his father. He could picture his old man parking his Plymouth Fury and closing the garage door with the engine running. He'd always resented his father for that. The way his father left it to his mother to find him—his skin rose red, a postmortem effect of the carbon monoxide.

For the first time, he could grasp why the old man did what he did.

Blake pulled out his sidearm, looking at the Smith's stainless barrel. He remembered plunking down five hundred for the pistol at the Wessel Gun Shop north of Eight Mile Road. He didn't like the department-issued Glock 17 with its 9 mm round. He wanted something smaller and lighter but with the punch of a .45. He remembered showing the pistol to the old dicks on the squad. They liked revolvers, but they didn't give him any shit about his semi-auto. They all worked well together in homicide. It was like a think tank, the way the old dicks would offer solutions when an investigation hit a dead end. Blake remembered Dr. George saying that tough guys don't ask for help.

No, he thought. But those old dicks? They loved to give it.

He looked at the Chief's Special again. Then slid it back into his waistband. Blake thought he may have fucked up by ever getting involved with Jason Perry. But there were a few things he could still do. He could retrieve the bottle of oxy from Jackie. He could keep Carla safe.

And he could help Valley Bureau Homicide.

He was almost to the salon doors when his phone rang. He was relieved to see Carla's name on his caller ID.

Blake stopped and said, "Where are you?"

"I'm in your car," she said. Her words sounded measured. He didn't hear any traffic noise.

"We got a problem," Blake said.

Carla said, "Yes, we do."

There was a rustling noise, the phone was being passed.

Warren Poole said, "That Dodge is sweet, Edwin. After I get roller girl all squared away, I believe I'll take it for a joyride."

43

THE TWO-STORY MOTEL ON VENTURA Boulevard aimed to snag tourists by advertising rooms at $69 a night within walking distance of Universal Studios. There were a dozen rooms but only three cars in the parking lot when Poole spotted it. He paid for three days in advance for a first-floor room with parking spot a few feet from the door. He asked the manager, a guy in a pair of dirty jeans and a flannel shirt, about room service. The manager pointed to a soda machine on the wall outside the office.

Poole said he meant housekeeping. "You know, the maid. I won't need that."

"We don't have one," the manager said.

Inside the room, the only amenity was an old tube television sitting on top of a dresser. Poole saw duct tape around the air conditioner and sheets that looked like they hadn't been changed in a week. The grimy bathroom window had security bars.

He thought the place was perfect.

Minutes after he'd snatched the woman, he'd pictured finding a dive motel. And boom, there it was right there on Ventura Boulevard. Warren Poole was starting to think there really *was* something to the book Dagney gave him. He remembered reading about visualizing positive results rather than dwelling on obstacles. He realized that after he left the Backdrop Lounge, he'd visualized making a big move on Blake. At the time he didn't know what that would be. But a half hour later it materialized when he spotted Blake's gal roll up in his car to her house and go inside. He'd also visualized her complying when he put a knife to her throat from the back seat when she drove away.

And she was.

She only began complaining after he took her into the motel room. She didn't like being put on the toilet, her ass on the seat, her arms behind her, her wrists tied together underneath the flush tank. She protested when he pulled her leggings down to her ankles. Near midnight, Poole wrapped her mouth with duct tape and said, "I'm going to grab some shut-eye, roller girl. But look at it positively. Nature calls? You're good to go."

A couple arguing in the adjacent room woke him on Sunday morning. He found his hostage asleep, her head resting on the wall behind the toilet tank. He decided not to wake her. He left the room and slid behind the wheel of the Challenger. Despite the rude awakening, he was still feeling positive as he drove two miles up Ventura Boulevard to an internet café.

A few minutes later, he was sitting in front of a computer. Now he was visualizing himself in Vietnam, hooking up with Tommy Donofrio, finding a nice crib with house servants at his beck and call. He applied online for the visa, just like Machine Johnny said he could. Then he checked out flights, looking for one in two days when he expected the visa would be approved. He was surprised to see he could get a China Airlines flight to Ho Chi Minh City, with one stop in Taipei, for only $540. Hell, it was cheaper than a short-notice flight to Toronto. He hadn't visualized that.

He reserved a flight.

Poole stopped at Peet's Coffee on his way back to the motel. He took a cup of joe and a breakfast sandwich to the patio. He watched the traffic pass on Ventura as he ate. The street noise didn't seem as loud as when he first arrived in LA. The slow crawl of the Monday morning rush hour matched his mood. He thought, no need to be in a hurry. Maybe later he'd take a drive to check out places to make the swap—people for cash. Or just go see some sights. Maybe do both at the same time. He felt good knowing Blake was in a different headspace now. He'd kept their talk short. He wanted the ex-cop to spend the night thinking about his girlfriend.

He wanted him wondering how the matter with the great JP was going to go now.

When he got back to the motel he sat on the hood of the Dodge, letting his face soak up some of the warm Southern California sun as he called Blake. He wasn't surprised Blake picked up on the first ring. He could hear road noise in the background. Blake in his car, he thought, probably frantically looking for his main squeeze. Right off, Blake threatened to hunt him down if she wasn't returned unharmed.

Poole had visualized him doing that. He listened, letting him vent.

Finally, Poole said, "No need to threaten violence, Edwin. Look, your roller girl is fine. Good broad, really. No trouble. You'll get her back. Presuming you hold up your end of the deal."

"And what deal was that?"

"The one we agreed to. You get Perry to step up. Fork over the half mil. You give me Jackie. I deliver both the mother and the kid."

"He can't raise that," Blake said. "At least on short notice. But we can get two-fifty. I know he's got that—in cash."

"That could work. That's one-twenty-five for me and one-twenty-five for you. One-and-a-quarter. That seems like a fair price for you to pay, doesn't it?"

"Fair fucking price for what?"

"For roller girl. She's no longer a breeder, but she's worth it, don't you think?"

Blake was silent.

Poole said, "I'm counting on you to close this one, Edwin. I'm counting on your influence with the man."

"First, I need to know she's okay."

Poole had visualized him asking that as well. "She's on the shitter," he said. "You know women. They don't like you busting in on them."

Blake said, "Poole, you listen to me—"

Poole slid off the hood. "No, *you* listen. Because this is how it's going to go. You go see Mr. Perry. Keep it pleasant. Have a couple of pops. Hell, or hang out in the whirlpool. You know, like you Hollywood people do. Me? I'll be in touch."

Poole hung up.

He slid the burner phone into his side pocket and surveyed the parking lot. He saw the day manager, a Mexican woman in stretch pants she had no business wearing, smoking a cigarette outside the office door. He noticed only one other car parked outside a unit. He decided the Challenger was too conspicuous.

He parked the Dodge behind the motel where it was obscured by a couple of big trash bins. He locked the car and walked to the vending machine outside the office. He fed it a couple bucks and pushed the button for a Minute Maid orange juice.

The woman was awake as he entered the bathroom. He held up the juice, saying, "Brought you some breakfast, roller girl."

She glared, her cheeks glowing red. She tried to speak through the duct tape, but he couldn't understand a word.

He ripped off the tape and said, "You want to pee first? Or do you just need some toilet paper?"

44

A YOUNG PRODUCTION ASSISTANT WITH a walkie talkie approached Blake as he walked out of the municipal center garage on his way to the LAPD Community Police Station in Van Nuys. Fifty feet away a film crew was shooting a scene in front of the old Valley City Hall. Blake stopped before the PA could say anything. He knew not to walk through a shot. He asked him what they were filming.

The PA said the name of a show for TNT that Blake didn't recognize.

"A pilot?" Blake asked.

"They're in their third season," the PA said. He paused, then added. "You in the industry?"

"Not for long," Blake said.

Blake walked to the police station, hesitating at its door. It was his second visit there in five days, but this time to a different unit, a different detective. The way he figured, once he was done talking to Paul Ricardo in Valley Bureau Homicide, once Jason Perry started covering his own ass, he'd never work in the industry again.

But that no longer troubled him.

It was about Carla now. Warren Poole had crossed the line. He needed to be collared. The only way to do all that was to engage the resources that waited behind the station's door. What Veronica had implied was right. He had to stop thinking like just another desperate Hollywood hack. He needed to start operating like a cop.

Cops in trouble call for backup.

A couple minutes later, Blake was waiting in a hard chair in a small third-floor waiting area outside the detective bureau. A uniformed officer behind a reception window had said she'd let Paul Ricardo know he was there. He'd left Jackie Rose in the Marina. She was no help to anyone now. He'd tried to retrieve the oxy. But she showed him an empty bottle and claimed she flushed the pills. He figured she probably hid them, but he was in no mood to tear the boat apart. Before he left, Blake came clean with her. Told her how he and Carla had found her daughter, how they'd been deceived. He told her Poole now had Carla, and that he was going to the authorities, whether she liked it or not. Cruising on the dope, Jackie didn't give him a hard time. Still, she wanted nothing to do with the police. So, he left her on the boat, telling her if she fled she'd be arrested and she'd never see her kid again.

After a five-minute wait, Paul Ricardo poked his head into the waiting area and asked Blake to follow him. He was wearing a blue dress shirt and dress slacks, his tie loosened, carrying a coffee in a LAPD mug. He offered Blake a cup, but he declined. As they walked through the homicide unit, he saw a half dozen other detectives in cubicles working their murder books. All wore ties, their sports coats and suit jackets hung over their chairs. Blake liked that they dressed up, though the cubicles reminded him more of an insurance office than his old gritty confines at 1300 Beaubien in Detroit.

Paul Ricardo asked Blake to take a seat at the table in the unit's interrogation room. The detective sat in a chair next to the wall, leaning back with it so it was on two legs. Blake knew Ricardo had been on the murder squad fifteen years, dealing largely with gang-related homicides in Valley turf wars with an occasional domestic killing in the mix. He was pretty laid back for a cop who chased down street killers in largely Hispanic neighborhoods. At least he was the last time they'd met.

Ricardo said, "I keep looking for that movie you were working on. What, they didn't like our material? Got plenty more for you if you want it. You know how it goes. The hits just keep on coming."

"They shot the film, but couldn't get distribution," Blake said.

"I'm not sure what that means."

"It means a company that distributes it into the theaters. The movie channels. DVD sales. They take a cut. Without that, not much happens."

"So, who saw it?"

"The actors. The crew."

"That's it?"

Blake nodded.

"That's a lot of work, a lot of money, on something that goes nowhere."

"Happens all the time."

Ricardo crossed his hands behind his head. "What brings you out here, Eddie? You want to see some murder books?"

"I'm not working a film," Blake said. "Or a show." Blake paused. "But I've got something you'd be interested in."

"Okay," Paul Ricardo said, drawing out the word.

Blake began, "So I get this call one day from a producer saying he's got a job for me . . ."

It took five minutes to work his way through what had happened: The friend of a friend. Meeting the ex-husband. Finding Jacqueline Rose. Her daughter being picked up. Then finding out the ex was a phony, that he was a hired gun from Vegas brought in by the producer.

Telling all in present tense.

When he paused, Paul Ricardo said, "That's got some twists and turns, Eddie. Sounds like it could be a hell of a movie."

"It's not a movie," Blake said. "The producer's name is Jason Perry. He's done some big shows and films."

Ricardo rocked a little in his chair. "Wait a minute. This isn't something you're putting together?"

Blake shook his head. "No, and I'm right the fuck in the middle of it."

"You're saying this is for real?"

Blake nodded.

Ricardo's hands came from behind his head and rested on his stomach. "Jesus Christ, Eddie. That sounds like a goddamn goat rodeo."

"There's more," Blake said. "Where the hired gun picked up the girl? I thought that might be of interest."

"What kind of interest?"

Blake recited the address of the dead dealer in Sherman Oaks.

Paul Ricardo leaned all the way forward, the back of his chair coming away from the wall. "How do you know this phony dad was there?"

"I watched him pick the girl up." Blake paused. "And later I saw LAPD on the scene."

Paul Ricardo blinked a couple of times. "You knew what went down in there?"

"Not right away. I found out when I turned on the news."

"That's my goddamn case."

Blake nodded. "Yeah. I saw that on the coroner's report."

"That's sealed."

"Not when I saw it."

Paul Ricardo got up and walked over to the door and closed

it. Blake's phone vibrated in his pocket. But he ignored the call. Ricardo returned to the table, pulling his chair closer to Blake. He leaned forward, resting his right elbow on the table, no longer a pal helping him out with a movie.

An agitated homicide dick now.

Ricardo said, "Let me get this straight. We work that scene almost a week ago. You *know* it's a goddam homicide. And you're just getting around to coming in here?"

"I know how it looks."

Ricardo leaned closer. "How it looks? A guy comes in here off the street with a story like yours, the first thing I'm doing is running his sheet. Figuring out who the fuck I'm dealing with. Do I need to run your sheet, Eddie?"

Blake pulled out his notebook. He wrote out Warren Poole's name and date of birth, ripped out the sheet and handed it to Ricardo. "Why don't you run the hired gun first?"

Ricardo looked at it for a moment. Then he stood, saying "I'll be right back."

Blake heard the door lock behind the detective. He spotted a small round dome in the ceiling, the room's video camera. He knew now that he was in the box. Given the circumstances he would have locked the door, too. He checked his phone. He listened to a voice mail from an unknown caller. It was a robot solicitor, a scam offering a free stay at a resort. Blake thought when this was all over that's what he was going to do. Not the scam. Take Carla somewhere real nice—presuming he got Carla back safely. Presuming she didn't dump him.

At this point, he couldn't blame her if she did.

Twenty minutes later, Ricardo returned. Another detective walked in behind him, a cop in his late thirties with a shaved head and a buttoned-up collar, his tie cinched. Ricardo introduced him as his partner. He sat across the table, looking at Blake with cold eyes.

Ricardo didn't take a chair. He leaned against the wall, his arms crossed. "So where is this guy Poole?" he asked.

Blake shrugged. "I don't know. Don't even have a number. He uses burners." Blake let a couple seconds pass. "But it gets more complicated."

"I'm all ears, Eddie," Ricardo had a sarcastic tone in his voice.

Blake explained how Poole still had the girl and was shaking down Jason Perry, looking to make a big score. He told him how Carla had taken in Jackie Rose to help her get clean and sober. JP wanted both the mother and the daughter. "But Poole can't close the deal with Perry because I've got the mother," Blake said. "Stashed on a boat in the Marina."

Ricardo uncrossed his arms, stepping away from the wall. "Let me get this straight. You're saying you're in on the deal? The ransom?"

"Poole thinks I am. And now he's got some leverage there."

"What kind of *leverage?*"

"He grabbed my girlfriend Carla. Last night. I've got to convince Perry to pay up. Poole delivers the kid. I deliver the mom. I do that, I get Carla back."

Paul Ricardo glanced over at his partner, who shook his head like the whole story sounded like bullshit. Ricardo walked over to the table, spun a chair around and straddled it with his legs, resting his arms on its back. He was only a foot from Blake now.

"So, Eddie," he said, "Let's just recap. You get involved with this nut job producer, who runs this goofy dodge with some Vegas guy with a sheet to get his old girlfriend back—for God knows *what* reason."

"He says he wants to get her off drugs."

"You bought that?"

"Sounded reasonable at first."

"Okay," Ricardo said, nodding. He continued, "But you find out the father really isn't the father. But a hired gun. And you and your gal friend pick up the mother at the Ventura lockup. Meanwhile, the kid is with this guy Poole. And now he's trying to shake down the producer for two-fifty k for delivering them both. But *you* have the mother."

"That's right."

Ricardo's brow furrowed. "A quarter mil for an ex-girlfriend and her kid? That's a shitload, even for a Hollywood fat cat. That doesn't make sense."

"It's more like blackmail. Perry is paranoid that this will all get out. Bad publicity. Screw up a megadeal he's got with Warner Brothers. Screw up what's left of his career."

"And this shakedown has gone on how many days?"

"Just a couple."

"And you were planning to do what?"

"I was trying to find out where the kid was. I was working for Perry."

"Are you now?"

"I wouldn't be here if I was."

"And if you did find the girl what were you going to do then? Fork over the mom and kid?"

"I was waiting to see how it all played out."

Ricardo glanced at his partner again, then looked back. "And then what? You were going to come down to our bureau and let us know about this little detail about Mr. Warren James Poole. That you happened to be sitting on a prime suspect in a homicide? Saying sorry, Paul, I just got kind of fucking busy, but I got something for you now."

Blake said, "I just did."

Ricardo addressed his partner. "We need to bring the clown Perry in." He looked at Blake. "You have the producer's address? House? Office?"

"Not on me."

Ricardo looked back at his partner. "Pull it. And run Perry while you're at it."

The young detective got up, heading for the door.

"You don't want to do that," Blake said.

"We don't?" He motioned to his partner to stop. "You already ran Perry's sheet, too?"

"No, I'm saying you don't want to pick him up," Blake said.

Ricardo stood up. "Then what the fuck are you doing in here, Eddie, laying out all this shit on me?"

Blake looked up. "'Because I've got a good way for you to collar Warren Poole."

45

A TWENTY-FIVE-FOOT-LONG LINE OF CUSTOMERS waited outside of Malibu Seafood, a no-frills eatery on PCH near Pepperdine University. Patrons ordered and then waited to pick up their fish and chips so they could sit outside on decks a couple hundred feet from the ocean. Blake avoided the crowded decks and took a seat at picnic table near the parking lot.

He wasn't there to eat.

Blake had spent all day Monday with Paul Ricardo working out how LAPD was going to move on the case. Ricardo said, "A ransom involved, I need to bring in SIS. That's the tactical surveillance squad attached to Robbery Homicide downtown. They have SWAT. They have high altitude airships. You won't even know a chopper is in the air."

Blake knew Ricardo was talking about the Special Investigation Section. He'd researched SIS when he was consulting on a pilot. By the 1990s it had earned the nickname as LAPD's "death squad." Around since the sixties, it had fought in more than fifty gun battles, killing more than three dozen suspects and wounding dozens of others. It was less controversial in recent years. Still, SIS detectives all carried .45 caliber Glocks and spent a lot of time at the range.

Ricardo told Blake, "Considering what Poole is up to, it's department policy that SIS be involved. But it's going to take at least a day, maybe two, to put the operation together."

Ricardo and his partner also visited the yacht in Marina Del Rey. Ricardo told Jackie Rose he wasn't concerned about the twenty thousand dollars she'd stolen. No complaint had been filed. But now she had a choice. She could go along with the operation to take down Warren Poole or he would inform the drug court that she was not cooperating with an ongoing homicide investigation. She spent most of the interview huddled in the corner of the salon's leather couch, twirling her hair between her fingers, largely unresponsive. But she didn't object. Blake guessed she was still making use of her hidden stash.

Jackie asked one question. "Are you going to arrest Jason Perry?"

Ricardo said he wasn't sure yet if the producer had violated any laws. If he did, his defense attorney would probably argue that he was an unwitting victim. "I can't make any promises, Mrs. Rose," he said. "If he doesn't care about the money you took, but continues to bother you, you can always get a restraining order."

Blake and Ricardo talked afterwards in the parking lot. Ricardo agreed not to interrogate JP until after he showed up with the ransom, going with Blake's suggestion that JP wouldn't cooperate if he knew police were involved. Still, Ricardo wanted to put the producer under surveillance. Blake wanted to talk to JP first. Make sure he was willing to fork over the money. Ricardo gave him twenty-four hours to get that done. And the homicide detective wanted to be notified immediately if Poole called and gave Blake a location for the swap.

By noon, Warren Poole still hadn't called. But Jason Perry was on time.

Blake watched his Tesla swing into the restaurant's packed lot and park illegally in a handicapped spot. As he walked toward him,

Blake couldn't help but notice his appearance. He was dressed in jeans and a solid flannel shirt. Gone were the long hair and the beard.

JP sat down across from him

Blake said, "I'm guessing you don't want lunch."

JP glanced at the seafood shack and said, "I don't wait in lines." He put his hands palms down on the table. "You said you have some news."

Blake nodded. "I've worked out a way to get what you want."

JP's eyes brightened. "Jackie?"

"I've got her."

"Where is she?"

"Well hidden from Poole. And you're right. She belongs in rehab."

"What about her daughter?"

"I've got a way to get her, too."

"Good. Good."

Blake leaned forward. "But, JP, that's going to cost you."

"I told you, I'll take care of you."

"It's not for me. You're going to have to pay if you want the girl, too. I've been in touch with Poole. Or I should say, he's been in touch with me."

"How is that?"

"He abducted my girlfriend the night before last. Tells me I'll only get her back if I deliver Jackie."

"Jesus Christ. There's no end to this guy."

"He's playing for keeps."

"He wants a goddamn million."

"I've convinced him to go lower."

"How much lower?"

"A lot. If I give him Jackie, he'll fork over both the mom and the kid for two-fifty cash. It could be on short notice. I'm waiting for a call back from Poole."

"Nobody can withdraw that from a bank without a couple days' notice."

"You don't have to. You've got it in your safe."

JP didn't respond. He looked down at the table, rubbing his temples, apparently realizing Blake had a better memory than he thought.

Blake continued, "Or, JP, you could involve the police. But if you don't, I don't think you have another choice."

JP looked up. "I don't want to do that."

Blake said, "The next step? What I *can* do for you? I can limit your exposure."

"What do you mean?"

"This guy Poole, you already know he's dangerous. He's already threatened to take people out. You show up with that kind of money, there's nothing stopping him from just taking the cash and eliminating all three of you."

"You could be there."

"That could get ugly. That many people, it gets chaotic. Like that show *Cops* where emotions take over. No, a situation like this must be well planned, controlled."

JP's brow furrowed. "I'm not sure what you're saying."

"I'm saying, I already have Jackie. And you want both the mom and the kid. So, you give me the money for the swap. I'll show up with the cash and get Poole to fork over the girl. Then I bring both mother and daughter to you. I'll tell Poole that's the only way it's going to go down. Take it or leave it. He'll go for that."

"What makes you think so?"

"He wants the money."

"But I should be there."

Blake leaned forward. "JP, this isn't in your wheelhouse. We're not talking about a movie set here." Blake discreetly pulled out his

Smith, held it against his ribs and opened his jacket, waiting until JP noticed it. "I dealt with these kinds of people in Detroit. I made a lot of big buys."

JP eyed the sidearm. "You're willing to put your life at risk?"

"No, I'm willing to take the sonovabitch out myself. Like I said, he's got my gal. At this point it's personal."

Blake slid the Chief's Special back into its holster.

JP locked his hands behind his head, looking off into the distance, thinking for a good fifteen or twenty seconds.

Finally, he said, "How do I know *you* won't take off with my money?

Blake looked at him like he had to be joking. "Because you gave me your word, JP."

JP squinted. "About what?"

Blake said, "That you're going to put me above the line."

46

DAGNEY ROLLED OUT OF BED at noon and headed straight to her coffee maker. As water dripped through her favorite dark roast, she padded down the hall to her office. The door was closed. She decided to let the girl sleep. The night before she was organizing video files for her website when Bella knocked on the office door and said she wanted to talk. They both lay on the futon and talked to nearly 5 a.m. There were tears, not all of them Bella's. Dagney had fallen to sleep and woken with the same thought.

The kid needed professional help.

Dagney glanced at her cell as she sat down at the kitchen table with her coffee. There were two missed calls from a blocked number earlier. She was hoping it was Warren and not the collection agency that had been hounding her about the balance she still owed for her breast reduction surgery. If it was Warren, she figured he would call back.

Soon, she hoped. She had a lot to say to Warren Poole.

Fifteen minutes later, she was in the shower when she heard pounding at her door, barely audible over the running water. She wrapped herself in a terry cloth robe and fashioned a towel turban over her wet hair.

She opened the door to Warren. She didn't see his car in her driveway or on the street. He had a brochure in his right hand and was slapping it against his palm. "I tried to call," he said. "You didn't pick up." He walked right past her into the living room.

She followed him, saying, "I just got up."

"Ever been here?" he said, handing her the brochure.

She looked and saw: HOLLYWOOD FUNERAL HOME—GENERAL PRICE LIST.

She handed it back. "You plan on dying soon?"

"It's part of a spread called the Hollywood Forever Cemetery. They're all buried there. Fairbanks. Valentino. DeMille. Peter Lorre. Jayne Mansfield. They even have that rocker, Johnny Ramone. There's a statue of him at his grave, playing his guitar."

"I've heard of it. You went there?"

"This morning. Figured while I'm here, I might as well see the sights. Best part, though, was Bugsy Siegel. He's behind a slab."

"You mean a crypt."

"It had vases with fresh roses. And lipstick on the marble."

"Lipstick?"

"Yeah, at least a half dozen lips. Left there by women kissing it. Valentino and Fairbanks didn't even have that."

Dagney studied Warren's eyes, wondering for a second if he was high, though she'd never known him to smoke weed. "What's next on the agenda, Warren? A star map? A whale watching cruise?" Dagney unwrapped the towel from her head, stroking her hair with it. She said, "What the hell has gotten into you?"

"You need to work on your PMA," he said.

She stopped drying her hair and squinted. "My what?"

"Positive mental attitude."

She remembered the acronym. "Oh, so you read the book."

Warren nodded, his eyes glancing around the room now. "Where's the kid?"

"She's asleep. We had a late night. We've been having some good talks."

"You need to get her up."

"Warren," she said, getting his eyes. "I'm not even goddamn dressed."

"I need to talk to her."

"About what?"

"I've worked things out with her mother. I'm going to be picking her up tomorrow morning. Get her back with her kid."

He started in the direction of the hallway to the bedrooms.

Dagney positioned herself in front of him, blocking his way. "Warren, it's nice not to hear you bitching. But this other thing, I don't know what you're into. But the girl has been talking"

"About what?"

"She needs help. And definitely not from the guy you're working for."

"She belongs with her mother. I'm taking care of that."

"Really? What, you're going to pick her up in the Ventura jail?"

Poole nodded.

Dagney tossed the towel on a nearby chair. "Bullshit. She's not there. We checked."

"We?"

"Yeah, we drove up."

"You took her to the goddamn jail?" His mood changing now, no longer the tourist with a PMA.

"She wanted to visit her mom."

Warren grabbed her arm, squeezing it hard. "You need to stay the fuck out of my business."

Dagney glared. "Take your goddamn hand off me. You put me in your business when you brought that poor girl here."

* * *

She blocked his way to the hallway to her office for a good five minutes, Dagney running her mouth. Saying the kid was damaged, that she had *abandonment issues* and had disclosed secrets. That she needed long-term therapy. It all sounded like a bunch of bullshit Dagney had lifted from the self-help books scattered around her house.

When she finally took a breath, Poole said, "Are you done?"

"Maybe," she said.

"Good." He pushed her aside and walked to her office door and reached for the handle.

It was locked.

Warren rapped on the door with his knuckles. "Bella," he said. "Open up."

There was no response.

Warren said, louder this time, "It's me, Warren. I have some news about your mom."

Dagney stood behind him, her arms folded. "It's okay, Bella. I'm here, too. Open up, honey."

Still no response.

He turned to Dagney. "You got a way to open this?"

"You need a tiny screwdriver."

"You have one?"

Before she could answer he slammed his shoulder into the door, a piece of trim flying across the room.

"You're an asshole, Warren," Dagney said. "A clueless asshole."

Poole's eyes went right to the futon. He saw its covers pulled back. He saw an impression on the pillow. There were some folded clothes on the side table.

But no kid.

What he saw was a window. Wide open. It overlooked the back-yard. He stuck his head outside, scanning in all directions.

He spun around. "Having some good talks, huh?"

Dagney was silent, maybe even pleased.

Poole's eyes went to the laptop sitting on her desk, a screen saver displaying geometric shapes. He walked over and touched one of the keys. The screen saver flashed to another image: Dagney as Diedre Gibson, on all fours. A black performer slamming her from behind. A white guy with his cock in her mouth.

He turned to Dagney. "Very nice. Working on a bright future for the kid, Dagney?"

She walked over. Saw it herself. Her fingers came to her mouth. "I never told her what I did."

Warren said, "Why tell when you can show."

"Fuck. I must have forgotten to sign out."

He grabbed her by the shoulders and slammed her into the wall, holding her there. "You stupid fucking slut."

"You're hurting me," Dagney said.

"Any idea where she might have gone?"

She shook her head.

He didn't like the way she looked away when she said it. He slammed her into the wall again.

"Bullshit." He dug his fingernails into her biceps.

"Goddammit, Warren, I said you're hurting me."

"It's supposed to hurt."

"Christ. I don't know. Maybe Venice. She said she had friends in Venice."

"Where in Venice?"

"She just said she used to meet them on the pier."

He let go and pushed her aside. He walked over to the window again. He was hoping he'd somehow missed the kid on his first look.

But all he saw was a fire pit and a tall cedar fence separating her yard from her neighbors'.

Dagney said behind him, "It doesn't matter where she went."

Still looking out the window, he said, "It matters the fuck to me. It matters to your twenty goddamn k."

He turned around.

Dagney standing there by her desk. Her legs in a stance, her robe spread open. She was brandishing a pistol. A *pink* pistol.

Aimed at his chest in a two-handed grip.

Dagney said, "You can keep your dirty goddamn money."

Poole laughed. "You expect to get my attention with a prop from one of your fuck flicks?"

She aimed it at the ceiling and fired off a round.

His ears rang. When it subsided, he said, "Join the NRA, Dagney. Take their training. Otherwise, you could hurt yourself."

She glared. "Already card-carrying, motherfucker."

He took a couple steps forward. "Dagney, put the fucking gun down."

She backed up one step.

Dagney said, "Out of my house. And never come here again."

He took another step forward. The door was closed behind her. She had nowhere to retreat. But he didn't like looking down the muzzle of the semi-auto. The hole in the barrel seemed dark and deep.

After another step he said, "How can we settle this?"

"Like I said, the girl needs help. We need to report to the police that she's missing. They'll find her. Get her to the right people."

"And if I don't, Dagney, what are you going to do? Fucking shoot me? You don't know shit. And not knowing shit, just what are you going to tell the police?"

"I know enough."

He took another step. One more and he'd be in arm's reach of her gun. "Look, let's just review what happened here. I bring you the kid and agree to pay you a sizeable amount of money. And for reasons that escape me, you go all motherly. I didn't know you had it in you. Until the kid cracks open your computer. Sees you fucking. Not one guy. But two. Salt and pepper, the black dude with his big horse cock up your ass."

"Fuck you, Warren."

He took another step. Within reach of the pistol now.

Poole chuckled. "You ever wonder why I never fucked you after you moved to LA?"

She didn't answer. But the gun was shaking in her hand.

"I'll tell you. 'Cause you started fucking niggers."

Poole turned his head and spit. Her eyes followed it to the floor.

He swiped the gun out of her hand.

He thought that would be it. That it was over now.

But she punched him underhand just under his ribs and drove her knee into his groin. He fell backwards, the back of his knees colliding with the futon.

On his back now on the mattress, her pistol in his right hand.

Dagney leaped on top of him.

He felt a fierce karate blow to his chin. Another to his cheek. He was still reeling from the dull pain in his groin. She slammed two knuckles into his forehead, her fingers parting around the bridge of his nose. She wasn't screaming like most women do when they fight. She was blowing breath out of her nostrils in short blasts with each punch.

Her hands went for his throat.

But he was able to come up with the pistol. He slammed the muzzle into the flesh between her neck and her chin bone.

And pulled the trigger.

She instantly went limp.

He pushed her off the side of the futon as she collapsed.

He eyed Dagney on the floor for a while as he caught his breath. It was a clean kill, he decided. Only a small hole under her chin. No exit wound. No blood splatter on the ceiling. He took a good look at the gun. It was a Taurus .380, designed for a woman. He didn't like the color, but he liked the way it felt, its compact size. It was similar to his Tomcat that Blake took outside the psych ward.

He slid the Taurus into his windbreaker.

Warren Poole walked to the kitchen. He took a bottle of kombucha from the fridge and rolled its cold surface over his chin and cheek. He slipped it into his windbreaker and grabbed a hand towel hanging from one of the kitchen drawers.

A few seconds later, he wiped down the doorknob to Dagney's office and the keyboard of her laptop. He returned to the front of the house and wiped down the front door after he locked it.

He left out the back door.

Five minutes later he was swigging the kombucha behind the wheel of his Camry, which he'd retrieved earlier in the day. He was thinking how Dagney had been hitting the gym for years, trying to keep herself in the porn game. He was thinking about her karate moves.

The bitch put up one hell of a fight. He had to admire that.

He was thinking about Dagney that way. Maybe even missing her—until he spotted the kid.

Walking in a fast gait on Santa Monica Boulevard.

47

BLAKE WOKE AT 6:30 WEDNESDAY morning, a half hour before he'd set the alarm on his phone. He'd spent the night on *The Closer*, waiting for a call from Poole that never came. Jackie kept to herself in the VIP state room. Blake slept on the couch in the salon. He figured she knew everything was changing with LAPD in the picture. He guessed she was tapping the last of her oxy stash, knowing her little yacht party was about to end.

Blake immediately noticed the sky when he walked out on the deck. The sun was just below the horizon and was painting cumulus clouds in scarlet and vermillion on the horizon. He spent a few minutes admiring the sight. He couldn't remember the last time he noticed those type of clouds or those colors in Southern California.

The sky was not all that led him to believe that Dr. George had correctly diagnosed his depression and the medication was working. The night before, he thought about his blues records back in his crib. He could use a little T-Bone Walker right about now. Maybe "West Side Baby" from the Black & White label. He knew he'd made some bad decisions since his meeting with Jason Perry thirteen days ago. But now he knew his brain had been misfiring for months before that. It was as if someone else was running his life. Someone he no longer recognized.

Someone who was finally gone.

His first thought was to call Dr. George and tell him. Instead, he made another call. Paul Ricardo answered in a groggy voice. "Heard anything?"

"Nothing," Blake said.

"Good."

"Good?"

"SIS has a team together. But RHD wants a sit-down to go over everything."

"I've given you everything. You can fill Robbery Homicide in."

Ricardo cleared his throat. "Eddie, I'm dealing with downtown's rules. I've set a meeting at the West LA station at 11 a.m. You won't have to come to the valley."

"What if Poole calls before then?"

"You'll have to stall him. They want to get surveillance going on Perry."

"You don't have someone sitting on him now?"

"SIS has to handle everything because a hostage situation is involved. Like I said, I don't make the rules."

Blake looked at his phone, saying nothing, knowing he was dealing with police bureaucracy now.

Ricardo said, "Eddie, you listening to me? Technically it's their show, but my ass will be on the line if this goes sideways. You know shit always runs downhill. If this guy Poole reaches out, wants to get it done, like I said, you have to stall."

"And say what?"

"I'm sure you have a pocket full of bullshit at your command."

After he hung up, Blake went below to check on Jackie in the VIP stateroom. She was asleep, or more likely nodded out. His first thought: What a time to be wasted. But his second thought was that her condition actually might be fortuitous. She was on cloud nine. That would reduce the chance of hysterics. That way Jackie Rose would be compliant during the exchange.

Warren Poole had to do some explaining to the kid after he asked her to get into his car. She didn't thank him for picking her up. But she got in.

The kid's eyes were red. "I thought you said Dagney was with the agency," she said.

"She is," he said. "Obviously they didn't do a good background check. I found out what happened. What you saw. I fully understand why you left."

"I thought I liked her."

"She was always good with young people."

"You said my mother was in jail."

"She was released a few hours before you tried to visit her."

"Why didn't you tell me?"

"I tried. Dagney didn't pick up the phone. She finally picked up yesterday morning. I told her I was picking you up. She didn't tell you?"

The kid shook her head.

Poole said, "I've been busy arranging everything."

"Arranging what?"

"Your mom is getting help. But they have certain restrictions. I couldn't arrange anything right away."

"To do what?"

"Put both of you back together. You're going to be seeing her soon."

He took her to dinner at Mel's Drive-In, telling her to order anything she wanted and suggested the strawberry shake with the whipped cream on the top. By evening, she was content spending the night at the BLVD Hotel, especially after he booked her a room so she'd feel comfortable in her own space.

After she fell asleep, Poole went back to the motel to check on roller girl. She spat a string of profanities when he removed the tape from her mouth. He pulled out the pink Taurus, gripped her hair and kissed her lips with the muzzle.

"You can do this party either way. You can stop running your mouth. Get up and stretch those pretty legs. Work out the kinks in your ass. Then you can have some carry-out. In-N-Out with fries and chocolate shake." He tapped the Taurus against her teeth. "Or you can continue to bitch. The tape goes back on. And you don't come off the shitter."

She opened her mouth to answer.

He pushed the barrel to the back of her throat. "You follow?"

She nodded quickly, her eyes riveted to his.

After she quietly finished her burger, he put her back on the toilet. He ripped off fresh tape and told her he she only had to sit it out one more night.

"Then what?" she asked.

"You behave, you're going home tomorrow, roller girl."

When morning came, he used his key card to check on the kid. She was sound asleep.

He drove to the internet café to check on the status of his Vietnam visa application.

He was approved.

He had a couple of calls to make and one more stop. The last call he planned that morning he wanted to make sitting in his hotel room. He wanted to sit in the swivel office chair, his feet up on the desk, he decided. Doing it real casual.

With a positive mental attitude.

48

THE CALL CAME IN AT 10 a.m. while Blake was in the galley, considering ordering takeout for breakfast.

Poole said, "Hollywood Forever Cemetery. Eleven a.m. Meet us at Johnny Ramone's grave. You can't miss it. Look for the statue of a guy with a guitar. Bring the mom. I'll have the kid and roller girl."

Blake said, "I need some time to get your money."

Poole chucked. "You mean our money. You'll be paid up, Edwin."

"And that means?"

"Just be there."

And he hung up.

Blake dialed Paul Ricardo. He told him he was not going to make the 11 a.m. tactical meeting. The exchange was on. He told the detective, "SIS needs to get off their asses and set up at the cemetery. And you better get a tail on Jason Perry. I think Poole is planning on having JP show up there with the cash."

Ricardo said, "Goddammit, I told you to stall him."

Blake detected movement in the salon. It was Jackie. She was barefoot and wearing only a bra and panties.

Blake covered the phone. "Get dressed. We're leaving in ten minutes."

"For what?" Her eyes looked sleepy.

"To get your daughter. And a heads up. JP will probably be there." She headed back to the stateroom.

Blake uncovered the phone. "Just get your goddamn people moving, Paul. I'll call after I get on the road."

Blake hung up and dialed JP. He didn't pick up. He checked his Chief's Special, ejecting the magazine to confirm it was full and then slamming it back home. He racked a round into the chamber of the Smith & Wesson. If LAPD didn't have its act together at Hollywood Forever, he vowed he'd take Warren James Poole into custody himself.

Ten minutes later, Jackie still hadn't reemerged from her state room. Blake pounded on the door. A couple seconds later, it opened. She was wearing running shoes and leggings under a loose, casual dress that Carla had bought her. She appeared cogent enough for what lay ahead.

Blake grabbed her by the arm and led her all the way to the Mini Cooper. He opened the passenger door and maneuvered her into the car, putting his hand over her head as she slid into the seat like he'd done hundreds of times before with suspects.

Jackie was silent as Blake navigated side streets through Venice, avoiding the heavy traffic on Lincoln Boulevard. He was only a minute from the I-10 when he reached for his phone to call Paul Ricardo. He didn't get the chance.

A call came in.

"Change of plans, Edwin," Poole said. "Where are you?"

"Santa Monica."

"Very good. I want you to get on the coast highway. You know, the one that goes along the ocean. Head north."

"Technically, that's west."

"Towards Malibu then. Point is, we're going to take the scenic route."

"We?"

"That's right, you and me. And you're going to stay on the phone so I can be your tour guide. That means you don't hang up. That means you don't make a call. Or switch to an incoming. You do that, you'll never see roller girl again."

Blake could hear road noise in the phone. Poole was in a car. He checked in his rearview mirror. He saw no sign of his Dodge or Poole's Camry. Blake looked over at Jackie. Her eyes were closed. Christ, he thought, she'd gotten into the oxy again.

He could see the ramp to PCH ahead. "PCH is a long way from Hollywood Forever," Blake said.

Poole said, "It's meant to be, Edwin."

Blake decided he had no choice but to comply. He had a green light onto the PCH ramp. A minute later he was heading toward Malibu.

"You still with me, Edwin?"

"All the way," Blake said.

"I want you to drive about twenty miles."

Blake said, "I'm going to put the phone down. Put you on speaker."

"Now why would you do that?"

"Because I don't want to get pulled over. Police will ticket you here for having a cell phone to your ear."

"Sounds reasonable, Edwin. So put the radio on. I want you tune it to one of those Latino stations. I'm in the mood for a fiesta."

Blake found one on AM, its DJ talking a mile a minute.

"That works," Poole said. "You can brush up on your Spanish. Let me know when you see the Malibu Pier."

Blake found the radio irritating. It was a Spanish talk radio. No music and the host's voice coming at him like a machine gun, Jackie nodded right through it. After a couple minutes he was able ignore the chatter and began thinking about where Poole had him going. The Malibu Pier was public, filled during the day with tourists and fishermen.

The sonovabitch was clever. It was no place for a gunfight.

Blake checked his mirror several times. Still no sign of a tail. His phone lit up twice, incoming calls from Paul Ricardo. He had to ignore the detective. Eventually, he spotted the Malibu Pier.

"Okay, I see the pier, Poole," he said. "But I'm not pulling over until I have your word that Carla and the kid are going to be there. And like I said, I don't have the money."

Poole said, "You're not stopping at the pier."

"This is bullshit."

"No, it's the second leg of the tour. A couple miles ahead, I want you to turn on Malibu Canyon. It's right next to the college out there."

"You mean Pepperdine," Blake said. "I'm putting the phone back down."

"You're doing just fine, Edwin. Let me know when you get to Mulholland."

He's taking us to JP's, Blake thought. It was all going to go down there. Not a choice he would have made if he was Poole. He hoped Paul Ricardo had moved fast and set up surveillance at the producer's house.

Minutes later, the Mini Cooper was climbing a two-lane road to higher elevations, snaking through Malibu Canyon. To Blake's left were steep mountains and signs warning of rockslides. To his right sheer drop-offs with no guardrails. Blake checked his mirror again. No one behind him. Ten minutes later the road leveled off, cutting through hills of chaparral, ranches, and a rustic state recreation area.

Blake spotted a stoplight ahead and picked up the phone. "Okay, I'm at Mulholland. I presume you want me to take a left."

Poole said, "You presume wrong, Edwin. I want you to keep going. Another mile or so. Look for Las Virgenes Canyon Road. And take a right. It's just after you turn. You can't miss it."

"Miss fucking what?"

"You'll see."

Blake poked Jackie.

She opened her eyes, saying "Where are we?"

"I'm not sure. But I need you alert."

"You there?" Poole said.

"I'm turning now."

"Good. Light some incense for me." Poole hung up.

Blake turned off the radio and dialed Paul Ricardo. He spat out his location, that the swap was about to go down. He was looking at an entrance sign in front of an open gate. It read:

HINDU TEMPLE.

Ricardo asked for details about the exchange.

"No time for that," Blake said. "You need to get some eyes out here."

"That's thirty miles through traffic," Ricardo said.

Blake snapped, "So send your goddamn chopper."

49

BLAKE DIDN'T SEE HIS CHALLENGER or Poole's Camry in the lot as he drove through the gated entrance and parked the Mini Cooper in the shade. He told Jackie to stay in the car.

Blake gazed up at the Hindu Temple, three stories of stark white stone graced with hundreds of ornate carvings. Gilded statues of Hindu gods perched near the top of its highest tower. Near the main vaulted entrance two shirtless monks in sandals and ochre harem pants fiddled with prayer beads around their necks.

Blake slid onto the hood of the Mini and waited. A Prius turned into the parking lot. Blake instinctively felt for his sidearm. But a young couple emerged and walked into the temple. A biker motored through the gate on a Ducati. Blake watched him park the motorcycle, walk to the entrance and take off his shoes before stepping inside.

The place was open to anyone.

Five minutes passed. Blake found himself scrutinizing the pair of statues in front of the temple's tower. He knew that was Lord Krishna with a flute in his hand, but it took him a while to remember the name of female figure posed next to him, Radha, his consort.

Carla told him about the pair back when she was into Kundalini yoga.

Blake heard the crunch of tires on stone before he heard the car or saw it.

A black Bentley. Its windows tinted.

It parked five spaces away but hardly stopped when its rear passenger door flew open.

Carla bolted out, not bothering to close the car door. She ran toward Blake. He slid off the hood of the Mini. She didn't stop running until she was in his arms.

Her voice trembled. "Jesus Christ. Thank God you're here."

He stroked her hair but focused over her shoulder, his eyes on the Bentley.

Jason Perry got out. He was wearing dress slacks and a pink-patterned collared shirt.

JP walked around the car to the front passenger door.

He opened it.

And Isabella Rose stepped out.

Blake turned to alert Jackie inside the Mini, but she was already out the door, standing, her hands tucked in her armpits, staring at JP and Bella.

The two of them walked casually toward the Mini, JP half smiling, a look of satisfaction on his face. He draped his hand over Bella Rose's shoulder.

Blake shouted, "Where's Poole?"

JP kept walking with the girl. "He had me meet him and pay up. He's probably long gone. But thank God he kept his word." After a few more steps he said, "Jackie, so good to see you."

They stopped about ten feet from Jackie. JP turned to Bella. "See, honey, I told you I'd get your mom back."

Bella wasn't smiling. Her eyes were darting around between her mother, Blake, and Carla.

Jackie drifted toward them, stopping five feet away. She said, "What the fuck do you think you're doing, JP?"

JP smiled and said, "I'm here to help. I'm here to help both of you."

What happened next would later remind Blake of the time the felon pulled the .357 heater on him during a traffic stop, the way everything unfolds like a jerky film at half speed.

It didn't start when Jackie pulled her right hand out of her armpit. It started when Blake saw a subcompact pistol in her hand.

Blake pushed Carla away and reached for his Smith. He wanted to present the .45 and give Jackie a command. His hand had just grasped the grip of the Chief's Special when he heard Jackie Rose say in a matter-of-fact voice:

"You goddamn sick bastard. You'll never touch my daughter again."

Then three shots. One after another.

Not from Blake. Blake scrambling toward the two of them.

JP fell backwards onto the pavement.

Jackie over him now, firing point blank into JP's chest.

Blake grasped Jackie from behind, pinning her arms to her side as one more shot went off into the pavement. He slid his hand down and gripped her right wrist, shaking it until the pistol fell to the ground. He recognized the sidearm as he kicked the gun away.

Poole's Beretta.

Blake glanced at Bella. She was frozen with her hands over her ears. He looked down at JP. The producer groaned once and then his jaw dropped, his mouth gaping.

Blake spun Jackie around.

Before he could speak, she cried out. "He didn't want *me*. He wanted my little girl."

The two monks near the entrance of the temple were no longer fingering their prayer beads. One paced. The other talked urgently into a cell phone.

Blake marched Jackie to the Bentley. She didn't resist. He put her in the back seat.

"Don't move," he said. And closed the door.

When he got back to Carla, she was holding Bella in her arms, the kid speechless, in a state of shock.

He held out the keys to the Mini Cooper. "Take your car. Take the girl back to the boat. I'll meet you there."

Carla hesitated.

"Carla, go. Either go now or spend the next eight hours at the police station. Not to mention dodging a bunch of news crews."

Thirty seconds later, he watched them drive off in her car.

Blake walked over to take a good look at Jason Perry. JP's arms were at his sides, foamy blood oozing from his mouth. His eyes were wide open as if he was transfixed on the statue of Radha and the Lord Krishna. He saw four bullet holes in his Ralph Lauren shirt. One oozed blood just under the trademark Polo horse over JP's heart.

Edwin Blake felt nothing for the man.

He walked back to the Bentley, intending to talk to Jackie and get the full story. But as he heard distant patrol sirens approaching in the canyon, he decided that wasn't his job anymore. He sat on the hood of the Bentley and thought about what Jackie had blurted out before she gunned Jason Perry down.

It all made sense. JP had groomed Isabella Rose and turned her into his sex toy.

Jason Perry was a pedophile.

50

THE STEAMY BACK SEAT OF the Los Angeles Sheriff's Department patrol car smelled of liquor and sour milk, apparently left by a nauseous drunk on a previous run. Blake, his hands cuffed behind him, watched Paul Ricardo pull into the temple lot in his department Crown Vic. He suspected county homicide wasn't far behind. It was their jurisdiction.

Jackie was detained in the back of another cruiser.

Blake watched Ricardo have words with two deputies. Finally, the homicide detective walked to the patrol car with one of them. The deputy opened the door but told Blake to stay in his seat.

Blake said, "Poole didn't show, Paul. Goddamn Perry did. The mother took him out. Apparently, he'd been molesting her daughter. I never saw it coming."

Ricardo didn't respond. He glanced at the temple and then JP's covered body on the pavement, his head nodding slowly.

Finally, he looked down at Blake. "Where did she get the piece, Eddie?"

"It was a .32 I took off Poole at the hospital. I hid it on the boat. The mother found it, I guess, when she was looking for dope. She must have concealed it under her dress."

Ricardo shook his head. "You didn't think it was important to tell me you had the asshole's gun?"

Blake didn't respond. He spotted a news truck pulling into the temple lot.

Blake looked back at Ricardo and said, "Paul, the deputies took my sidearm."

Lines appeared in Ricardo's forehead. "Jesus Christ, Eddie. Why do you think you're sitting in the back of a goddamn cruiser? They're going to take you to their Malibu station. Probably want to do a GSR kit."

Blake knew he wouldn't pass the standard test for gunshot residue on his hands. He said, "I'll fail it. She put one into the pavement when I was shaking the pistol from her hand."

"And where's the kid? Your gal?"

"I wanted to spare them."

"From what?"

Blake nodded in the direction of the news truck, a male reporter in a blue jacket stepping out of the van's door with microphone in his hand. Blake said, "You'll have no problem getting their statements."

Ricardo stared at him for a few moments. "I'll see you at the station."

The deputy slammed the door.

Two hours later, he remained cuffed as he waited inside an interview room in the sheriff's Malibu station. He'd been waiting for an hour. Finally, a sheriff's homicide detective came through the door. He had silver hair and a black mustache, his suspenders parted by his protruding middle-aged stomach. Paul Ricardo was a few steps behind him.

The sheriff's detective took a seat across from Blake, Ricardo in a chair off to the side.

"I'm detective George Bullard," he said as he dropped Blake's driver's license and conceal carry permit on the table.

Blake said, "Can you take off these goddamn cuffs?"

Bullard smirked. "They hurting you?"

"Only my pride. In case Detective Ricardo didn't tell you, I spent twenty-five on the fucking job. And it wasn't writing paper on surfers and barking dogs in Malibu."

Bullard smirked again. "Yeah, I heard something about that. But first why don't you tell me what happened?"

It took a good half hour, starting with the first meeting with Jason Perry and ending with shaking the pistol out of Jackie Rose's hand. Bullard hit him with questions along the way when the narrative sounded illogical. The detective couldn't seem to wrap his head around JP's master plan to find Jackie and Isabella Rose.

"It sounds preposterous," Bullard said.

Blake said, "Look, I didn't invent this town. I only live in it. Half the people in that business are batshit crazy. Don't tell me you don't know that."

Bullard nodded. That seemed to strike a chord.

Blake held up his hands, signaling to remove the cuffs.

Bullard looked back at the LAPD homicide detective. Blake could almost swear Paul Ricardo was enjoying seeing Blake cuffed and interrogated.

Finally, Ricardo nodded. "We've got two cases, detective. Two jurisdictions. Sounds like Eddie's solid for yours. And I'm going to need him as a witness to connect Poole to the dope dealer homicide."

Bullard turned back to Blake. "We spent two hours with Mrs. Rose. So far, your story checks out, at least on the shooting."

The detective stood up, reached across the table, and unlocked the cuffs.

Blake looked up and said, "I'd like to get my sidearm back."

Bullard didn't respond.

Paul Ricardo was heading for the door of the interview room.

Blake yelled. "You going to have a goddamn car sit on my place twenty-four seven, Paul?"

Ricardo kept walking.

Detective Bullard pushed his ID and permit across the table to Blake. "You expecting more trouble, cowboy? I would think you've had your fill."

It was dark when Blake walked out of the station with only his phone and his wallet. A deputy who returned his personal items said he knew nothing about his weapon.

Blake called Carla as he walked across the parking lot, letting her know he'd grab an Uber and would be headed to the yacht. She wanted details about the investigation. But Blake saw Paul Ricardo in the distance, leaning against his unmarked department car.

He told Carla he'd catch her up later.

When he got close Blake said, "Can you give me a lift to the Marina, Paul? Carla and the kid are there."

Ricardo said, "Haven't I already done enough heavy lifting for you, Eddie?"

"You can get your statements."

Ricardo sighed. "Get in."

There was an accident somewhere ahead on PCH and no alternate route. Ricardo put on the Crown Vic's flashers mounted near the top of his windshield and crawled along the berm alongside a five-mile backup. They didn't talk about the case. Blake didn't ask him about his gun. He figured it was being held until the residue test came back.

"Fourteen-hour day, Eddie," Ricardo said. "My wife's been giving me all kinds of shit about the overtime I've been putting in lately. She wants me to transfer to a desk job."

Blake got the message.

Thirty minutes later, they'd hardly spoken most of the ride.

Ricardo pulled into the yacht's parking lot. He slid the Crown Vic into park but left the engine running.

Blake said, "You're not coming in? And Poole is still out there somewhere."

Ricardo looked at his watch. "I phoned in an APB back at the sheriff's. It's goddamn 11 p.m. And I still need to swear out an affidavit to get an arrest warrant. I'll see you here first thing in the morning with my partner."

"Thanks for the lift," Blake said. He turned toward the door, reaching for the handle.

"Eddie?"

He looked back at Ricardo. He was holding Blake's Smith & Wesson and its loaded magazine in the palm of his hand.

Blake took the Chief's Special, slammed the mag home and chambered a round.

Ricardo gave him a thumb's up.

Blake said, "Like I said, Paul, thanks for the lift."

51

CARLA WAS SITTING IN ONE of the chairs in the salon, Bella asleep on the sofa. Blake spotted Carla's clothes in a trash can. She'd showered and changed into a jogging suit, trying to shed any remnant of Warren Poole.

"Did he assault you?" Blake asked.

"He roughed me up," she said.

"That's not what I meant."

"I don't want to talk about it." She held a finger to her lips, her other finger pointing at Bella sleeping and motioned Blake to the salon doors.

Blake followed her to the aft deck. Before they could sit, Blake heard a distinctive rumble he recognized coming from the direction of the parking lot. Exhaust pipes. They sounded like *his* pipes. He turned and saw the taillights of a Dodge Challenger passing the entry gate. It slowed and then sped away on Mindanao Way.

Blake turned to Carla. "Did you tell Poole about the boat?"

"I didn't tell him a damn thing."

"I think that was him," Blake said. "Get the girl."

"And do what?"

"Go to the last slip. Break into a boat if you have to. And stay there."

Thirty seconds later, he escorted them off the yacht, his eyes searching the dark parking lot until Carla and Bella disappeared onto the deck of a distant sailboat.

Blake returned to *The Closer*'s salon and killed its lights. He closed the electric window drapes, casting the room into near total darkness. He sat in the swivel chair that faced the two glass salon doors leading to the aft deck.

Blake dialed Paul Ricardo's cell.

The detective's voice mail answered.

Blake whispered a message. "You need to turn around. I think Poole just cased the boat."

Two minutes later, he detected footsteps on the dock planks. He heard the boarding door open on the starboard deck. Blake slid the Chief's Special into the space between his leg and the arm rest. Out of sight. But accessible.

When the footsteps reached the deck, Blake could feel his heart pounding. He took a deep breath, telling himself he had the tactical advantage. But the steps he heard also told him the intruder was wearing leather heels. Last he saw Warren Poole he was wearing rubber soled Hush Puppies.

Blake thought, maybe it isn't Poole. Maybe he saw someone else's Dodge. How would Poole know the yacht's location among hundreds of slips? Maybe it was *The Closer*'s owner, coming to check his boat.

He had to be prepared for that. Not shoot some rich guy on his million-dollar toy.

Blake shut off his thoughts and concentrated on the footsteps. They were on the slim outer deck now, moving the length of the boat. They paused for a couple seconds at the bow, then came back port side until they stopped on the aft deck.

Whoever it was lingered just outside the salon doorway.

Blake's first thought was to reach for his gun. Aim it at the entrance. But his second thought was to leave it concealed. In the dark salon he had the element of surprise.

The salon doors opened to a backlit silhouette.

The silhouette walked in a few steps. A sliver of light shining through a space between the drapes illuminated the silhouette's face and hand.

A pistol there. A pink pistol.

In the hand of Warren Poole.

He didn't see Blake in the darkest corner of the room.

Blake said, "That's a pretty gun, Warren. You roll a hooker for that?"

Poole took a couple more steps forward and stopped. "Yeah, I'm embracing my feminine side."

"You've been here too long," Blake said. "Soon you'll be hitting yoga classes. Creeping on California girls." He let a couple seconds pass. "You're more resourceful than I thought. How did you find the boat?"

Poole reached into his windbreaker and pulled out a piece of scrap paper and tossed it on the floor. "You need to clean your car more often, Edwin."

Blake thought, the slip's address. He'd tucked it under the Challenger's visor. Blake said, "Speaking of that, where's my fucking Dodge?"

Poole took a couple more steps. Halfway across the salon now, about fifteen feet away. "We never made a deal on the car. You're going to have to pay for that. Like you did for roller girl."

"Pay with what?"

"The *kid*, Edwin. I have some unfinished business with the kid."

"About Sherman Oaks? Valley homicide already has enough to put you away."

"I told you. I didn't kill that guy."

"Then who did?"

Poole said, "The kid."

Blake chuckled. "Now that's a creative defense."

"It's the truth. The guy was in a death rattle when I showed up. Ask her. My guess is he was tapping her after her mother didn't show up. I was the good Samaritan. Even wiped down the gun. Told her if she kept her mouth shut she'd be all right." Poole laughed, "Damn, Edwin. I heard the news. JP checking out and all. Ms. Jackie in custody. Think about it. The kid is a chip right off the old block. Or is it the other way around?"

Blake didn't believe him. But it didn't matter. "Even if your bull-shit checks out, they catch up with you, you're going to be going away for twenty or thirty."

"Not gonna happen," Poole said. "I just need to have a little heart-to-heart with the kid."

And take out the only living witness, Blake thought. He inched his hand next to his leg, feeling for the Chief's Special with his fingertips.

He wanted to keep Poole engaged. "So, if I give you the kid, where do I get my car?

"When we're done I'll leave it one of the short-term lots at LAX." He paused. "So, where is she?"

"She's not here."

Poole pointed the gun. "Then take me to her."

"You're not going to shoot me."

"Is that right?"

"You shoot me you'll never find her."

Poole hesitated. Like he hadn't thought of that. As Poole was thinking out a response, Blake heard a sound everyone who lived in LA knew well.

Poole heard it, too.

"Guess what that is?" Blake said. "LAPD calls it an airship."

Unexpectedly, the chopper's blinding spotlight engulfed the yacht, penetrating the gaps in the salon's curtains and sending shafts of light across the room like a laser light show.

Poole spun toward the portside window.

Blake drew the Chief's Special and rolled onto the floor, coming up with the gun in a two-handed grip.

The salon returned to pitch black.

Blake shot anyway.

He didn't wait for the result. He scrambled up four steps to the galley and took cover behind a cabinet and countertop, waiting for his eyes to adjust to the dark.

Poole was nowhere in sight.

52

WARREN POOLE HUDDLED ON THE swim deck, using the transom as cover as he took stock of his surroundings. The LAPD chopper had moved on, its blades still thumping as its spotlight scanned boat slips on the other side of the channel. His eyes went to the narrow side deck, the small boarding door there. It was the only way off the yacht. He decided there was no way the ex-cop was going to let him walk off like a guest returning from a day excursion.

It wasn't his nature.

He tried to visualize how it would go. Blake comes out the double doors, doing that cop sneak and peak. His pistol in a double grip. His finger extended on the side of the trigger guard, showing that cop trigger discipline. When he emerges he's twenty feet away.

From the cover of the transom Poole could drop him in his tracks.

Poole glanced at the chopper as it banked over the apartment buildings across the channel. He found himself thinking about the book Dagney gave him. His favorite line: that in every adversity was the seed of an equal or greater benefit. The *benefits* were waiting for him across the Pacific. He had 250 grand, a visa, and a ticket to Ho Chi Minh City. Maybe he shouldn't have stopped at the boat. But it was right on his way to LAX. And the kid was a loose end. She was the only one who could link him to Dagney rotting away in the bedroom of her bungalow.

After a couple of minutes, Poole concluded Blake wasn't coming out the double doors. He surveyed the back deck, thinking he could make a run for the side door. But then he spotted a stairway in white fiberglass in a dark corner on the deck. So that's where Blake was, he concluded. Above, waiting for him with a full view of the boat and the entire dock.

Waiting for him like Bogart waited for Edward G. Robinson in *Key Largo*.

Poole removed his leather shoes. He climbed onto the main deck, crawling on his hands and knees. When he arrived at the stairway a canopy over the deck shielded him from above. He rose, crouched, and studied the way it curved around above. He climbed the first few steps, gripping the Taurus with both hands.

Poole could sneak and peak, too. He'd seen it in the movies.

Blake took the interior steps from the pilot house to the flying bridge. The LAPD airship was hovering on the other side of the channel. No help to him now. Blake spotted a couple of empty lounge chairs on the forward deck. He peeked over the side of the flying bridge and saw the boarding door. It was closed. If Poole fled, he decided, he wouldn't have bothered to latch it.

Warren Poole was hiding somewhere on the boat.

The only view Blake did not have was the aft deck below. Most of it was covered by a fiberglass canopy with a rubber dinghy tied down to its surface. Blake crouched and quietly stepped from the flying bridge onto the canopy. He was halfway across when he saw Carla on the dock.

Walking toward *The Closer*.

He wanted to shout out. Instead, he waved his hands over his head, trying to get her attention.

The voice came from behind him. "That's the mariner's distress signal, Edwin. I learned that in the marines. That cop chopper can't see you."

Blake spun around into the combat stance.

Poole was in a two-handed stance, too. He was at the threshold of the flying bridge, his pink pistol trained on Blake's chest.

"Toss the gun, Poole." Blake said it like a police command. "And lay face down."

Poole chuckled. "You're having a flashback, Edwin. You're not on the street anymore, barking orders at some Motor City punk. This, I believe, is what you call a Mexican standoff."

Blake kept his focus on Poole across the Smith & Wesson's front sight. "Police are on their way, Warren. That chopper, that's called an area sweep. The pilot has a good description. You'll be easy to spot from the air with that shiny spot on the top of your fucking head."

Poole took a step forward, glaring. For a moment, Blake thought he was going to fire.

Instead, he said, "I'll make you a proposal. I forget about the kid. You toss *your* gun. You put up *your* hands. I go my way. And we never have to do this dance again. You have my word."

"You track record is shit when it comes to that."

"True. But since coming to LA, I've been on a path to self-improvement."

Blake could feel blood pulsing in his grip. He thought, what's with that chopper? Paul Ricardo must have got his message and sent the airship. But where the fuck was the patrol response?

And where the hell is Carla?

Blake spotted a dark figure silently emerge on the flying bridge behind Poole.

Finally, he thought. Paul Ricardo. Or maybe a uniformed cop.

But it was neither. He didn't know who it was until he saw Warren Poole launch forward, airborne, clean off his feet.

Revealing Carla behind him. Her forearm skyward—the big follow through of Ronda Rumble's signature can opener.

Poole fell forward, landing face first on the starboard side of the dinghy. But he bounced off the inflated pontoon and was back onto his feet.

Lifting the pink pistol.

Blake pivoted and shot.

Poole's body shook. He glanced down at his chest and then back up with a look of disbelief. When he tried to raise his gun again Blake emptied the Smith's magazine.

Six .45 caliber, hollow-point rounds into his torso.

Poole staggered backward. Then fell from the canopy.

Blake rushed to the starboard side and looked down. His body was wedged in the open boarding door. Poole was motionless, dead or dying, the pink pistol still clutched in his hand.

Blake, adrenalized, spun around toward Carla. "Why the hell did you come back?"

Moments later, he realized he'd yelled the words as if she'd made a mistake. He walked over and held her. She was shaking. He was, too.

"Why did you come back?" he said again, this time softly.

"I thought I could help."

He held her face in her hands and looked into her eyes.

"I'm glad you did," he said.

53

EVERYONE HAD BEEN UP ALL night. Everything had become even more complicated because Marina Del Rey was the sheriff's jurisdiction. Paul Ricardo told Blake he'd dispatched the airship after he received his voicemail. But the sheriff's small Marina station, not a mile from *The Closer*, had failed to respond with a patrol car. Instead, the two sheriff's homicide detectives handling Jason Perry's murder arrived at the yacht around midnight, well after two cars from LAPD's Pacific Division. The sheriff's dicks interrogated Blake and Carla separately at the Pacific station for three hours, Paul Ricardo's partner joining them. Ricardo and a youth officer questioned Isabella Rose.

Now Blake and Carla were sitting on a wooden bench with a handcuff rail in the Pacific station. They were not in cuffs. Neither was Isabella Rose when they saw the female LAPD youth officer escort the girl toward them in the hallway, Paul Ricardo trailing.

It was nearly 7 a.m.

As the group passed, Carla reached out as if to touch the girl. But Bella stared straight ahead and kept walking. Ricardo stopped.

Blake looked up and said, "You find my Dodge?"

"No sign of it."

"I saw it drive by."

"He must have ditched it. In case you missed it, we've been a little busy. I'll put your car on the wire."

"What next?" Blake asked.

"You're both free to go. But expect some follow up from the DA on the Hindu Temple shooting."

Carla was watching Bella as she disappeared around a corner. Carla looked up at Paul Ricardo. "What about her?"

"She's being taken to CJH, Central Juvenile Hall, detention."

Blake looked up at Ricardo. "You check her prints with the Sherman Oaks weapon? Poole claimed he wiped down the gun."

Ricardo said, "Don't need to. She gave herself up. That asshole had it right. Rossi had been having his way with the kid for a couple of days. She found his piece and popped him when he tried it again."

"I was sure Poole was lying," Blake said.

"He's still a killer. She told us about a woman Poole used to watch her. Over-the-hill porner named Dagney Allen. The kid disclosed Jason Perry's sexual abuse to her. But Allen never told Poole. Apparently to spare her the humiliation. I had Santa Monica PD do a health and welfare check on Dagney Allen. I just got off the phone with them. Kind of ironic isn't it, Eddie?"

"How so?"

"You may have left homicide. But homicide hasn't left you." He paused. "She's history. Signs of a struggle. Shot to her head. We ran the pink Taurus. It's registered to her."

Blake nodded. "That's why Poole showed up in the Marina. The kid could tie him to his only homicide. Like I said, he bragged about not leaving witnesses."

Ricardo shook his head. "Still a dumbass. We found visa papers and a plane ticket to Vietnam in his jacket. He must have shipped

Perry's money there. Or had it wired. All he had to do was catch his flight and we'd never have nailed him."

"Even with a homicide charge?"

"That's what I mean by stupid. Vietnam has no extradition agreement. I guess he didn't know that."

Carla looked up. "What's going to happen to Bella? She's just a kid."

"Juvenile division is handling it now. She'll get a hearing. Considering everything, her story, if it checks out, I doubt she'll be doing juvie time."

Carla asked, "And what about Jackie?"

"That's the sheriff's case, though we'll be having some input. Depends what jurors think. I'm betting she'll plead out."

Carla said, "I wonder if we could take the girl when she gets out."

Blake knew that was coming. Carla hinted at it earlier while they waited.

"Call me this week," Ricardo said. "I'll put you in touch with her worker. But truthfully, I'm not sure how social services is going to look at this whole thing."

"What *thing?*" Carla asked.

Paul Ricardo chuckled. "Oh, I don't know. Extortion. Kidnapping. Ex-cop operating without a PI license. Two homicides and the standoff on the boat. With Eddie in the picture it's not exactly the stable environment social workers like to see."

Ricardo buttoned his sports jacket and looked down at Blake.

"Stick to the movies, Eddie," he said. "You'll be doing us all a favor."

54

THEY TOOK AN UBER TO Carla's Mini Cooper parked in the lot across from the boat slips. Carla snuggled next to him in the back seat.

"I guess this means you're not dumping me so you can slide through social services," Blake said.

She rolled her eyes. "Anyone ever tell you that you are high maintenance?"

Blake kissed her. He held her chin between his fingers and said, "Like I've heard you say, be careful who you point the finger at. Three more are pointing back at you."

"Fuck you, Eddie," she said.

The Uber driver, a red-headed, rocker-looking guy in his twenties with hair halfway down his back, glanced at them in the mirror.

"Don't worry," Blake said. "That's her way of saying I love you."

The car dropped them off next to the Mini Cooper. Blake tipped the Uber driver ten bucks, got out and looked across the lot. He could see a coroner's van and two sheriff's department vehicles parked next to the security fence. Beyond that he saw yellow crime scene tape surrounding *The Closer*.

"C'mon," Blake said. He began walking towards the boat. "Let's get your clothes."

Carla lingered. "Eddie, not now." But then she caught up.

They entered through the gate and stopped at the tape. Poole's body was gone. The side deck was stained with blood. Sheriff's detective Bullard stood on the aft deck. He spotted Blake and walked to the starboard railing.

"Still a secured scene," he said.

"Carla left some clothes," Blake said.

"She can pick up her things when we're done."

"You inform the owner?" Blake asked.

The detective shook his head.

"We can take care of that," Blake said. "But I'm just wondering. Where did my round land in the salon?"

"That's evidence," the detective said.

"Not evidence against me. If it was, I'd still be sitting in the box."

The detective turned, looking like he was going back to work.

Blake shouted. "Detective, I just want to be able to tell the owner what kind of damage I did to his goddamn boat."

Bullard stopped and turned around, staring at Blake for a couple seconds. Finally, he said, "The teak panel. By the door. Your .45 made a clean hole."

Blake gave him a thumbs up. He took Carla's hand as they walked back to the car.

Carla insisted on driving. Leaving the lot, Blake said, "Your old teammate is going to be pissed."

Carla turned to him. "I doubt it."

Blake said, "Keep your eyes on the road, Carla."

She looked back at the road. "She'll love it. She'll be telling the story for years at every party she throws on the boat."

Blake saw another parking lot off Mandanao Way. "Let's look for my Dodge. It's got to be close."

"I need coffee. There's a Peet's right across Lincoln."

A few minutes later, Blake wheeled into the parking lot of the strip mall containing the coffee shop. He spotted a *Los Angeles Times* box. He handed Carla a ten. "Coffee is on me."

"You bet it is," she said. "That sonovabitch Poole took my purse."

As Carla stepped into Peet's Coffee, Blake fed three quarters into the box and pulled out a Thursday morning edition. He saw a front-page headline about Jason Perry's murder. The story below it detailed the expected arraignment of Jacqueline Margaret Rose and identified her as JP's estranged girlfriend. Blake did not see his name. He didn't see anything about what had gone down last night in the Marina.

Carla emerged carrying two coffees to go.

He showed her the headline. "No mention of me. Or you."

"That's too bad."

They started toward her car. "That's not even funny."

Carla handed him his coffee. "Eddie, your Hollywood people love this shit. When this all comes out, your phone will be ringing off the hook. You're a walking crime show."

Inside the Mini Cooper, Blake plucked an antidepressant pill from his shirt pocket and washed it down with a coffee chaser.

He glanced at Carla. "I wonder how long I'm going to be on this stuff."

Carla said, "You're back, Eddie. For now, stay with it."

They spent a good ten minutes parked, sipping coffee. Blake said they both needed a good vacation. Maybe Hawaii or the Bahamas. Carla wondered if the TV commercials about those Sandals resorts were for real, always showing a couple on an empty beach, the whole resort to themselves.

"I know a place like that for real," Blake said.

He told her he knew a forensic psychologist he'd worked with on a pilot who had a house in Tortola in the British Virgin Islands. "He told me I could rent it anytime. Water and air both eighty-five degrees. He says it overlooks the bay where Blackbeard the Pirate used to ambush the Brits."

Carla put the Mini in gear, backed out and headed for the lot exit. "Sounds like our kind of place," she said. But her eyes were not on the road ahead.

"Stop!" Blake said.

She slammed on the brakes as a large bakery truck pulled out in front of her. It hesitated halfway out of its parking spot, the driver giving Carla a look, and then turned and drove away.

Revealing Blake's Challenger in the adjacent parking space.

"Pull in," Blake said. "I've been carrying my spare keys since that sonovabitch ripped off my Dodge."

He spent a good half minute standing outside the car, his eyes scanning the interior.

"What are you waiting for?" Carla said.

"Technically, I should call this in," he said. "Let the sheriff's techs process it." He looked at Carla. "But fuck it. They should have sent a patrol car last night."

Blake popped the locks with his key. He opened the driver and passenger doors and looked through the interior. The paperback *Success Through a Positive Mental Attitude* was on the passenger seat. He saw something on the floor behind the back seat.

A couple seconds later he handed Carla her purse.

"You're a good man, Edwin Blake," she said.

Blake walked around to the trunk and opened it. Inside he saw a carry-on suitcase. He was going to slam the lid shut and deal with that later when he saw something else—a box partially concealed behind it.

A FedEx box with Ho Chi Minh City address.

"What's that?" Carla asked.

"The label has a customs declaration," Blake said, reading it. "Used paperbacks valued under fifty dollars."

"He didn't exactly strike me as a big reader."

"There's a FedEx store right around the corner."

Blake lifted the box, feeling its weight. "That probably was his next stop."

Blake used his car key to pierce the packing tape. He opened the flaps and saw a dozen paperbacks. Most had cover art of attractive women and muscular, shirtless men. Blake lifted the books out, exposing more paper underneath.

Neatly stacked piles of paper. They were hundred-dollar bills, their bundle wraps removed.

"Jesus, Eddie," Carla said, seeing the cash, too.

"What?"

"What are you going to do with that?"

"I'm not into romance novels," Blake said.

He picked up a stack of the bills, looking at the portrait of Benjamin Franklin. He'd never noticed it before, but it struck him that Benjamin Franklin was smirking.

Two hundred and fifty k. Jason's Perry's get-out-of-town stash.

Carla's eyes widened, seeing the money now. "Jesus, is that JP's?"

Blake nodded.

"Damn, Eddie," Carla said. "Like I said, what are you going to do with that?"

Blake glanced at her, saying, "JP has no heirs. I should probably hand it all over to one of his suits. My guess, he's got a small army of lawyers."

Carla squinted.

Blake's eyes went back to the box. He picked up another bundle, thumbing through the bills like a dealer breaking in a deck of cards.

Turning to Carla, he said, "But I think I'll wait for my second thought."

ABOUT THE AUTHOR

LOWELL CAUFFIEL is the best-selling author of nine books and an award-winning veteran investigative reporter. His research has taken him everywhere from the President's private living quarters in the White House to the dangerous confines of urban dope dens. Cauffiel's three crime novels have explored diverse characters and settings that range from a Detroit shakedown crew in *Marker* to the glitzy, corrupt underworld of the National Football League in *Toss*, which he co-authored with former Superbowl quarterback Boomer Esiason. His five nonfiction crime books have covered a monstrous, homicidal patriarch in the *New York Times* best-selling *House of Secrets*; a pair of female serial killers in *Forever and Five Days*; and a calculating criminal justice instructor who tried to design the perfect crime with the murder of his TV anchorwoman wife in *Eye of the Beholder*. Cauffiel's first true crime book, *Masquerade*, the story of a Grosse Pointe psychologist's deadly double life, was a national best seller. He has appeared in more than two dozen documentaries about his books, including appearances on the BBC, A&E, Court TV, Oxygen, and Investigation Discovery. He has written, produced, and directed documentaries for the Discovery Channel and as executive producer developed the feature film *Stockholm*, staring Ethan Hawke. Cauffiel now lives in Los Angeles where he creates shows for cable, broadcast, and streaming networks. Learn more at LowellCauffiel.com.